I'll Remember You

Deborah Packer is an actress/writer with a Master's degree in Speech and Drama from the University of Michigan and has worked on stage, TV and film in Toronto and Los Angeles. She has also written and performed sketch comedy and completed two screenplays. I'LL REMEMBER YOU is her first novel.

I'll Remember You

BY

DEBORAH PACKER

ISBN: 978-0-578-88154-6 (paperback)

For my dearest parents, Helen and Murray, whose love, support, humanity and courage in the face of adversity gave me the strength and inspiration to write this story.

For Thom Koutsoukos, my brilliant actor/husband. His enduring love, constant support and endless patience encouraged me every step of the way.

"For thy sweet love remembered, such wealth
brings, that I scorn to change my state with kings"
William Shakespeare

Prologue

Miami Beach May 1942

The night air was thick and foul with the smell of oil, smoke, and burning flesh. The explosion had pierced his eardrum with such intensity he could no longer hear the rhumba music blasting from the brightly lit tourist hotels along the beachfront. *God damn Nazi cowards!* It seemed so unreal, yet familiar. The hotel owners were slow to answer the call to dim their lights, making the merchant ships and tankers easy marks for the prowling Nazi subs.

Only a moment before, PFC Murray Pickarowitz had been innocently guarding Haulover Beach, serving his two hours on, four hours off in what many soldiers dubbed monotonous duty, and *they* were young, unarmed seaman on a liberty ship. He had heard about the U-boat attacks ever since arriving for basic training in April. One ship after another. So many men. So many lives. And, now in the quiet night, marked only by the ring of the hotel orchestras, he could hear their screams.

As he rushed toward the water, pieces of them began to wash ashore. A merchant seaman lay face up in the shallow water, his body covered with oil. Murray bent down toward him. Suddenly—here it was. The flash of a long-forgotten time and place. A memory branded with a vengeance on his psyche.

—⁓—

Lomza, Poland —a child of three running terrified as bombs, shrill and piercing, strafe the city. He and his frantic mother – caught in a daylight raid. Nowhere to hide. And, around the corner, the German soldier lying in the street, his arms outstretched, crying for 'wasser' The child leaves his mother's side and moves closer, his eyes riveted to the soldier's face. No face, really. Just a bloody mass of pulp. Nothing to distinguish it as human—except that **sound** *coming from deep within the bowels of his belly —a distinctly human cry for water. The pleading to a boy of three as his mother quickly whisks him away.*

—⁓—

He had crossed the ocean, a nine-year-old desperate for a better life. He would awaken many a night in his safe Brooklyn apartment, wet with perspiration, unable to catch his breath. The memory would fade as the boy grew into a teenager. It was baseball at Ebbets Field, kosher hot dogs at Coney Island. He would learn to use his fists on the mean Brooklyn streets. In the thirties, the WPA put him to work when work was hard to find. Now, here he was — a soldier in training for *another* war. He had expected to go into the infantry. *Why not!* He had boxed in some small-time matches in and around New York. Strong and agile, he could fight the best of them, and he knew it. But, he had just turned twenty-nine. Instead, they sent him to the Air Corps. Now, he was doing sit-ups and learning to use a rifle on a beach in Miami.

His pulse was racing as he gazed at the lifeless body floating in the blood-stained water. The seaman never had a chance. Oil had engulfed his lungs. Murray closed his eyes. A tear brushed his cheek. He felt an intense agitation. So, he hadn't shaken it. He never would. Devastation and death, his only world from the time he was two, had inadvertently shaped him more than he could ever hope to understand. A child's trauma in Lomza had unfolded as plain as if it had happened yesterday. And soon, he'd be going back to *it*.

He continued to scramble alongside the other soldiers and emergency workers searching for life among the cans of food, flour, whiskey, wood, and human debris floating ashore that night in Miami Beach — the rhumba music still blaring as the burning hull that was once a ship lay grotesquely silhouetted against the illegal lights of the beach hotels.

Chapter One

*B*obbie Feinman drew a deep breath as the ancient train dragged into the Miami station. Locked for two days in an overcrowded railway car with hormone raging young recruits, screaming babies and her depressed friend, Eunice, she was drowning in a relentless cacophony of noise and despair.

As the train whistle bellowed its final toll, she had a sudden urge to scream out, but an innate sense of propriety tempered the moment.

What kind of pea-brained idiot was she to have asked Eunice to join her on this journey? She felt sorry for her. *That* was her problem. She was always feeling sorry for people. Eunice had been grieving over a traveling salesman ex-boyfriend who cared more for his 1938 Packard than her. Bobbie thought she might appreciate an opportunity to recuperate in sunny Miami Beach, away from the bleakness of her male-impoverished life. And Eunice readily agreed. But, their vacation hadn't even started, and Bobbie was thoroughly exhausted and yearning for some quiet time alone.

Outside the window — a sea of soldiers, dazzling in their freshly pressed uniforms, marched proud and tall near the slow moving train. As it screeched to a steam-belching halt, she could feel her heart pounding. Just *what* had she gotten herself into?

Eunice jockeyed for a better position, snatching a small pair of binoculars from her bag. "If this is heaven, sign me up!"

Bobbie stared at her in disbelief. For two whole days, this redheaded time bomb had been crying her heart out, her life in utter ruin. This was some recovery!

Suddenly, a wave of air-starved passengers grappled for the doors. Eunice's eyes remained fixed on the exalted faces of the soldiers just outside her grasp. Bobbie sat stiffly in her seat, her face drained — too wilted to make a run for the exit. She watched, uneasy, as suitcases sailed carelessly through the air. *What should she do?* If she stood, she risked a major blow to her head. But, as a small space opened, she heard a voice crackling inside her. *Get the hell out of here!* She jumped up, grabbed her small valise, signaled to Eunice, and the two joined the rest of the tired herd beating their way out of the train, onto the platform and toward a line of taxis.

God, how she hated crowds! At fifteen, she had accompanied her father on a business trip to New York and inadvertently stepped out of the Hotel Astor on Broadway just before twelve o'clock midnight. It happened to be New Year's Eve. Her small-town teenage exuberance turned to mortification as she found herself consumed by a mass of holiday revelers. Dragged almost two blocks by this mind-less swarm of humanity shoving its way nowhere, she sur-vived the experience barely, vowing never again. And now, here she was, in the throes of another unruly mob. She gently pried herself loose from a monster of a beach um-brella as its indifferent owner elbowed his way past her. "Whose idea was this, anyway," she moaned.

Eunice raised an eyebrow. Miami Beach had been Bobbie's suggestion. She would have preferred New York City.

She wiped huge beads of perspiration from her face. Her dress hung wrinkled and damp in the penetrating heat of the morning sun. Any minute she might heave the remains of the chicken sandwich packed three days ear-lier and eaten the night before. How would they ever find a taxi in all this mess? Unbearable! She had to do some-thing! A careful smile crossed her world-weary face, and from deep within her belly came such an earth-shattering scream that even *she* was surprised by its ferocity. In a sec-ond, she had fallen to the ground in a perfectly choreo-graphed faint.

Eunice's face went white. "Oh my God! I can't believe this. Bobbie! Bobbie! Are you all right? Bobbie! Talk to me!"

She thought she'd give it an appropriate amount of time before allowing Eunice into her little scheme, but Eunice's reaction required her immediate attention.

"I'm acting," she whispered under her breath, one eye slightly ajar.

"What?"

Frustration pierced her face. *Couldn't Eunice see what she was trying to do!* In a pinched growl, her lips tense, "I said I'm...ACTING!"

"What? Oh. OH!" Eunice turned toward the crowd. "HELP. HELP. MY FRIEND JUST FAINTED. SOMEBODY HELP!"

Two startled GIs appeared and obediently knelt down beside the prostrate Bobbie. As one began mouth-to-mouth resuscitation, the other applied quick and hard whacks to her back. *What was this? Some new kind of resuscitation technique? What was she supposed to do now? Just lie there until they managed to break every bone in her body?* Panicked by the potential for real injury, she started gasping for a breath.

"I guess all the hustle and bustle's too much for her," suggested Eunice, feverishly batting her eyelashes. "She's just a small-town girl from Michigan, you know, and really not used to—"

"Where am I?" Bobbie cried, her eyes pleading with the two unsuspecting soldiers to stop their life saving heroics. She'd be dead if she left her fate to Eunice.

"You okay, Miss? You sure gave us a scare."

Ha! Nothing like the scare they just gave *her.* She smiled weakly and offered her most pathetic sigh. "I guess I'll be fine, but we'd be mighty obliged if you could…" She took another comforting gulp of air, slightly pushing the drama. "call us a taxi?" She winced. *Mighty obliged! Who was she kidding with that fake southern drawl. They'd never fall for it!*

Energized by their own gallantry, the young soldiers

jumped up to the curb, wildly waving their arms. Three taxis magically appeared. The GIs lifted Bobbie's battered body from the cement platform, helping her into the first cab as Eunice jumped in on the other side.

This was *some* ruse, and she couldn't take any chances. She carefully rolled down the window and leaned her head out toward her trusting benefactors. "You've been so kind. How can we ever thank you?"

As one of the soldiers began to suggest a way, the driver put his vehicle into gear and sped away, throwing the girls to the floor of the cab. Undaunted, they picked themselves up and waved back to the GIs in humble appreciation. Victory permeated the air.

"Bobbie, that was absolutely amazing!"

"Thanks, kiddo. No big deal." Bobbie's face glowed with the success of her subterfuge—no one more surprised than she. A degree of self-reliance and daring belied her small-town upbringing, but an innate sense of honesty and justice made some of her risk taking rather troubling. *What would her father think of her antics? Feigning a faint to get a cab!* Not much. Of that, she was sure. Certainly nothing he would have taught her to do. This *skill* was a consequence of her dramatic leanings as star pupil in Miss Bensett's forensics and elocution class where she could emote to her heart's content and receive heartfelt compliments from her classmates. It was her one gift, and it made her feel special. The only Jewish girl in a high school of Protestants and Catholics, she spent much of her school years trying to fit in, reinventing herself to suit the image of what she thought they wanted her to be. Otherwise, they might forget themselves and call her a dirty Jew — words she first remembered hearing as a five-year-old after her father moved his family from Cleveland to the small town of Holly in the early twenties. She would vanquish their taunts by being the nicest person in the world as well as a great actress. *Their mean, spirited outbursts would melt into great affection and no one would ever be cruel to her again.*

The cab driver cocked his head back. "Am I supposed to guess where you're headed?"

What a rude man. "Miami Beach, please. Just drop us at the first small hotel you come to."

A cynical smile permeated his sun-worn features. "Unless you got a place to stay, missy, there ain't no way you're gonna find a room. The entire Air Corps has taken over — converted the hotels to army barracks. You might as well forget it and go home."

Go home? Back on that horror of a train? "Please, just drive on," Bobbie urged. "We'll take our chances."

"Suit yourself missy, but you'll be sorry."

The cabbie, bloated with disdain, drove them across the Intercoastal, dangerously weaving in and out of traffic, dodging an endless trail of cars and military vehicles as if on a joyride — with Bobbie and Eunice as his unwitting captives.

From the back seat of the speeding taxi, the girls clung to one another and attempted to sightsee. The steel blue of Biscayne Bay looked serene and inviting if only they could enjoy it. Bobbie was grateful she hadn't eaten any breakfast that morning. Certainly, she would have lost it all on the cab's upholstery. *It would serve the driver right! Missy, indeed!*

Collins Avenue was brilliant with the patter of marching soldiers. Traffic in some places had come to an almost complete halt. The girls could draw a breath and perhaps finally appreciate the beauty of the palm trees swaying against the warm wind coming off the Atlantic. But, as Eunice's eyes hungrily followed the scores of servicemen along the route, Bobbie noticed with growing alarm the many "No Vacancy" signs that hung like omens on the small hotels lining the avenue. The cab driver's warning was right. *They'll never find a room* — her vacation would be a complete bust, and she'd have to suffer another trip confined to that prison train, listening to Eunice wail about her miserable, deprived life! *No! They must find a place! Please God. Let there be something!* Her eyes poured over every inch of street as she studied each sign and hotel along the route. Then, before her — a *miracle!* She felt a pounding in her chest. Her heart skipped a beat as she let out a shriek of unequivocal relief. "STOP HERE!"

The taxi came to a screeching halt outside a small weather-beaten building. Again, the girls picked themselves up off the floor of the cab.

"Twenty bucks!" roared the driver, his eyes glowing with delight.

Eunice's face went pale. Twenty dollars! That was half of her vacation money!

Bobbie felt herself go hot with rage. She had just

about enough of his rudeness and antics behind the wheel of that cab. Reaching into her handbag, she produced two crisp dollar bills. "Thanks for a lovely drive and the good conversation," she purred, handing him the money. She signaled a "let's go" to Eunice and reached for the door. Together, they jumped out of the cab and rushed toward the hotel. The man's screaming invectives only fueled Bobbie's boldness. "OH, AND KEEP THE CHANGE!" She turned a proud head toward Eunice. "Twenty dollars. Some nerve! Who does he think we are? A couple of southern hicks?"

Eunice tossed her a look. "No. A couple of midwestern ones."

—⁂—

Behind the desk of the small hotel sat a matronly looking woman, thin black hair plastered like cement on her small, angular face, viciously fanning herself with a piece of cardboard. Her eyes narrowed as she watched Bobbie and Eunice approach. "No rooms!" she grumbled.

Bobbie felt a rush of indignation. "But that sign!"

"Every day, it's the same thing! I got to have a room! Give me! Give me! Give me! Hell. Don't you know there's a war on? A million soldiers and they're all on the beach! Go back where you came from, girlies. I got my own problems."

Bobbie stood her ground. "But why do you have the sign out if you don't intend—"

"Jesus, Mary, and Joseph! What do you all want from

me? I don't need this abuse. Leave me alone, you hear! Damn war! Damn soldiers!" Her arms flailing, she jumped out of her chair and disappeared into a back room, continuing her unprovoked tirade. A sense of despair enveloped the girls' once hopeful faces. They turned and walked out.

A contingent of soldiers marched past as they began their long trek up Collins Avenue. Bobbie had never seen so many in one place, at one time. Like in the newsreels. Strong, brave young men, smiling for the cameras, displaying their V for Victory signs. Suddenly, one of them dropped to the ground in front of her. Instinctively, she ran toward him. As his buddy helped him back into line, the soldier acknowledged her concern with a look of regret.

Bobbie's stomach tightened. "This whole trip could be a big mistake."

"You must have lost your mind," offered Eunice. "The whole Army Air Corps is here! Your mistake and my lucky day!"

As the soldiers marched around the corner at 14th Street and out of sight, Bobbie felt a twinge of discomfort. There was such a *neediness* in that GI's eyes. She kept silent. She couldn't begin to make sense of it, so how could she hope to explain it to Eunice —a woman whose life had found new meaning since stepping off that train.

The noonday sun began to strike with the full brunt of its force. Perspiration raced down their faces. Their dresses molded uncomfortably to their overheated bodies. Three hours of constant searching and — nothing. Maybe they should forget it and go home. Suddenly, an oasis in the middle of a desert! A hotel. With a vacancy sign! Like a madwoman, Bobbie rushed toward the door. Eunice hurried to keep up – when their eyes caught sight of something just to the left of the sign. Bobbie felt a familiar ache. There it was again. The reminder that she was…different. All the stable events of her young life melted away and, in a moment, she was a stranger in a strange land. It was all coming back. Those times she had returned home from school crying, troubled by unprovoked malice in people who didn't know her – children too young to even understand the meaning behind their cruel gestures and harsh words. As her family became a more familiar part of the town's landscape, the perceived *horns* which marked them as different began to disappear. Her father, Morris, became a pillar of the community, loved and respected for his generosity and integrity. Then, came the 1930's. An obscure radio priest by the name of Father Coughlin began spewing his anti-Semitic poison over the airwaves, his preaching all the more frightening because his bully pulpit was a church only thirty miles away. It wasn't long before she saw it again —the loathing looks, the whispers behind her back when they thought she couldn't hear. It would continue, at times die down, then begin again. Maybe it was Coughlin parroting Hitler and castigating the *Jewish bankers,* or the screeching paranoia of the German Bund rallying its local supporters – or the KKK parading their own special brand of hatred in front of the Turner house. Ed Turner, her father's Negro friend, had a small farm on the outskirts of town. It was the only place they were allowed to live. *Keep a low profile. Don't make waves. Dad's got a business here.*

Then came Pearl Harbor, and everything seemed to change. Roosevelt had spoken eloquently against racial and religious discrimination in a stirring State of the Union Address. Employment was rising. The wartime economy demanded it. *Now, things will be different. We're at war against a tyrannical enemy. Everyone will be united in one noble and glorious effort! No need to feel resentful and blame her and her family or Ed Turner and his.*

Bobbie's attention returned to the menacing placard that hung unfettered like an odious blemish on the pristine Miami landscape. She felt taunted by the smugness of its cheap message. **No Jews or Dogs Allowed.** The sign reeked with what she already knew. Nothing had really changed. It was easier to think so. Miami Beach simply mirrored the bigotry of the times, no matter what was happening in far off Europe.

She raised her head with unspoken resolve and walked into the hotel. Eunice followed, hopeful Bobbie might somehow swallow her pride and beg for a room.

—⁓—

The lobby smelled of must. The chipped paint on the crumbling brown walls cried out with decay. A pasty-faced man of sixty eyed the girls as they walked up to the front desk.

"May I help you?"

Bobbie took a deep breath. "We have a reservation."

"I see. Your names?"

"Christian. Mary Christian," said Eunice.

Bobbie hesitated as she looked into Eunice's desperate eyes imploring her to mount another great acting job and put them out of their misery. But, within the cracks of Bobbie's bruised child ego, came a voice soaring with conviction. "I'm Bobbie Feinman. That's F-e-i-n-m-a-n. My father is Morris Feinman from Poland. Been in this country a number of years. Perhaps, you've heard of him?"

The desk clerk curled his upper lip. "I see. I'm afraid we have nothing available."

Bobbie pulled her five-foot, six-inch frame over his desk, offering her sweetest smile. "That's just fine. Because, you know what, Mister? I wouldn't give you two cents for this flea bag, anyway."

"Bobbie, maybe we could —"

"Let's go, Eunice!"

Intrigued by the nerve of this wretched twosome, he tossed them a wicked smile. It wouldn't cost him anything. Certainly not his pride. "You might try that Hotel Wellington down on Fourth Street. They cater to people of your persuasion. I don't make the rules here. Personally, I don't care what you are."

A trickle of a smirk crept over Bobbie's face. "Thank you. That is *so* reassuring." Her head held as high as she could stretch it, she turned her back to the man and walked briskly out the door, leaving a dejected Eunice her only recourse —to scurry behind.

—⁓—

They wandered the streets of Miami Beach, solemnly passing more "No Vacancy" signs, neither speaking to the other, each locked in a war of wills. The afternoon sun was still torturing them with its hopeless intensity. Yet Bobbie was feeling curiously redeemed. A small sense of justice had been meted out. How proud her father would be that she didn't cower and beg. Sure. They were sapped. They were roomless. But they would survive this minor inconvenience. *Something would materialize.* Buoyed by a renewed sense of purpose, she even offered to carry Eunice's bag, but Eunice refused to allow her the satisfaction. And, as they continued their trek up Collins Avenue, bogged down by luggage, sore feet and blistering temperatures, Bobbie decided. Vacancy or not, at the next hotel that wasn't restricted, she'd use her dramatic skills and *demand* a room.

—⁓—

A large, wrinkled woman in a flaming red wig sat at a very unkempt desk. A cigarette with a long ash dangled precariously from her mouth. Two small dogs, whose wrinkled faces mirrored her own, sat perched on top of the desk snarling as the girls approached.

Bobbie was hopeful. The hotel wasn't restricted and no sign was out. Certainly, an immediate bribe was in order. "They're adorable."

The dogs growled louder, their teeth locked in a gritting display of their presumed authority.

"Cut it out!" the woman snapped.

With calculated ferocity, the dogs lunged at Bobbie. She jumped away, missing their spiked claws by inches.

"Mommy said CUT IT OUT!" yelled the woman.

Whimpering in defeat, the animals quickly moved off the desk – their tails between their legs.

"Suppose you'll be wanting a room?"

Eunice took a thankful breath, but Bobbie's eyes remained riveted on the dogs. She knew their rage was blunted only temporarily. They were waiting for another opportunity. She could feel it. *Poor little dears with their matted fur and cold eyes. That old crow of a mistress must be a master in the art of mean.*

"You bet we want a room!" cried Eunice. "We had no idea how busy this town is!"

The woman's face softened. "Yes. Isn't it wonderful? How many hours?"

Bobbie's eyes narrowed. "Hours?"

"Five bucks an hour. That's the rate."

The girls exchanged cautious looks. Bobbie allowed herself a moment away from the dogs' steely gaze. The small, makeshift lobby was bereft of furniture. The only light allowed in through a glass ceiling cast a decadent shadow over the torn upholstery on a chair rigidly standing against a peeling wall. *Very unnerving.*

Suddenly, they were drawn to a flimsily dressed, overly made-up woman leading an energized captain past them and up the stairs – his hands groping her bountiful breasts as she screamed with delight. They soon disappeared into one of the upstairs rooms — the door slamming hard behind them.

"Thank you," smiled Bobbie, "but, I don't think so. Shall we go, Eunice?"

Eunice stood resolute.

"Eunice?"

"Okay. Okay."

"Too bad." offered the matron, a mocking glint in her eyes. "But maybe we'll see ya again!"

Eunice looked back wistfully as Bobbie dragged her out the door.

The Wellington, a modest little residential hotel off Ocean Drive on Fourth Street, was home to an assortment of unusual guests. Some had fled the snow-plagued northern winter. Others, with a more pressing agenda, had escaped the war in Europe with at least their bodies intact. Classical music played daily over a small Victrola behind the main desk. To its refugee boarders, the hotel was a welcome sanctuary, an asylum away from a lost home and a horrible past. The lobby was simple. The furniture, comfortable looking but worn. The desk clerks, a husband and wife, had fled France two paces ahead of the Nazis, their current employment compliments of the Jewish Agency, which had successfully placed a number of exiles before the U.S. immigration policy shut the door tight.

As the girls straggled in, they noticed the heavily dressed couple who stood mute and stiff before them. Unusual attire, Bobbie thought, for Miami Beach.

The wife, a haggard, unhappy looking woman of forty, scrutinized the girls, then whispered to her husband, *"Putain"*.

Bobbie winced. Her limited high school French had given her an unwelcome insight. *They think we're whores! Sticks and stones* — "Look. We're two simple girls who got off the train this morning from Michigan, and we're exhausted. We've got to have a room. We've been all over town."

Her husband, a gaunt, gray-haired gentleman with dark circles under his eyes, looked upon the girls with fatherly concern. "I am so sorry. We seem to be full. Perhaps, you could come back tomorrow."

Eunice swooned into the desk. But, like a heat-finding missile, Bobbie exploded. "TOMORROW! Where are we supposed to sleep, TONIGHT! Tell me that? In the STREET? My friend here—" She grabbed Eunice's arm and swung her around toward them. "She needs a room! She has to…meet her husband and tell him… about the baby. He's due to be shipped out any day. WHAT'S SHE SUPPOSED TO DO?"

Her hands hugging her stomach, Eunice let loose a heavy sigh, relishing if only for a moment the sweet image of her phantom pregnancy. She had underestimated her friend's tenacity. Bobbie had finally come through, and Eunice was more than ready for the ride.

—∿—

Murray Pickarowitz sat in the lobby watching with growing interest. Intrigued by its many refugee guests and their stories, he had visited the Wellington a number of times. Today, he had brought a couple of young female friends from Brooklyn to meet two soldiers he had known, casually. Now, his curiosity was ignited as he observed this young woman with long, raven hair so desperate for a room. He was touched by something deeper, far beyond the superficial appeal of her good looks. It was her perseverance. Her insistence against the odds. Her concern for her friend. Her willingness to fight.

—∿—

Bobbie drew an anxious breath and waited for the couple's response to her latest performance. Masterful, to be sure, but would they believe her? Or would Eunice's pathetic overacting make them suspicious.

The husband stared at Eunice's belly for a moment, then turned to his wife. "Don aux le chambre derriere la cuisine."

"Impossible," she argued. "Cette trop petite. Il'n y a pas un fenetre la."

"Cette un chambre. L'faire!" Exasperated, he turned back to Bobbie with an apologetic smile. "If you do not mind, we have something, but it is very tiny and there are no windows."

"Sounds ideal!" she chirped.

"Perfect!" cried Eunice.

The husband handed the keys to his wife who, grudgingly, led the girls through the lobby and down the hall. As Bobbie passed PFC Pickarowitz, she noticed him smiling at her —a friendly, sympathetic smile. Usually guarded, she smiled back, acknowledging the moment to Eunice in a momentary lapse of her well-preserved propriety. "Now, there's a guy I could go for."

"You and a half million others."

She glanced back for a final, dangerous look. *He was still smiling!* As she turned to follow Eunice, she smashed into the side of the narrow corridor. She thought she heard a crack, and for a moment, the room was in a spin. *Panic! Oh God. What an idiot!* In a flash, she fled down the hall, holding her battle-scarred head in her hands.

Murray's eyes lingered on the hallway before surrendering to the animated company of his friends. But his thoughts kept returning to the resourceful young woman with the big brown eyes who had responded to his smile with a gentle one of her own before banging her head on a wall and disappearing into the hallway of the hotel.

Chapter Two

B obbie lay awake, tossing and turning. Their tiny room faced a narrow back alley. Without windows, there was no ventilation, and the air smelled of spoiled fish. Mating cats echoed in the quiet of the night, their screams mimicking the cry of children. And those camp-style beds! Certainly, the tiniest she had ever seen; the mattress so thin she could feel the floor beneath her body. Then, there was the matter of Eunice's sleeping habits – a pattern of repetitious snoring, followed by a descent into a strange gibberish — at times yelling out with such ferocity that Bobbie felt her heart might jump out of her chest. She thought about waking her, but as soon as she'd get up and walk toward her bed, Eunice would sigh, fall back into a deep sleep and start snoring again. It was the first time they had shared a room together. Her luck! Two sleepless nights on the train and now this. Perhaps she'll suggest that Eunice stop consuming so many of those silly romance novels, conveniently forgetting *she, too,* had brought one along. *If only she could read!* But the one light switch over her bed might wake Eunice. So she stared at the ceiling cracks, methodically counting one – two – three, until somewhere around five hundred and fifty, she finally succumbed to a fitful sleep.

—⁓—

A new day – and Eunice jumped out of bed, refreshed and ready for whatever it might have in store. "Hurry up, sleepy head," she admonished. "I feel the lure of adventure stirring. Let's get to that beach!"

Bobbie could hardly keep her head from dropping into her cereal bowl during breakfast. A day on the beach could be just what she needed – a few hours to unwind and relax, feel the gentle breeze off the ocean, and maybe catch a few winks.

They took towels, lotion and their cheap romance novels and hurried to the wide-open area on Fourth and Ocean Drive. But Bobbie's hopes soon sank as she scanned the stretch of coastline. Her long-awaited refuge seemed to be a popular spot for hundreds of daytime trysts.

Eunice removed her wire-rimmed glasses and sat posed like a bathing beauty while Bobbie marveled at the daring of an overzealous twosome sharing a tempestuous embrace only feet away. This very public display of affection made her blush. Why was she such a prude? After all, there was a war on. Tomorrow was uncertain. Not that she was judging them. She almost envied their freedom, their recklessness. Feeling like an intruder, she lay her towel down on a patch of sand and placed her sun hat over her face.

"I think I'll take a little walk," announced Eunice. A

stroll might make her more accessible to the small collection of unattached soldiers.

Thank God, thought Bobbie. "Good. You do that. Go and enjoy herself. No need to hurry back. I'll just be here, sleeping away." She watched her needy friend strut down the beach, missing the prostrate couples by inches. *Poor Eunice.* At twenty-two, abandoned at the alter by a man who promised her the moon, the sun, and a myriad of stars. An announcement of their engagement with the obligatory picture of the happy couple appeared in the local paper two days before the wedding. A number of women, to whom he had obviously promised the same, came forward — more than a few already claiming to be his wife. Bobbie thought the experience might make Eunice cynical and distrusting. Yet, she continued to attach herself to the wrong kind of men, and Bobbie saw danger. What Eunice needed was inspiration, some time to reflect. So, Bobbie suggested she immerse herself in a number of books — Shakespeare, Dickens, D.H. Lawrence, Jane Austen, Proust. Three months later, Eunice had become deeply melancholy, and Bobbie felt personally responsible. She had single-handedly turned her friend into a shrinking violet. So much for introspection and the spark of great literature!

The passing years did little to encourage wisdom, as Eunice's recent debacle with the traveling salesman confirmed. Now, Bobbie watched her walk the beach, desperately inspecting every male along her route. Eunice was ready and much too willing for her next fatal fling.

Suddenly, Bobbie's attention was drawn to a familiar figure flexing his muscles in the water, three women around him blithely snapping photographs. *The soldier from the hotel!* She quickly averted her eyes and tried to immerse herself in her book. But it was no use. She looked toward the water and regarded with modest fascination how the corners of his eyes crinkled when he laughed. How the women seemed to glow in his attention. How well-developed his muscles — *Don't get involved with a soldier!* Her father had warned her a long time ago. Magazines were full of stories about distraught young women throwing themselves off bridges and hurling themselves out of ten-story windows. It made a deep impression, and she had promised herself she'd be smarter than that. Thousands of soldiers might be meeting thousands of girls, but wartime romances were hardly sure bets. At least, that's what her dad told her — *over and over.* She hadn't expected to find Miami Beach full of soldiers. Why hadn't someone warned her? She simply wanted to escape the frigid Michigan winter. She never could tolerate the cold.

She heard a voice – that irritating inner parent that constantly plagued her and ruined her daydreams. *Probably one of those lover-boy types who steals your heart and leaves you miserable and alone in one of those slimy hotels near some far-away army base!* No. That was in that stupid novel she was reading. *Don't get involved with—* Of course, her younger sister, Fay, was engaged to a soldier. But that didn't count. They had known each other way before he signed up.

"Get the stars out of your eyes, kiddo! He's nothing but trouble."

Eunice's stinging declaration startled her. She hadn't expected her back so soon, sure she would have tripped over some poor, lonely guy just waiting to mess up her life again. "Some authority you are, Eunice Nussbaum. Gushing over every male you've seen since we came here!"

Still, Eunice had a point. The soldier seemed much too dangerous with his wavy black hair, piercing blue-green eyes and athletic build —*but he has such a gentle face, such a sweet smile!*

Suddenly, Eunice was giving her an exuberant kick. "May day! He's coming over!"

Keep calm, she told herself. He was just a soldier she had seen in the hotel. Someone who had smiled at her and watched her — *walk straight into a wall. Oh God, no!* Like a flustered schoolgirl, she lay back down on her towel, scooped up her novel, and shrouded her face.

—⚈—

PFC Pickarowitz had noticed Bobbie as soon as she arrived on the beach. How might he go about meeting her without looking too foolish? She could be married, perhaps visiting her soldier-husband.

His old friend, Sadie, a well-endowed woman of fifty, observed right away his interest in this young woman with a white carnation in her hair. A powerhouse of a woman, Sadie – a dyed blonde whose hair was pulled so tight in a bun on top of her head that her face took on the appearance of constant surprise — had owned a bakery in

Brooklyn for years before moving herself and her girls to Miami. Having buried two husbands, she wasn't looking to marry again, but she had great plans for her two young twin daughters of nineteen years. "Murray, *bubala,* get the lead out of your pants. Go up and introduce yourself for God's sake." Her deep-throated Brooklyn accent suggested years of cigarette abuse.

"I don't think so, Sadie."

"I don't think so, Sadie! What's the matter all of a sudden? I'm ashamed, ASHAMED of you. Since when are you so afraid to—"

"I got my reasons."

"Yeah. Yeah. You got your reasons. You know what I think of your reasons?" She made an obscene gesture with her arm. "Now, do me a favor. Get over there before I do something crazy and embarrass my beautiful children."

—⟋⟍—

When Murray finally approached them, Eunice was affecting a bathing beauty pose, and Bobbie's face was pressed tight against her book.

"Hi, girls."

Bobbie emerged from under her novel. "Oh! Hello there." She could feel his eyes studying her.

He took a deep breath. "I admired your spunk yesterday with the desk clerk."

She felt her face go red. She hoped he wouldn't notice. "It's called desperation."

He nodded, as if to signal his understanding. "I'm Murray."

"Helen, but everyone calls me Bobbie."

Eunice managed a soft but deliberate grunt.

"Oh, and this is my friend, Eunice."

"I'm just here for a few days," Eunice offered. "But Bobbie's staying for three weeks!"

Bobbie winced. *Why did she have to tell him that!*

"Great day for the beach, huh?" continued Eunice, undeterred. "Of course, I don't really swim at all. See, when I was a kid, I almost drowned in a bathtub and—" She stopped. Neither of them seemed to be listening. "You know. I think maybe I'll just get my feet wet. Okay, Bobbie?"

"Hmm?"

"I said I'm going to drown myself. You mind?"

"No, of course not. Go ahead. Have a nice time."

Eunice rolled her eyes, gathered herself up and headed toward the water.

For a long moment, the soldier stood silent. His apparent shyness surprised Bobbie. She would have thought he'd be more sophisticated.

He began to shuffle his feet back and forth in the sand. His discomfort gave her courage to overcome her own.

"Would you like to sit down?"

"Thanks." As he made a place for himself, he looked around as if inspecting the beach for the first time. "This place. It's like a paradise."

"Paradise. I don't know. If the heat doesn't get you. I've seen fellas dropping like flies."

"Yeah. That's a big problem here. I felt like I couldn't breathe when I first came down, but I got over it."

She shifted uncomfortably as he continued to stare. Silences embarrassed her. She would chatter on about the most inane things simply to avoid them. She wasn't a child. Twenty-six was well past the clumsy stage, unless you led a somewhat sheltered life in a small town. The depression had kept her out of college. Money was tight, and her father had already put his oldest daughter through the University of Michigan. She went instead to a small business school in Detroit and continued working in her father's dress shop, learning the ins and outs of the clothing trade while her mother privately worried her second born might be headed toward spinsterhood. Fay, five years younger, was already engaged and might marry first. Bobbie certainly didn't care, but it seemed to be a major concern to her mother. Most of the girls married right out of high school. She never did understand the rush. She prided herself on being a working girl and, although she still lived at home, actually enjoyed her independence. She had a few boyfriends but no one special. No one she would consider spending the rest of her life with. She liked to joke about the guy she lost because she was too shy to tell him she needed to go to the bathroom. Coming home from a date one night, she ran into the house so quickly, he never called again. Of course, she wasn't about to call *him*. She had her pride. Probably too much. Many boys thought she was aloof. They hadn't understood that she was afraid. And, though many considered her beautiful with her long, silky black hair, aquiline nose and prominent cheek bones, she always thought of herself as a plain Jane.

"What do you do?" she asked. "I mean, besides marching up and down the beach?"

He smiled. He hated marching. "Physical instructor. Did some amateur boxing a few years ago. Guess they figured I'd know how to train. What do they know. Truth is, I'm not very good at it, this soldier stuff." *Why had he confessed such a thing to a total stranger?*

"A lot of these guys really seem to get into it."

His face contorted. "Most of them have no idea. I was born in Poland. Had sort of a —ringside seat."

"Poland?" She looked surprised. His accent was definitely New York.

His forehead wrinkled. "I was only three, but my town was bombed pretty badly. There was this German soldier lying in the street. He didn't have a face."

For a moment, he seemed lost in a bad memory, and Bobbie lowered her head. Their discussion had turned much too serious. An innocent question had made her privy to something intensely personal.

"We came to America a few years later. I'm one of the lucky ones, considering what's—" His voice trailed off. He glanced out at the ocean as if the beckoning waves could offer some solace from a private hell raging within.

Say something, Bobbie thought. *Anything.* "Now, you'll go back as an American G.I."

Murray cast his eyes toward the sand. "Go back, yes."

As soon as she had spoken, she reproached herself. This

soldier had seen things far beyond anything she could possibly comprehend and she, *supreme idiot,* had to go and remind him that he was *going back!*

Murray's face suddenly relaxed. His eyes crinkled with sublime curiosity. "Where are you from, Bob?"

Bob? No one had ever called her Bob. Her nickname was Bobbie. The family called her that from the time she was a little girl, possibly an Americanized version of *bubie* or more likely, an expression of her father's disappointment that their second born wasn't a boy. "Detroit, now, but I spent most of my life in a little town called Holly. Five thousand people if you count the ones in the cemetery."

He laughed. She had a good sense of humor. He liked that.

Thank God her faux pas hadn't completely alienated him! She could relax a little, grateful she had finally made him laugh. Yet, the soldier seemed so unpredictable, mercurial even. "What about you? Where do you call home?"

"Brooklyn. Toidy toid and toid by da wada woiks!"

"Oh, yeah? So, tell me, Mr. toidy toid, how did a kid from Poland pick up that accent?"

"That's an easy one, Bob. From the bleachers at Ebbets Field, watching the Bums play. Biggest thrill of my life." He fidgeted, staring out at the water, again.

Why couldn't she be clever instead of smiling back in that disgustingly sappy way. Suddenly, she looked up. The three women who had been with him in the water were standing in front of them, staring down at her with strange looks on their faces.

Curious about this young woman who had turned her outgoing friend into some inhibited jackass she couldn't recognize, Sadie, her hands cemented to her hips, offered up a generous smile. "So, don't I get an introduction?"

Murray looked up. "Sadie! Bobbie, this is my old friend, Sadie, and her daughters, Fern and Sophie."

Bobbie's eyes narrowed. She had seen the two younger women somewhere before. All three seemed rather heavily made up, eye shadow generously applied, red blush covering every inch of their bounteous cheeks. And those hairdos! Both girls had their blond hair piled high on their heads, held with a number of ribbons and combs. Unusually glamorous, she thought, for the beach.

Sadie snatched a card from the bosom of her water drenched bathing suit and handed it to Bobbie. "It's a pleasure to meet you— ah, Bobbie, right?"

"Right. Nice meeting you, too."

"You know—" she began, leaning in, her well-manicured right index finger almost piercing Bobbie's face. "You've got some figure. I happen to work at a store on Lincoln Road. The joint has great clothes. You wouldn't believe the prices. Come visit. We'll have a ball." She moved away with her daughters, waiting for Murray to join them.

Murray stood and wiped the sand from his hands. "Got my own bungalow with a few hundred other guys down the road at the Sea Isle. So, I'll probably see you around."

"Yes, guess you will." She felt a surge of disappointment. Her heart began to flutter as he looked over to Sadie, then back to her. *Maybe, he'll suggest a meeting.*

He hesitated, then offered a casual wink and walked away, leaving Bobbie to wonder what she might have said to discourage him. Perhaps, he was involved with — Now, she remembered. Fern and Sophie had been sitting with him in the lobby of the hotel the evening before. She hardly noticed them, then. She was so captivated with—

"BOBBIE! THIS IS SOME HUMAN BEING. LET ME TELL YOU. WORTH A MILLION BUCKS!" From a few hundred feet away, Sadie was waving and pointing toward Murray as he stood, laughing and shaking his head.

Bobbie acknowledged Sadie's eager display of affection for Murray with a cursory smile and a wave of her hand, but she felt herself go red. Everyone on the beach seemed to hear it as well. It seemed obvious to her that Murray wasn't that interested, or he would have suggested they get together. Just as well. *Don't get involved with a*— She lay back down on her towel and watched gloomily as the foursome walked up the beach and out of sight.

Eunice returned, circling like a vulture. Bobbie saw the prying blood lust in her eyes.

"So?"

"So…what?"

"You said last night you could go for him."

"I was only joking, Eunice. I didn't mean it. Didn't you say he's nothing but trouble? Isn't that what *you said*?" She was feeling exposed, unprotected. God, how she hated feeling like that. It was a sign of weakness, of vacillation. She felt trapped by emotions she couldn't understand or express. Something was nagging at her, mocking her.

"Look, let's get this straight. I'm here for a rest. That's all! I refuse to put myself in one of those situations. So, YOU CAN JUST WIPE THAT SILLY SMIRK OFF YOUR FACE!" She closed her eyes, trying to calm herself. When she opened them, everyone on the beach seemed to be staring. *That's just great. They lie around in various stages of lovemaking. No one cares. No one even notices. I raise my voice just once and they all gawk!* She turned to Eunice, attempting to preserve a small piece of her fragile dignity. "I'm going in the water. You coming? Or would you rather stay and burn up?"

"I already went in, Bobbie. You were a little too occupied to notice. So, I'll just stay here. You forget. I'm not a real redhead!"

"Who could forget!" In marked defiance, Bobbie walked toward the water, her head held high, refusing to yield her pride to the still gaping onlookers. *Keep it steady. Don't trip. They'll all be watching!* Maybe, she should do something crazy. Turn around and bow. *Thank you all. And now, for my final number!* That would show them. Why should she cower? She hadn't done anything to be ashamed of. Let them stare. Those hypocritical busy bodies. No sir! She wasn't going to give them the satisfaction of even a glance. Besides, she had a bigger problem. A test of will. Of survival, really. That weak, pathetic heart of hers was throwing curve balls, and she had to fight it with all the strength she could summon.

Chapter Three

*H*e walked back and forth along the tumble of sand. A wide-open area, Haulover Beach was still vulnerable to attack, and Murray couldn't forget what he had witnessed here. The brave men who lost their lives. Hundreds more would die before the Navy finally provided the tankers and merchant ships with escorts. Much of this area continued to be fenced off. A year earlier, tourists left in droves, horrified by the number of bodies that had washed ashore. Those who risked bathing off Miami's beaches in those days got drenched in oil. Murray did his swimming in the Sea Isle pool. Now, the Coast Guard was patrolling and the tourists were back. But, today, something else was worrying him. German espionage. The FBI had been busy checking reports of hundreds of sightings. If there were spies coming ashore these days, the military tried to keep the information from getting out and causing panic. Frayed nerves, especially at night on sentinel watch, could cause many a G.I. to toss his supper. Murray was learning to live with it.

He was still into his two-hour watch. A warm breeze off the ocean had offered a slight respite from the oppressive heat of the day. He was feeling an urge to break out. He kept lapsing into the memory of a lovely young woman he had seen only briefly at the Wellington and spoken to on the beach. Normally private, he found himself opening up about something he had never spoken about to anyone. His heartfelt attraction to her disturbed him. It was a futile and unrealistic emotion.

The force of his feelings almost overcame his doubt, but he had backed out of an opportunity to ask her for a date. Now, he had to do something — anything to shatter the gloom of that decision. His attention turned to the callow fellow, probably no more than eighteen, walking past him on rounds. A puckish smile crossed his face as he motioned the boy over.

"What's up?" the young soldier asked.

"Did you see something?"

The boy looked out over the water. "Just a cutter."

"No. I mean over to the left." Murray pointed in the direction of some flares, to a short blink of light followed by a longer blink.

The youth looked toward the flares, then shrugged his shoulders. "It must be one of ours. The Coast Guard's got it covered."

Smug little bastard! Murray leaned in, his voice low and determined. "You know, where I come from, you grow up real fast. Have to keep your eyes open and watch your back." He glanced toward the gentle waves rocking the shoreline, then glared at the boy as if to impart some special information only *he* was privy to.

The soldier's eyes widened. "You're saying we might really see us some Krauts...in Miami Beach?"

"You didn't hear about the four spies they caught coming ashore south of Jacksonville a few months ago?"

"Yeah. I think I did."

It hadn't been a lie. The military police did catch four Germans. Of course, no one knew what heinous espionage they were about to commit. Prior to their capture, they had only managed to eat their way through a number of excellent restaurant meals and amuse themselves on a particularly lucrative spending spree in New York City.

Murray moved away, leaving the boy to ponder this new piece of delicate information.

"Hey, wait! So, what do we do if —you know—"

Murray hesitated. "You know... any German?"

The boy shook his head.

"Kommen sie hier, Fraulein. Now you say it."

"Kommen sie...hier, fraulein"

"Great! Mit der hosen in die hant."

"Mit der...hosen...in da hant."

"Terrific. That's it!"

"That's it? What's it mean?"

Murray leaned in, again, savoring the moment. "Doesn't matter what it means except— if someone answers back, you've got problems." He walked slowly back to his post as the worried young man furtively examined every inch of ocean within his view, carefully repeating *"Komen sie hier flaurine mit der hasen...hosen in da...der...hant"* as if the life of every soldier in the military depended on it.

Murray fought to keep himself from laughing. It had been a moment of sublime release from a desolate routine. He hated sentry duty. He was alone and thinking too much. Often, in the dark, he would hear it again. That deafening, gut wrenching sound. First quiet, then devastation. Bombs falling indiscriminately on his town. At Ellis Island, he made himself a vow. No more death and destruction! He threw himself into learning English and baseball and American history. The harsh realities of life on the uncharitable streets of Brooklyn had its own special challenges for an immigrant kid. Now, he was a naturalized American citizen and a soldier. The child's naive pledge no longer had much meaning.

He continued walking his beat, watching the apprehensive child-soldier desperately trying to learn *'Come here Miss, with your panties in your hand,'* a line Murray picked up from an old commander who probably dallied in Germany a little too long after the Great War.

He felt a tinge of guilt. Had he trampled the kid's idealism? *So, big deal.* Maybe, he'll give more thought to what he might find when he gets *over there.* Besides, if Murray came clean, confessed he was only having some fun, he could risk a fight. It wouldn't be the first skirmish he'd encountered since joining the army. Usually, he was defending himself against some simple-minded country boy. As a child in Poland, he had confronted enough venom to last a lifetime. He had expected the misplaced hate would stop when he came to America. But, it persisted, and like an open wound, festered in a climate of suspicion on the streets of New York and now, in the Army Air Corps.

—∿—

A pathetically sunburned Eunice left her tiny hotel room against Bobbie's strict orders and ventured out into the lobby. Maneuvering herself into a chair, she screamed out in pain. Max Renault, a thin, dignified looking French refugee in a tattered, loose fitting suit, looked up from his newspaper.

"Redheads," smiled Eunice. "We burn very easily."

Max raised a skeptical eyebrow and returned to his paper.

Bobbie lumbered into the hotel, tired and irritable. She had spent half the morning walking around in blistering heat looking for something to relieve Eunice's sunburn. It was Sunday and many of the drugstores were closed. She finally found a mom and pop store about ten blocks away.

When she discovered Eunice restlessly perched on a chair, her annoyance peaked. "Why didn't you stay in bed? You'll only feel worse."

"I'm not staying in that excuse of a room. I'd rather die!"

Bobbie retrieved a tube of ointment from her purse. "Here, miss smarty pants. Rub it all over, and for God's sake, do yourself a favor and stay out of the sun!"

"But I'm on vacation. What am I supposed to do?"

"How should I know? Why don't you try reading a book or something."

"A book?" A book I can read in Detroit."

Bobbie plopped herself down on one of the comfortable lobby couches. This trip had been a painful mistake. She had sought a little rest and comfort. Instead, she was getting little or no sleep and playing nurse maid to a spoiled, self-indulgent child of thirty. She quickly snatched the gothic romance from her handbag, yearning to escape into some easy reading and maybe, give that over-active brain of hers a rest. She considered most of these novels quite tiresome; silly, brain-dead young women falling into the most unbelievable situations. Of course, *this* particular story appeared a little juicer than most. She had found it quite by accident while browsing for something more challenging at a second-hand bookshop. The blurb on the cover of the book caught her attention right away. The heroine, a small-town librarian, travels the world on a pirate ship, then falls into a Turkish opium den after being sold into slavery by a big producer who had promised her a movie career — and that was it. Bobbie was hooked!

She had just settled in, ready to explore the next sordid chapter, anxious to lose herself in a pagan world of intrigue, when out of the corner of her eye she saw *him* entering the hotel with two other soldiers. A momentary flush came over her. She moved to cover her face. Mustn't let Eunice see, not after her hysterical outburst on the beach.

Her eyes followed as he approached a table in the back of the room and greeted two young women with the loving enthusiasm of old friends. *Fern and Sophie, Sadie's girls! They certainly do get around.*

"I wonder what lover boy is up to," observed Eunice.

"My God, haven't you anything better to do with your life?"

"What life? I'm here in Miami Beach with a million soldiers, and I look like a beet. I got no life."

"You don't look like a beet, Eunice. A tomato maybe, but not a beet."

If she could just finish this one chapter—*who was she kidding!* She kept her head down, focusing on the white of the page and waited. She'd simply depend on Eunice's roving eye to sound the alarm and draw her attention back to the activity at the other end of the room. She prayed she wouldn't have long to wait.

"Okay, kiddo. Here he comes!"

Bobbie lifted her head with a dramatic flair. "Eunice! Will you stop making such a big deal."

Murray kissed Fern and Sophie on their cheeks, then headed for the front door. He was genuinely surprised to see Bobbie sitting in the lobby. She appeared so completely absorbed in something she was reading. *Don't bother her.* He felt trapped between a deep desire and a deeper fear. Finally, he decided. It was reckless, but he had to do it. As he approached, he noticed her sunburned friend staring at him. "Looks like you really enjoyed the beach."

"Redheads, you know. Never could take too much sun!"

Bobbie looked up from the margin of her book. She and Murray exchanged warm smiles before their attention was drawn to the voice of a newscaster beaming over the radio at the front desk.

President Roosevelt reported today that operations to drive our enemies into the sea of Tunisia will not be long delayed. The allies will gain control of the strait across the Mediterranean and will invade Europe at more than one point. The battles to come will be costly, he says, and we must have calm courage at the home front. Now, we will resume our current programming.

Bobbie had been watching Murray during the broadcast. He appeared deep in thought. She hesitated, not wanting to intrude. "Do you... have any idea when you might be leaving?"

He turned to her, his face rigid. "No. No... I don't."

She lowered her head. Once again, it seemed she had miscalculated, said the wrong thing.

Murray's eyes suddenly shimmered with hopeful resilience. "Listen, Bob. Maybe we could go dancing sometime. Kick up our heels. What do you say?"

He's so unpredictable. Hurry up. He might change his mind! "That would be very nice."

He looked down at the hands of his grandfather's old Gruen. It had always given him a sense of calm. "Great. Well— I've really got to go, now. But I'll call you later."

Later? When later? What does he think? I'm going to hang around Miami Beach forever! "Sure, I'll look forward to it," she said, masking her disappointment with a friendly smile.

He offered her his now familiar wink, then turned and exited the hotel.

Eunice saw a faraway look in Bobbie's eyes. "You've got a big crush on that one."

Bobbie turned back toward her with a look of surprise. "What in the world are you talking about, Eunice?"

"Don't play coy with me. You're here three weeks. That's almost a lifetime. What have you got to lose?"

Poor foolish Eunice! What did she have to lose? Why, merely her pride and her heart! Their second meeting and —*nothing.* She looked away, unwilling to surrender her most secret thoughts to Eunice —and certainly not to herself.

Chapter Four

*W*hen Uncle Sam sent him to Miami Beach for basic training, Murray thought the Army had either gone swell or crazy. Boot camp was rough, but not as rough as life in Brooklyn. Growing up on the streets of Brownsville in the late twenties, he had been a part of a number of neighborhood skirmishes. His accent and clothing didn't especially endear him to a band of Irish youths. And, with a gang on every street corner, learning to use his fists was a matter of survival.

The enforcement branch of the mafia syndicate later known as Murder Incorporated happened to set up base near Pitkin Avenue. Bugsy Siegel, Lucky Luciano, and a band of well-dressed tough guys were common sights in the old neighborhood. Some of them were especially kind to the rag-tag street kids who followed after them admiring their handsome clothes and nice cars. Murray's mother warned her son to stay far away. But she couldn't stem his curiosity. Often, he'd pass them on the street and stand in awe of their seeming abundance and self-assured demeanor. Those first years in Brooklyn were heady times for a kid whose earliest recollections were those of war.

He read everything he could get his hands on about his adopted country, and after school took odd jobs that earned him spare change, which he obediently gave to his mother. He never really knew the man he called *Tata*.

—m—

Isadore Pickarowitz had been a baker and union organizer in Lomza when he married the sixteen-year-old Sarah Epstein in 1909 against the wishes of Sarah's father, Aaron, a well-known teacher at Lomza's famous Yeshiva. Within four years, she had mothered three children – Samuel, Murray, and Rebecca. A family tragedy would alter the course of their lives. Their fourth child, another son, was born prematurely, living only three months. Isadore was heartbroken. Things had not been easy in Lomza. Years of anti-Semitic decrees would lighten up, then begin again, making a secure life all but impossible. Now, it was decided. They would go to America. Money was tight, so Isadore would go first. Sarah and the children would follow as soon as he was financially able to send for them. But, when Isadore departed, war clouds were amassing. Within three months, Europe was embroiled in a World War, and Poland was under siege. While he struggled to make a living in New York City, his family endured years of dark cellars, intense bombing, and the horror of watching Russians and Germans killing each other right before their eyes. By 1915, the entire Russian sector of Poland, including Lomza, was occupied by the invading German army. Only eighty miles north of Warsaw, the city was swollen with refugees flooding in from surrounding towns. For Sarah and her family, it was a constant battle to stay alive. For Isadore, life had become a no man's land of worry, guilt, and fear. Finally, the armistice was signed. The bombing stopped, and the soldiers went home – leaving the scattered remnants of humanity to pick up the pieces and rebuild their lives. The burdens of the war years forced even greater economic hardships on the country. Anti-Jewish boycotts began. Aaron's Yeshiva was burned to the ground, and the family became impoverished. It would be three more years before Isadore could finally scrape together the fare to bring his wife and children to America. Sarah's mother, father, and two brothers followed a few months later.

It was 1921, and Murray was nine years old. He had lived through war, famine, pogroms, and decrees. Yet, he managed to grow into a hopeful, intelligent young boy, unusually mature for his age. And, he was excited about the prospect of coming to America and getting to know the strange man his mother kept referring to as *tata*.

The family first settled into a tiny, cold water flat in Queens before finding a small walkup in Brooklyn's Brownsville area. Another son, Benny, was born in 1922. Years of toil and worry about his family had aged Isadore. His eighteen-hour days in the bakery would make it impossible to find the time to relate to the young boy who so desperately wanted his love and guidance. At thirty-two, Isadore was a beaten man. Four years after the family was reunited, a stroke left him paralyzed and unable to work. For seven years, he would sit in his rocking chair at the window of their third-floor tenement watching life go on without him. Sometimes, he would express fear or admonition as he watched his children play in the street below by pounding on the window with his one good hand when he felt they might be in trouble. In the quiet of his desolate sanctum, his eyes would scan the neighborhood should any misguided ruffian appear and try to start a fight with his boys. Frustrated that he couldn't protect them, he felt outright pride when he saw Murray, only four years earlier a bedraggled nine-year old off the boat, negotiating his way through the mean streets of Brooklyn and asserting himself with a mean left hook. From that time until his death seven years later, Isadore's hopes and dreams for his children, and especially for the cunning, street-smart Murray who favored him in looks, remained forever hidden inside his damaged brain.

With Isadore no longer able to support the family, Sarah went to work full time in a commission bakery. The work was exhausting, the hours long, and the store always damp. Murray constantly worried about her health. The oldest son had left the family nest at seventeen to marry. His priority was caring for his young wife who required much of his attention. So, Murray, now the man of the family at fourteen, made a fateful decision. Although he loved school, he would quit and help his mother in the bakery. The added income would help pay the bills and take care of his ailing father, his sister, and three-year-old brother, Benny. Sarah's parents, now living in Cleveland, offered help. Her father, Aaron, had found a good job at a local Yeshiva and managed to put his two sons through college. He had offered to bring Murray to Cleveland for his education, but Sarah felt conflicted. Proud and immensely protective, she labored over the decision. Murray was a strong, sometimes mercurial, curious, thoughtful and independent spirit. Her father had a stern, dictatorial nature, and she worried that her son would not flourish in his custody. She went against her natural inclination and turned her father down. Although disappointed, Murray never judged her motives. Who could understand the strange emotional world of adults with their deep-seated fears and expectations. *Ma must have a pretty good reason or else I'd be going. Next case!* Privately, he wondered what could have been if he had been allowed to go to Cleveland. Perhaps, he'd be a lawyer or maybe a historian. He always loved history, especially American. For now, it seemed, he was destined to make his way in life without an education.

Coming home from PS 66 one day, Murray had a fortuitous encounter with an Irish kid hanging around his father's shoe shop across the street from the family's third-floor tenement on Douglas Street. The boy had the reputation of the being the meanest, toughest kid in the neighborhood, and Sarah had more than once warned her son to stay away from him. But this day, Murray was in no mood to suffer the kid's taunts. *Yid wimp. Kike! Yellow-bellied Jew boy!* As Isadore sat helplessly perched at the living room window, he watched his second born give the kid the licking of his life. When Sarah heard about the fight, she reprimanded her son but that evening, a smile lingered longer than usual on Isadore's normally frozen face. Murray's prowess wasn't lost on the other neighborhood toughs, and the Irish kid never bothered him again.

Murray started working out at a local gym. It might help him cope with the frustration of having to leave school. A couple of small-time boxing promoters happened by and started watching him. Amazed by his strength and agility, they wanted to take him under their wings. Murray was grateful for the attention, but he was still a teenager and Sarah was unwilling to see her son get busted up in any ring. It wasn't until he was eighteen that he actually boxed in some events around New York. Although they were amateur matches, he turned quite a few heads with his strong left hook and sudden right jab. The sweet smell of money, although small potatoes next to what the pros were making, was enticing – especially to a kid who never had any.

In an attempt to build some kind of relationship with his father, Murray would sit with Isadore after each bout and recount in vivid detail every one of his punches. Isadore could only nod and stare. Murray wondered just how much his father really understood. One night after getting his nose bloodied and broken in a match that lasted the full nine rounds, Sarah put her foot down. *Find another job, bubala!*

Isadore's condition became more precarious as he continued to suffer tiny strokes. Silent in their treachery, they slowly took away what was left of his ability to comprehend.

In 1932, he finally succumbed at the age of forty-six. Murray was particularly saddened. As he watched his mother struggle through the depression, he came to believe that his father had, through a tragic set of circumstances, let them all down.

During those first years after Isadore's death, Murray found a number of odd jobs to help the family. There was the back-breaking work in the garment district, pushing heavy clothing racks from building to building, and a summer job waiting tables at Grossinger's resort in the Catskills where he received room and board and worked for tips. He moonlighted as a bodyguard for a movie theater owner who had thoughts of trying to make a match with his beautiful, young daughter, but Murray wouldn't have anything to do with her. A spoiled, demanding brat with too much makeup— that's what he saw. With his arresting good looks and his infectious upbeat personality, there would be many girls who had special feelings for him. He never had the time to get serious about any of them. He had a family to support. His kid brother, Benny, idolized him and saw him as a ladies man, but Murray winced at that label. He liked women and enjoyed their company but a *ladies man?* That implied an artifice, a lack of respect, and Murray could never abide those macho types of guys. Always with his hands in his pocket even when money was tight, he remained a devoted son and brother to his mother and siblings. No matter what job he attempted, he always pushed himself to do better. His family was counting on him. His father's death had instilled within him a strong desire to succeed as well as an expectation of his own early demise.

Thanks to Roosevelt and the recently formed WPA in 1935, he landed a job as a painter in a renovated government office on the fourteenth floor of the Woolworth Building in downtown Manhattan. It just happened to be the headquarters of Thomas E. Dewey, newly appointed Special Prosecutor to combat organized crime. Murray was fascinated as well as curious. He did some digging and found out that Dewey's team of prosecutors included a large number of young, bright Jewish lawyers. At that time, Jewish attorneys had difficulty landing jobs in many restricted New York law firms although they had graduated from major law schools. Dewey had also chosen as his Assistant Prosecutor, a brilliant black attorney by the name of Eunice Carter. The team was selected not for political reasons – but on their own merits. Dewey, Murray decided, was a real *mensch!*

Some of the mafia figures were from the old neighborhood. Often, Murray would take the subway down to Foley Square and watch as the explosive drama of the trials unfolded. Bugsy Siegel, Louie Lepke, Lucky Luciano, Abe Reles, Hymie Weiss. Dutch Schultz. He had known a few of them, casually – sometimes pass them on Pitkin Avenue, even say hello. When Dewey's G-men took the stand, he would hear them talk of the all-night candy store under elevated subway tracks in the sleazy intersection of Saratoga and Livonia. He'd remembered hearing about it as a kid. Called Midnight Rose's, it was considered a special kind of place or else lots of grown-up guys had some sweet tooth. Maybe, they were involved in illegal activities. Still, it was hard to believe that they could have done everything the G-men had accused them of – Racketeering – Prostitution – Extortion – Narcotics – Murder! Right under his nose! He hadn't seen much – except once he remembered hiding in the back of the bakery where his father first worked as two toughs started beating up on the owner. He never understood why, but he had been told to keep his mouth shut. He always felt guilty about that – thought he should have done *something*. He hadn't been privy to any of the mob's activities. What does a kid know? He wondered why those 'Young Turk Mafioso,' as the press labeled them, had chosen that kind of life. Poverty? The lure of easy money? He was poor too – always scraping around to make a buck. Inherently, he knew the answer. *Those bums wouldn't be in this mess if they had Ma for a mother!* Sarah was the ship that steered him away from all that wasn't quite kosher. His moral compass, he called her. And, like it or not and sometimes, he didn't like it at all – he usually listened to his mother.

—ᵐᵐ—

In 1936, Murray was best man at his mother's remarriage to Kalmon Semonovich, a burly good-hearted tailor who made her laugh and treated her as if she had been woven in gold. Her new husband brought financial stability and much-needed cheer to her life. Now, she could start to enjoy some of the pleasures she had missed in those early years of Isadore's illness. A hint of rouge appeared on her pale cheeks, and her thin, graying hair with the help of a bottle, became red again.

Murray was relieved and grateful for his mother's new-found happiness. Now he might be free to travel, to see more of the country that so fascinated him as a boy. *Life outside of Brooklyn!* Maybe, he'd visit California and get into the movies!

However, in 1939, Hitler invaded Poland, and suddenly the anxieties of his childhood crept back into his world, no matter how hard he tried to push them away. In September of 1940, due to the Selective Service Act, he registered for the draft, carefully following the news of the war in Europe. He agitated over the growing situation with the Jews, thinking about his childhood friends from Lomza; wondering if any of them had been able to escape. He never talked about it with his mother. Those thoughts were best left unspoken. No need to stir up memories, especially now that Sarah seemed so happy.

In April of 1942, the Air Corps came calling. Now, a year later, he was an athletic instructor. Given his boxing skills, this assignment — training young recruits — was a perfect fit, and Murray was happy for a one-way ticket out of Brooklyn. Although he hated the regimentation, the endless marching, the abusive, small-minded officer types he had to suck up to — *keep your eyes open and your mouth shut* — he was in paradise. From the hard Brooklyn streets to Miami Beach! Not a bad assignment. Others complained about the food and the demands of military life, but these home-front requirements were the easy part. He knew something the eager, young recruits in his charge did not know. He was going over, but he wasn't coming back.

—ᴡᴡ—

About four blocks from his barracks at the Sea Isle, Murray was putting the newest inductees through calisthenics. Silently, he observed their futile attempts at simple maneuvers, one – two – three – four – half quarter – full – recover. *These guys are pathetic! Falling flat on their faces from simple knee bends!* Transforming a civilian into a soldier was not an easy assignment. Calisthenics had been no problem for him. He could do a hundred pushups on his fingers. Undaunted, he continued to call out the routine as the out-of-shape young recruits labored to follow.

Suddenly, an official black car drove up and stopped just feet away from the beach. Two captains and a colonel emerged and stood on the sidewalk talking among themselves and pointing to the soldiers. Murray strained to hear. As a medium-sized, mustached man in uniform exited the car, Murray and the others joined in a communal gasp. *Clark Gable!* Murray adored him; had seen every one of his films at the Lowe's Pitkin Theater where he worked as an usher in another of his hundred or so teenage jobs. In those first difficult years after the stock market crash, he would find the movie house a much-needed escape from the dog days of the depression. He would sit in the darkened theatre, captivated by a seemingly wealthier America that didn't know about poverty and despair. *Hollywood must be a hell of a town! Doesn't look too hard, this acting stuff. Big deal. I can do that!*

His idol was now standing ten feet behind him, and Murray was visibly nervous.

Suddenly, the colonel called out to him. "Corporal, bring the men to attention."

Murray was taken aback. *Corporal! He wasn't a corporal.* He had been promised his stripe months before but was put off with excuses. He had his own suspicions about why it hadn't come through.

Murray saluted. "Yes, sir! Atten-hut!"

The recruits obeyed. *That they could do!* He felt a momentary flicker of relief.

The physically imposing colonel moved himself into place, facing the recruits. "Men, as you already know, this is Captain Clark Gable. I'd like you to show him how the U.S. Army Air Corps is going to be handling itself when old Uncle Adolph gets a visit." He turned to Murray with a firmness of chin. "Proceed with drill work and demonstration."

Murray raised an eyebrow. *What's with this jerk? I'm an athletic instructor, not a drill instructor!* Sure, he knew how to drill, but that wasn't his job. *Oh well. Big deal.* For a moment, Murray's attention turned to Gable. He had remembered an article in the *Stars and Stripes* about the actor signing up for the Army Air Corps a few months after losing his wife in a plane crash. Murray wondered what he'd be doing in the military. The poor guy had to be over forty by now.

"**Private First Class!**"

Murray turned abruptly toward the colonel. "Yes, sir!" The old man had finally roared his true rank, but Murray was struck by the condescending tone of his voice.

"**Proceed!**"

He took a deep breath. *Oh boy!* "Yes, sir! Company, fall in!"

The miserably inept novices tried their best as Murray reversed a couple of the commands. What did *he* know? This wasn't *his* job!

The soldiers, already flustered by Gable's presence, started bumping into each other as Gable and the officers watched in muffled horror.

"First day out," offered the colonel, turning to Gable in his most apologetic voice.

The others nodded in agreement.

Gable winced, pointing to Murray. "Yeah, but what's **his** excuse?"

Murray groaned. Suddenly, all eyes were on him as drops of perspiration formed a small ridge on his brow. His days as physical instructor in paradise were definitely over. He'd be demoted and sent away to some lonely outpost in the cold, frozen north where he'd be made to do penance by repeating the drill work over and over until he got it right.

Suddenly, Gable started to laugh.

The officers looked at each other, puzzled, ready to pounce on this clueless Pfc who had the audacity to embarrass them with his poor knowledge of drill commands! Now, they regarded the movie star captain with dumb surprise. And, in a matter of seconds, *they* were laughing too.

Murray could feel his blood pressure rise. In another time, if some guy was making fun of him, he might have reacted with his fists. All he could do now was stand at attention like an idiot with a passive look on his face and let them have their fun. This was the U.S. Army. Officers were laughing. That had to be good, considering the alternative.

Again, the colonel turned his steely gaze toward Murray. "As you were."

Their amusement over, Gable and the officers piled back into their dark sedan.

Relieved, but just in case they were still watching — Murray let out a simple command. "Company. Right face. Forward. March." As the recruits started moving in a less than perfect line down the beach, he turned back to watch Gable's car speed out of sight. A mighty weight had been lifted. He had managed to fool them all, again.

Chapter Five

*H*er hope of finding some peace and relaxation stalled. Eunice developed a fever. Feeling guilty about calling her a tomato, Bobbie hung around the hotel attending to her friend's every need. Her daily gin game with Max, the kindly French refugee she befriended, helped ease some of the boredom. It didn't hurt that she usually won. Secretly, she was hoping Murray might come around. But what was the point? *Don't get involved...*

After three days, Eunice's fever finally broke and her tomato face peeled off. Bobbie felt emancipated. After a hectic afternoon exploring the pricy stores on Lincoln Road, the girls sat in a Collins Avenue soda shop trying to cool off. Outside, rows of nimble young soldiers were confidently marching to "I've Got Sixpence" as the heat of the day bore down on them with oppressive rage, tearing at their fortitude, demanding their submission. Bobbie cringed as she watched a number of boys collapse from exhaustion. She kept searching for Murray among the sea of faces, reprimanding herself for allowing him to dwell in her thoughts.

She saw a pathetic look in Eunice's eyes as she observed

her sipping her double-dip ice cream soda and staring wistfully at the passing troops. *Why did she have to look so needy?*

Suddenly, Bobbie's attention was drawn to two soldiers standing in front of the window, one motioning a desire to join them. Eunice seemed to be beckoning him with a wink and a nod.

"**What** are you doing?" cried Bobbie.

"What does it look like?"

"Are you nuts? What will they think of us?"

"With any luck —that we're they're types!"

Eunice's glasses came off, and in a flash, the soldiers were inside the restaurant standing in front of their table. Bobbie felt a growing apprehension as the one swarthy soldier leaned in.

"You girls want some company?"

"Can't say no to the U.S. Army!" Eunice grinned.

"Army Air Corps, honey, and don't you forget it!"

As Eunice coyly gestured for them to sit, her hand casually brushed against a glass of water, spilling the contents all over Bobbie's brand-new sun dress.

Bobbie began wiping furiously as the two men pulled up chairs around the table. She regarded them with a cool restraint. Both were captains. The second soldier didn't seem too dangerous, really. A thin, nervous looking man, he sat cowering uncomfortably beside his more aggressive buddy.

"My name's Frank. Frank Russo. He's Harry."

Harry Sweet grunted a weak hello. Bobbie sensed that coming into the restaurant wasn't *his* idea.

"I'm Eunice. She's Bobbie."

Bobbie smiled, reluctantly. After all, hadn't Eunice put up with *her* flirtation? How bad could it be? They'll all have a nice talk. Eunice wouldn't be unhappy anymore, and Bobbie wouldn't feel guilty she had suggested Miami Beach.

As the minutes passed into an hour, Bobbie realized it wasn't going to be easy to walk away. Frank reveled in Eunice's attraction to him, and Eunice grew radiant with his attention. Bobbie sat stoically, exchanging a mutual sense of discomfort with Harry until a waitress with a decidedly superior attitude appeared at the table.

"You boys plannin' on orderin' or just lookin'?"

Frank raised an eyebrow. "Maybe we'll order, or maybe we'll look. You got a problem with that?"

"Frank." Harry reprimanded in a quiet voice.

"Like maybe it's against the law what we're doing?"

The waitress leaned over the table, eyeballing him. "Like I said, you orderin' or lookin'?" *Too hot headed,* thought Bobbie. *I bet this jerk hauls off and smacks her one. Definitely not a good match for Eunice.*

The waitress continued staring at Frank. Bobbie felt her comfort level beginning to drop.

"Give me a tongue sandwich on rye." he finally announced.

Bobbie took a deep breath. *Okay, maybe he's not so hot-headed, after all.*

"Tongue on rye!" She glared at Harry. "And you?"

Harry looked up, meekly. "You got any bromo seltzer?"

Frank regarded his friend with inquiring concern.

"Sorry. Frank. I got a bad stomach."

The waitress rolled her eyes, shook her head and walked away. Bobbie wished she had brought the Alka-Seltzer tablets she left in her room.

As Frank leaned in toward Eunice, Bobbie saw in his face – a roadmap of lust and passion.

"I'm sorry. Did you lovely girls **want something**?"

It was his manner. Coarse, inappropriate, suggestive. *What did he mean? Did we **want something!***

She had to speak up. It would be better in the end. Eunice would thank her later. "I don't think so. In fact, we have to be going."

"What's the hurry?" Frank demanded.

"There's no hurry, Frank!" cried Eunice.

"Good. So, how about us showing you girls around town?"

Bobbie was undaunted. "You just ordered a tongue sandwich."

"So. How about it," he continued, ignoring her and fixing his gaze on Eunice. "We could show you Haulover Beach and maybe take in the dog races. Got a two-day pass. Might as well make the most of it."

"Great!" Eunice shouted, throwing up her hands.

"You're just going to leave your tongue sandwich?" Bobbie persisted.

Frank stared hard at her before turning back to Eunice. "What's with her and the tongue sandwich?"

"There's a war on," offered Bobbie. "Can't let food go to waste!"

"She's just joking, aren't you Bobbie?" Eunice's eyes were smoking.

"Well, actually, I'm not—"

"Joking, huh? Okay. Good! It's settled, then. Let's go."

A pained look hardened on Bobbie's face. "Go... where?"

Frank proceeded to pull the chair out for Eunice. As she stood, her hand again brushed the side of Bobbie's water glass, tipping it over. Bobbie struggled to keep the cool liquid away from her dress, and for a split second, she wondered if Eunice had done it on purpose. *No. She's just so enamored with Captain Big Shot, lover boy, she doesn't know what she's doing. Besides, her glasses are off – a definite peril to everyone around her.* "Look," Bobbie began. "Why don't you all go ahead. I have a slight headache and—"

"Okay, fine." said Frank.

"No, Bobbie. You have to come too. Doesn't she Frank?"

Frank grunted. Who needed a dame like that around cramping his style!

Bobbie saw it – that pathetic look in Eunice's eyes. She was a sucker for that look. *Why does she need me around? She'd have a much better time without me.* She looked over at Harry – the picture of boyish innocence – then back at Frank glaring at her, hoping she would disappear. Suddenly, it all became clear. She would go along to save Eunice from doing something stupid. She nodded an okay and saw the flash of disappointment in Frank's eyes.

As he and Eunice rushed out of the shop, Bobbie looked over at Harry, waiting politely for her to make a move. *Oh God! How do I get into these situations. I'm just a pushover!*

Bobbie and Harry obediently followed them out the door.

—⚹—

They walked endless stretches of beach and later attended the dog races. Bobbie averted her eyes during most of it. *Poor, overworked greyhounds, huffing and puffing their way around the track. What kind of life is that for a dog?* Frank explained that the dogs loved to run. That they were born to the sport. *Yeah, sure. Like chickens love a lion's den!* She hadn't made a fuss. In fact, she hadn't said a word all afternoon because Eunice seemed so happy, but this little adventure would be her last. So, when Frank suggested they go to a friend's apartment for a drink, Bobbie was ready. Her headache had become quite unbearable. She needed to get back to the hotel. But Eunice would have none of it. They'd get her an aspirin, and she'd be fine.

Broken by the force of Eunice's urging, Bobbie relented – again. She'd hang around to make sure her gullible girlfriend didn't turn into another wartime statistic.

—⚹—

Frank and Eunice had disappeared into the bedroom of the unadorned apartment. The modest furnishings suggested its use as a communal retreat. As the easy sounds of Glen Miller wafted through the closed door, Bobbie's imagination was going wild with thoughts of late-night assignations and lurid sex scenes played out between soldiers and their willing concubines.

She sat trapped on a sloping cloth couch in the living room. Harry hadn't uttered a sound all afternoon. Now, the words were pouring out.

"See, I didn't want to jump into this marriage. Don't get me wrong. She's a great girl, and I love her, but what if something should happen to me? We've got this kid on the way and everything. Of course, I'm thrilled about that, don't get me wrong. I always wanted a kid. I was an only child. It was kind of lonely growing up. Pop wasn't home much, and Ma never spoke about him. It was as if he never existed. Of course, he always made sure there was food on the table..."

—⁂—

Two hours later and Bobbie had a terrible urge to run screaming from the apartment, but she couldn't be rude. Harry needed to talk.

"I think the biggest problem was that I never really knew my father. I used to envy the kids that played baseball with their dads. He was on the road a lot. He'd come home once every few weeks, and they'd start going at each other. I never remember a quiet moment when Pop was home. That's probably why I was so scared of marriage..."

It was almost eight o'clock. Her body had gone rigid as

she struggled for an excuse to leave. She hadn't gotten up, not even to go to the bathroom. Harry was so intense about everything, so absorbed in his angst, she thought he might hurt himself. She'd come back from the bathroom, and there he'd be – with a knife to his throat! She couldn't risk it. He needed desperately to open up, and it was her duty to listen. *Such a sweet man. What in the world does he have in common with Frank?* Of course, she and Eunice weren't exactly peas in a pod. *Eunice!* Her thoughts suddenly turned to what her friend might be doing behind the closed door of the bedroom. Her stomach tightened and she looked longingly toward the front door. *Get me out of here!*

"I haven't been able to see her in months. The doctor doesn't think she should travel. I might ship out and never see her or my kid again." Harry hesitated, finally looking over to his new-found friend. "So, what do **you** do, Bobbie?"

The sky had suddenly opened after a dreary storm. This unexpected reprieve was a sign. *Enough is enough.* "Listen, Harry, I'm just beat. Do you think you could get me a cab?"

"Sure, but what about—" He gestured toward the bedroom.

She attempted to stand, but her knees had locked from being so long in one position, and it took a moment to get her bearing.

She walked into the long hallway of the apartment. Eunice's dress and one shoe lay in a heap on the floor leading to the bedroom. She braced herself, then returned with a hollow feeling in the pit of her stomach. She was probably just hungry. She hadn't eaten all day. Maybe, it was tension. It would always begin in her stomach. She was being ridiculous, worrying about Eunice. Certainly, the woman knew what she was doing. She felt conflicted about leaving, but what else could she do? Open the door on them? What if they were in the middle of — she'd never forgive herself, and Eunice would probably never speak to her again – which wasn't such an unappealing thought. Still, she couldn't remember ever seeing her friend so lighthearted — not even with that jailbird boyfriend who dumped her at the alter eight years before. She mustn't be judgmental. Passion made people do peculiar things. Of course, she wouldn't know. She'd never felt that way except in some school-girl crushes. She prided herself on the knowledge that her heart never ruled her head.

"Look, Harry, do me a favor, and see that she gets back to the hotel."

"Sure. Don't worry. Frank's a good man. She'll be okay."

There was something so real about Harry. The concern for his wife — the way he unburdened himself to a stranger without feeling embarrassed or apologetic. She thought him somewhat of a sap when they first met. Suddenly, she felt a kinship and a respect. It was a lesson. She had always been a good listener, but passing judgment was something she fought against but sometimes couldn't help. Harry's words appeared honorable. She had to believe him. What choice did she have? More importantly, she wanted desperately to leave. Her teeth were floating, her stomach was growling, and her head was spinning. She turned and gave him her sweetest smile, grabbed her purse and flew out of the apartment.

"By the way, thanks a lot for listening," he said, trying to keep up with her. "Hope I didn't go on too long."

"Oh no, Harry. It was all very interesting."

—⁓—

The clock on the bed stand pointed to midnight. Bobbie lay awake consumed with guilt. Why hadn't she insisted they leave together? But Eunice was a grown woman. What could she do? Walk in that bedroom and demand she come to her senses? What right had she to interfere, or even assume it was so bad? Just because *she* didn't have the guts to do the same. Nowadays, there were two kinds of women. The V girls, who'd do it with anybody, and the nice girls who wanted to but didn't. Eunice was somewhere in between. Secretly, she envied that part of Eunice's nature that could be so trusting, so open, especially after a string of disappointing love affairs. Bobbie was too circumspect, forever analyzing her thoughts and feelings. On the one hand – but then on the other – until she squeezed the life force right out of it. A blank canvas pleading to be drawn with more definition – much too logical – smart, but small town. *What a pathetic combination!* She remembered part of a poem she had learned in high school – "A ship with a furled sail at rest in the harbor. In truth, it pictures not my destination but my life." A ship going nowhere. *Afraid of taking chances? Afraid she might get hurt?* Quick courtships were common nowadays. Gone were those old taboos of family consent and long engagements. The war brought different priorities. But, in moments of passion, promises were made — and broken. *There's the rub!* She had read too many tragic stories. The newspapers were filled with them. She sat up remembering the promise she had made to her father. And, in an instant, the burden of her distracting thoughts lifted. Once again, good sense prevailed! *No sir! It wasn't going to happen to **her!***

Chapter Six

B obbie had worried, needlessly. Eunice not only survived the night but thrived as she began spending as much of her waking and non-waking hours as possible in Frank's company, and Bobbie relished the opportunity to finally be on her own. It had been almost a week since she had seen Murray. The image of him sitting in the sand, locked in that childhood memory, whirled around inside her head. Perhaps, he had forgotten her; maybe he already shipped out. She found solace in her daily gin games. An older, divorced man had asked her on a number of occasions to join him for dinner. She declined, preferring the company of Max and his refugee friends. They responded to her interest and concern, needing to remember, often afraid they wouldn't be believed. She would listen to them recount, in harrowing detail, stories of escape and hardship. Max, she learned, had fled within a day of the German invasion of France, going into hiding in the south of the country, then traveling by foot into Spain before the Jewish Agency helped him locate family in the States. He saw himself as one of the lucky ones. Safe harbor had become impossible now. He spoke to her about the disappearance of vast numbers of Jews not only from France but from other countries as well. He felt encouraged by a mass rally planned later that week in Madison Square Garden, earnestly hoping it would awaken Roosevelt and the State Department to do something for the hundreds of thousands of people still trying to escape.

—⚭—

One morning as she sat in the lobby reading, Bobbie was drawn to the stifled voices of the desk clerk and his wife arguing in their native French. Although she tried to ignore them, their unusual behavior was constantly drawing her back.

Sitting nearby, Max looked up from his paper and noticed the concern on her face. "What's the matter, Bobbie? Can I be of help?"

"The desk clerk and his wife. They seem so—"

The wife hit her fist hard on the desk and ran from the lobby into the interior of the hotel. As some of the guests looked over, her husband looked toward them and smiled. "Forgive my wife. She is very high strung and not feeling well today."

This seemed to satisfy the others, but Bobbie couldn't get the incident out of her mind. Something quite terrible had happened. She saw it in the passionate manner of their altercation, yet she couldn't understand it from her limited high school French.

"They are disturbed because of what they have just read," Max explained, handing her his newspaper.

Her eyes scanned the bold-faced article at the top of the page. "America's most muscular man, nineteen-year-old James Doty, a strapping youth with bulging biceps and barrel chest, was rejected for army duty —" She looked up, confused. "because of a heart murmur? I'm sorry, Max, I don't see what —"

"I am afraid you are looking at the wrong story, my dear." He pointed to a much smaller article further down the page.

As she perused the piece, her face reddened. "This doesn't make sense, Max. Why would this be—"

"It's quite simple. The Rumanian government wants to sell seventy thousand Jews to the allies at fifty dollars a head. Your government thinks it is too dangerous to receive so many refugees from an enemy country."

"Too dangerous? How could they be a danger?"

"They think they might be spies."

"Spies! But that's ridiculous!" Bobbie looked back at the agitated desk clerk pretending to busy himself with some paperwork. She felt her stomach go queasy. She turned back to Max. "Do they have family there?"

He leaned over to her, an echo of regret in his voice. "It seems that all of their family are there."

She was burning with an undefined rage. It was the closest she had come to personally understanding some of what was going on in Europe, and she felt overwhelmed by a feeling of helplessness. She knew some of the facts, already. Max had simply put a human face on them. Jews were a relative minority in America, a little more than three percent of the population, and they had no real voice. Many supported Roosevelt. A few even had prominent positions in his administration, but it didn't translate into power. She had listened intently as Max spoke of atrocities and mass executions in Eastern Europe. She read the same reports at the beginning of 1943 — reports that made their way into the newspapers, but were relegated to the back pages and given such small priority that she couldn't bring herself to believe them. Certainly, if it were true, Roosevelt would do *something!* She felt the room spinning. She quickly ran to the front door and opened it wide, taking in some fresh air. She watched a contingent of confident young men marching down the street, singing another cheery Irving Berlin song. Her head throbbing, she slammed the door and ran back to her room, tears streaming down her cheeks.

—⟶—

Murray lay in his damp, uncomfortable pup tent on bivouac. Though swollen and hurting from a number of insect bites, he couldn't stop thinking about the girl with the carnation in her hair. By now, she may have left Miami. *No.* He wouldn't let himself believe that. It was all he had to hold on to this night. He had to think positive in order to keep *other* thoughts from taking over. He had planned to ask her to a USO dance, but his unit was called to the

Everglades for almost a week of intense training. *Why did the Air Corps have to spring everything on him? Why couldn't they be more civilized?* Most of the men found it quite wretched, wading through alligator infested swamps with carnivorous mosquitoes pouncing with delight. He had volunteered for a couple of difficult maneuvers not because he felt brave but because he was confident no one was going to get killed. There would be no shot-off faces of half dead men begging for water. Of course, he hadn't anticipated those damn mosquitoes! A few guys in the unit seemed to resent his enthusiasm. They thought him guilty of an exhausting amount of energy. Of course, he couldn't wait to go over and help fight those *Nazi bastards,* but he knew he didn't have what it took to be a good military man. The numbing ritual, the loss of identity, the surrendering of mind and body, not to mention the marching — the endless marching! Twenty to thirty miles every day and they never leave the beach! One hundred and twenty-eight steps per minute. He had counted! *What in hell did that have to do with battle, anyway?* He had always been his own man, never good at taking orders. Now, he had to sublimate that part of himself in order to survive. And, he was, after all, a survivor.

It was raining and damp in the Everglades that final night of bivouac. He closed his eyes and felt the gentle touch of Bobbie's delicate cheek brush against his sunburnt face, her body wrapped tight around his mosquito-bitten legs, and for now, he was safe and warm.

—⁂—

Ten o'clock. Bobbie lay on her bed. She had been feeling a deep sense of apprehension ever since the incident with the desk clerk and his wife. Maybe, too much knowledge wasn't so good after all. It would have been better not to ask. Not to know. She felt drained. Her head throbbed with a deep, unspecific ache. She had a sinking feeling as if she had been somewhere too horrible, yet nowhere at all. She was a small-town girl, protected, even coddled. Now, it seemed a harsh intruder had cruelly taken away her innocence.

The constant static of the radio jolted her out of a deep sleep. She looked over at the clock on the bed stand. Two a.m. Eunice hadn't returned. It was her last night in Miami Beach. Her last night with Frank. In just hours, she'd be leaving to catch the train back to Detroit and her assembly line job at the Willow Run defense plant. She had become more confident, more self-assured than Bobbie had ever seen her — all because some wise guy soldier appeared to genuinely care about her. How would Eunice handle her separation from Frank? She hadn't spoken much about him since that first day. Bobbie wasn't one to pry, but it seemed unlike her to be so guarded. Perhaps, she was afraid to reveal too much. That it might somehow encourage the evil eye. *No.* Eunice wasn't the superstitious type. Bobbie was usually the cautious one — so careful, so protective that she figured she'd never find anyone to love her. Yet she longed to feel cherished. To have someone tell her how wonderful she was. Too much of a romantic with a little of the cynic thrown in, that's *her* problem. Who was she kidding? How could she ever hope to find *that* kind of happiness. It only existed in novels, and most of them ended tragically – *Madame Bovary, Anna Karenina* — she'd read them all. As for the soldier she had met, casually; she hadn't seen him in days. He must have shipped out. She had searched the newspapers looking for something that might give her a hint. She thought of going to the Sea Isle Hotel. Wasn't that where he said he was staying? *No. Leave it alone.* After all, she only saw him for a few minutes on two occasions. What right did she have to even think — *Don't get involved..* She heard on the radio that the Russians were pushing back the Germans at Stalingrad, and the allies were starting night raids over Berlin. How difficult for families of soldiers, always wondering, waiting for word. She felt torn – wishing she had gotten to know him better, grateful she hadn't. Soon, she fell back into a deep sleep.

—⚡—

Three o'clock. She awoke to the sound of the key turning carelessly in the lock. She watched Eunice slowly enter the room. "God, Eunice, you scared me for a minute. You okay?"

"I'm…fine." She walked over to her bed and sat down, staring at the wall.

"Heard on the radio tonight – they're starting daylight raids on Berlin."

"That's nice."

"Maybe, the war will be over before we know it."

"Maybe." She lowered her head and began to weep.

Bobbie's stomach tightened. She jumped out of bed and ran to her side. "Eunice, what's the matter?"

Eunice's eyes were heavy with tears. "I know you think I'm nuts, but I loved him."

Stay strong. Don't panic. "No, I don't think you're nuts."

"Yeah. You do. But I didn't mean this to happen."

Oh God. Here it comes. Bobbie tried to take her hand.

"Don't patronize me, Bobbie," she said, pulling away. "I'm not a baby. The worst part is, he'll never know how I feel."

What is she talking about? "You two didn't plan to — He didn't say anything about—"

"He didn't meet me tonight. I waited for almost an hour. Finally, I went to his hotel." She hesitated, unable to form the words. "They told me…his company shipped out. Gone. Just like that. He knew he'd be leaving, and he didn't even say goodbye. Not even a note – can you believe that?" She broke into a deep wail.

Bobbie struggled to make sense of it. That day in the soda shop had been mostly forgotten in the joy of Eunice's rebirth. They seemed so happy together. Even Bobbie had been fooled. What kind of comfort could she give? What could she say? I told you so? This was hardly the time for a reprimand. She suddenly felt a deep loathing for the soldier. "Where did you go Eunice? It's after three."

"To a movie. Yeah. Can you believe it? I sat through two movies, but I can't seem to remember what they were."

Say something. She's in such pain. "I'm so sorry about this, Eunice, but maybe he didn't know he was going to ship out."

Eunice raised her head. Her red eyes suddenly twinkled, begging for an affirmation of her deepest wish. "What are you saying? You think he really didn't know?"

"Sure. Sometimes, for security reasons, they don't tell the guys when they're going to ship out. I read it somewhere." She had read it somewhere – in the desperate stories of women left behind, the literature of broken hearts that had filled her head with so much apprehension. Anyway, it sounded plausible. *Dear God. Please let Eunice believe me!*

Eunice's brow furrowed. She sat in silence – her head perched thoughtfully in her hands. After a moment, she looked up.

Stay strong, thought Bobbie. *Don't let her see your doubts.*

"I know what you're trying to do, and I appreciate it. Don't get me wrong. But it kind of serves me right for getting mixed up with a soldier. You tried to tell me, but I wouldn't listen."

Bobbie winced. A stranger had bared his soul to her on a beach, and something within her stirred. If Eunice only knew that she'd give all she possessed for a chance to see him just once more. "Don't rush to judge him, Eunice. Maybe, someday, he'll come back for you. You just never know."

Eunice brightened, and Bobbie felt a small measure of relief. *We all could use a little delusion,* she thought, trying to vindicate Frank's actions and justify her own little white lie. The problem was that she had read too many of those magazine articles and remembered all too well. Her first impression was right. Guys like Frank don't come back. She took a tissue from the small pocket of her nightdress and wiped the remaining tears from Eunice's mascara-stained eyes.

"You know what, kiddo? You should try to get some sleep. Things always look better in the morning. I'm sure it'll all work out. Frank will probably contact you when he gets settled. But, you've got a train to catch, and if it's anything like that cattle car we took coming in, this will be the last sleep you get till Detroit."

The memory of their harrowing trip to Miami seemed to break Eunice's mood. A tiny smile crept onto her face. "Thanks Bobbie."

"For what?"

"For putting up with my craziness. I guess I've been acting pretty much like a fool."

Bobbie's eyes welled up. She wanted to scream out — *You're not alone!* That *she*, Miss Goodie Two shoes, Miss *don't get involved with a soldier* Feinman had been an even bigger fool. "Don't you think that, Eunice. Not for a minute. You are nobody's fool! All I know is — we're both a little crazy. That's for sure. Must be something in the Miami air, don't you think?"

The girls sat together in the silence of the night, each absorbed in the prison of her own private thoughts.

—◊◊◊—

Eunice was up early and packed her one small suitcase in record time. Considering that neither of them slept much, Bobbie was surprised at her energy. They stood together on the steps of the hotel as the taxi pulled up. If Eunice had been thinking about Frank, nothing more was said.

"Promise, Bobbie, you'll call me as soon as you get back?"

"I promise. You're sure you're going to be okay?"

Eunice laughed. "I'm fine. Never know who you're going to meet on a crowded train!"

They embraced. Eunice jumped into the cab, rolled down the window and waved a hearty goodbye. Bobbie watched the taxi disappear up Collins Avenue. And, all the time, she thought **she** was the actress!

Murray's face suddenly flashed before her. She closed her eyes and gasped for a breath. A survivor wrenched from a burning ship just in the nick of time! What happened to Eunice could have happened to her. *Thank God Mama's joining me in a couple of days.* Her mother would be her buffer —her protection from these silly, girlish fantasies. She sank down on the hotel steps, her head reeling with dark thoughts of what might have been.

Chapter Seven

Wearing a wide-brimmed sun hat, Minnie Feinman emerged from the train, grateful to be alive. She had survived the journey. The rest would be easy. Her best friend, Bertha Shatterhoff, begged her to come to Florida for her granddaughter's wedding. Minnie hated train travel, especially nowadays, but she finally relented. *So, how bad could it be?* She would suffer it —the train ride **and** the wedding —for her friend.

—⁓—

After pogroms in Poland made their lives a living nightmare, young Minnie, her father, stepmother, five sisters and one brother emigrated to America in the late 1890s. Forty-five years later, she had managed to hold on to her accent and, more importantly, her sense of humor. Most of her teenage years were spent in the New York sweatshops. At eight cents an hour, on a good day if she worked twelve hours, she could make almost a dollar. Her handsome second cousin, Morris, who escaped to America to avoid the Czar's army, also worked in the shops. With his industrious nature, he would be her ticket out of the harshness of her new life. He wasn't such a wonderful dancer, but you can't have everything! Besides, he told a good story, and he was from Kikol, her hometown. *So, how bad could it be?* Four children later, she had comfortably settled in to her pre-scribed role of wife and mother, subordinating her fun-loving personality to that of her strong-willed husband. Yet, Minnie still enjoyed a good dance and a good joke, and she could dream with the best of them.

Bobbie spotted her mother in the crowd. "Mama!" She ran over, tenderly embracing her. "How was the trip?"

Minnie shrugged her shoulders. "I'm not saying it was so good. I'm not saying it was so bad. It was...a trip."

A skinny, young private walked over and tipped his hat. "It was great meeting you, Mrs. Feinman, and thanks for the advice."

Minnie started to giggle. "For me, it was good too! And you're very welcome."

The soldier bent over and planted a kiss on her cheek, then strolled away. She blushed as she watched him go.

Bobbie stared after him, then turned back to her mother with a subtle grin. "I'm not saying it was good. I'm not saying it was bad?"

"Okay, so it was more good than bad."

She struggled with her mother's small but weighty suit-case. "So, what advice did you give him?"

"Since when do I give advice? I listened to him. That's all."

Bobbie threw her a knowing smile. It had been ten days

since she had seen her — ten days and a myriad of emotions. But now, everything would be okay. Mama was fun to be with, but more importantly, she had good sense.

Bobbie decided she wouldn't say anything about Murray, not yet. *What for?* Dragging the cumbersome case, she escorted her coy and clever little mother to an awaiting cab.

—⟋⟍⟍⟍—

Murray and his buddy, Joe, crept discreetly onto the lawn of one of the small beach hotels just north of the Rony Plaza. This night there was a full moon. It was Murray's first effort with a partner, and he wanted to make sure everything was perfect. He couldn't risk getting Joe in trouble, too. They huddled behind a hedge and spoke in whispered tones. Murray's eyes carefully scanned the area directly in front of the hotel.

"It's clear, Joe. I'm gonna go."

"You sure it's okay?"

"No problem. Let's do it!"

Murray quickly moved from the cover of the hedge and hurried up to the side of the hotel. After one more look around, he ran over to the "No Jews or Dogs Allowed" sign that hung to the left of the big palm tree and signaled Joe to follow. Together, they gave the sign a hearty yank. Murray was surprised that it offered so little resistance. Not like the other times when working alone, he struggled and was almost caught. He thought about it before accepting

Joe's offer to help. If the military found out, there would be hell to pay. But he had been bothered by those signs when he first came down to Miami and decided they had to go. If the army couldn't take care of it, he would — and, four hands were always better than two.

"See what I told you, Joe? Nothing to it. Let's get the hell out of here."

The soldiers ran across the lawn, disappearing into the night.

—◊◊—

Bobbie pleaded with the desk clerk and obtained a more spacious room with a window. Though not exactly an ocean view, it at least offered more light than the stuffy, depressing little room she had shared with Eunice.

After a day of unwinding from the perils of her trip, Minnie was now prepared in her yellow, lace outfit and matching hat to take on the Shatterhoff wedding. She would have preferred spending the evening with her daughter rather than the old ladies she'd probably be seated with at the dinner party afterward. Without her husband there, who was going to ask her to dance? Probably, some aging pensioner without his teeth.

—◊◊—

Mother and daughter stood patiently outside the Wellington waiting the arrival of Bertha's nineteen-year-old nephew,

Myron. Minnie had mentioned that he couldn't see very well even though he wore glasses. Bobbie tried to persuade her to take a taxi, but Minnie wouldn't hear of it. Her friend would be insulted. How dangerous could it be, riding with the boy? He only drove five miles an hour.

"I only hope they got something good to eat. It shouldn't be a total loss."

"You don't mind that I'm not going, Mama?"

Minnie shrugged her shoulders. "Why should we both have to suffer? Just stay in the hotel, and don't talk to any strange men."

Bobbie smiled. *Strange men?* She still hadn't mentioned anything about Murray.

Minnie had noticed a couple of older men from the hotel glaring at her daughter, and she was convinced that at least one of them had unhealthy intentions. Of course, Bobbie hadn't been aware of anyone with unhealthy intentions, but how could she argue with Mama? Maybe she was thinking of Max and her other card playing buddies, all in their late sixties. Minnie had been advised of their daily gin games and that Max was fanatical in his quest to steal at least one win.

—⁓—

Wearing heavy, horned-rimmed spectacles so weighted they kept falling down his nose, his pink jacket shimmering in the late afternoon sun, Myron Shatterhoff drove his battered looking 1935 Ford up to the hotel, maneuvering to the edge of the curb in such a precarious manner that a man standing on the sidewalk had to jump away to avoid being hit.

"*Oy gevalt,*" offered Minnie.

"Hello, Mrs. Feinman!" Myron yelled, oblivious to how close he had come to killing someone. "Sorry I'm late. You won't believe what happened!"

"Myron, darling," she replied with a sigh. "I'm afraid I would. So, this is my daughter, Bobbie."

Bobbie glared at him with immediate dislike as she helped her mother into the car. "Mama, are you sure you're going to be okay? Maybe we should—"

"I'm fine. You shouldn't worry. Although…."

"What, Mama?"

"A little prayer wouldn't hurt."

Mama's humor, but Bobbie couldn't dismiss her own uneasiness as she watched Myron attempt to thrust the car forward half a foot. It chortled to an abrupt stop. *That's it! Mama's getting out of there!* She vaulted like a leopard toward the car.

Myron managed to find the elusive gear and shift correctly.

"Sorry about that, Mrs. Feinman. I think I've got it now."

"You shouldn't worry, Myron darling. I don't drive either." She turned around in her seat, rolling her eyes and offering Bobbie a brave wave as they sped off at five miles an hour— smoke billowing from the engine in protest.

Bobbie had felt a vague apprehension all day. Seeing her mother driving away with this *idiot* only fueled her discomfort. She was desperate for a game of cards and ran back into the hotel to find Max.

—⁓—

Max enjoyed his gin games with Bobbie. They were a mighty challenge, and she was certainly a formidable adversary. He sensed all evening that something was troubling her. She seemed distracted. Still, it didn't stop her from winning most of the games.

Around eight o'clock, after a particularly quick gin that had surprised even her, Bobbie looked up for a moment. She felt flushed, and her hands started shaking. *It was an apparition! He hadn't shipped out!* Her heart began pounding so loudly she looked to see if her card partners heard it.

—⁓—

Murray walked into the hotel, his eyes scanning the room. When he saw her, he hesitated, preparing. *Not yet!* He walked to another part of the lobby and started a conversation with a couple of soldiers he pretended to recognize, continuing to eye her from afar.

Bobbie furiously sorted her cards; her fingers nervously placing and replacing them in different patterns in her hand.

Murray circled back. *Now!* He walked over to her with a big smile on his face. "Hi Bob. What's cookin'?"

She looked up, feigning surprise. "Well, hello again. Nothing much. What's cookin' with you?" She was grateful she was able to project such a matter-of-fact tone. *What an actress!*

Murray cleared his throat. "I was wondering. There's a new USO show in Flamingo Park. I thought you might like to go. Lots of terrific music…"

She had been reconciled, thinking he was on a troop ship headed for England. Yet, there he was! Standing before her! Asking for a date! She heard herself answer. She had no control, none at all. "Sure. I'd love to. That'll be great fun!"

Murray was taken aback. He hadn't expected it to be so easy. It had been over a week. He didn't know if she'd still be there or even interested in seeing him again. "Terrific! Good. Okay. So, shall we go?"

Bobbie gasped. *He means right this minute!* In all the tumult, she had forgotten about her card game. Carefully, she turned to Max. "Would you mind?"

Max raised an eyebrow. *Does he mind! Ha!* Maybe now he could find a less adept partner and win a game. "Go, Bobbie. Do me a favor."

Two other players sitting at a nearby card table, both casualties of her phenomenal luck, nodded in agreement.

Bobbie turned to Murray with a laugh. "I guess he doesn't like the way I play. You mind if I leave a note for my mother?"

"Your mother?"

"Yeah. Eunice went back home. Mama came down for a wedding."

Bobbie tried to concentrate on her message to Minnie but her hands were clearly trembling. She hoped he wouldn't notice. When she finished, she handed the note to the desk clerk as Murray offered her his arm. She smiled and willingly obliged. *A perfect gentleman!*

As they started to walk out of the hotel, Murray noticed a number of hotel guests, including Max, watching them. He leaned over and whispered into Bobbie's ear. She laughed and nodded.

Both turned toward the awaiting throng and bowed. Max, whose fascination for the game of gin had been momentarily interrupted, began to clap his hands. The other guests joined in, expressing their mutually felt approval.

Bobbie looked at them, surprised and embarrassed. *The entire lobby was applauding! Had everyone noticed?* Perhaps, she hadn't been as private about her feelings as she had thought. Maybe — not the great actress she had assumed.

—⧑—

Flamingo Park on this calm Miami evening served as a perfect backdrop. The ocean breeze had cooled off the brutal heat of the day, and the moon glistened as the dynamic orchestra let loose with some of Bobbie's favorite melodies. *It was so...*she tried not to let herself think it...*romantic.* Murray's agility on the makeshift dance floor amazed her as she struggled to keep up. He twirled her with such frenzy and danced with so much joy, she almost went limp from excitement. *After all this time. To spend a couple hours* *together!* Of course, any night out would be terrific after her last ten days with Eunice. That's what that faint parent voice kept telling her, although she was hardly listening to it now.

The show over, they took a leisurely walk down Ocean Drive. She wanted to put her arms around him and thank him for coming for her, for taking her away from the gloom of the past few days, but something inside kept pulling her back. "Really enjoyed the evening."

"Yeah," he said, beaming. "What did you think of that orchestra, huh?"

"A great orchestra."

"Almost as good as Benny Goodman's."

"You're some dancer, Murray! I had trouble keeping up."

He smiled. He loved to dance. Ever since swing became the craze of the country, he had been going to one dance hall after the other. "You're not so bad yourself, Bob. You can even follow me!"

"You don't need a partner."

"Yeah, that's what they say — but it's always nice."

They shared a laugh. She liked his sense of humor. *That's important,* she thought. *That is, it would be important if...*

Murray leaned over and placed a sweet kiss on her cheek. All the blood in her body was rushing straight to her face! Did he notice? She passionately wanted him to kiss her on the mouth. What was he waiting for?

He began checking the doors of cars parked on the

street. Finding one unlocked, he opened it and quickly motioned for her to join him inside.

She hesitated. "Aren't we taking a big chance, Murray? What if the owners—I mean, what would it look like if—"

"Hurry up, Bob!"

She couldn't think straight. *Oh God!* She jumped into the passenger side of the well-appointed Nash and slammed the door. For a moment, there was silence as she sat rigid. "Well. Here we are. I guess this finally gives us a chance to talk." *A chance to talk?* Who was she kidding? All she wanted was to feel the warmth of his lips against hers. They were finally alone, and she was sounding like some mindless teenager on her first date.

He sensed her apprehension as he moved toward her, gently placing a kiss on her forehead. He leaned back waiting for her reaction.

Had she misjudged his interest? *A kiss on my forehead?*

In an instant, they were in each other's arms. How it had happened, she was afraid to think. For all she knew, she could have made the first move. It wouldn't surprise her. Was she being too easy? Oh, hell, what did it matter. This was the most fun she's had in years. Somewhere inside, that obnoxious parent voice was blabbering away, but she refused to listen. Her own thoughts rang out clear. *Enjoy it, you stupid fool. Stop analyzing everything!*

The car horn suddenly discharged with a shrill, almost blood-curdling shriek. Murray hit the steering wheel hard. It refused to budge, so intent it was on destroying their evening!

Oh God, Talk about embarrassing. They'll be clapped into jail, and Mama would have to come bail them out!

With a similar thought in mind, Murray threw her a look. The two of them jumped out of the car and started running. One long block away and out of breath, they felt comfortable enough to glance back. The car horn was still blasting, but soldiers and their girls were walking by – unconcerned, preoccupied.

Murray looked over at Bobbie. A glimmer of a smile crossed her face. Soon, they were laughing.

"You've got some guts, Murray Pickarowitz."

"Nah, that wasn't a big deal. We'll just have to find some other place."

"I don't know if I can take much more excitement in one night."

He gazed into her eyes and marveled how her hair shimmered in the moonlight.

She thought she saw a troubled expression on his face. "What's the matter? Did I say something wrong?"

"No, Bob. You were just fine."

She was just fine! What was happening to her? What has she gone and done? *Don't get involved with a—*

—⟞⟝—

She unlocked the door to the hotel room, careful not to disturb her mother. She pulled her hair back, straightened her slightly rumpled dress and entered.

Minnie watched as Bobbie moved stealthily through the room, knocking over a chair and banging her head against the bathroom door.

"Mrs. Shatterhoff's granddaughter made a lovely bride."

Bobbie jumped. "Mama! I'm so sorry to wake you. I was at a USO show with a soldier. a friend, a very nice—"

"Did I ask you where you were?"

"I left the note at the desk."

"I got the note."

Minnie reached for the light switch over the bed. For a moment, they regarded one another in silence.

"So, did you have a nice time, Mama?"

"Don't ask. The groom was an hour late. They couldn't find the ring. Our Myron forgot to bring it. So, he goes back to his house to get it, but he can't drive so fast, as we already know, and he can't see in the dark. So, what does he do? He drives to the wrong place. The wedding? It was two hours late, and the dinner? It was cold. And that's all I know." She paused. "So, you maybe had a better time?"

A better time? She was about to burst! *No. Stay calm.* "Very nice, Mama. I actually had a...very nice time." The seconds ticked away. Bobbie waited for the inevitable.

"So...who's this soldier friend?"

"His name's Murray". *Don't say too much.* "He's... from Brooklyn." She moved into the bathroom to wash and brush her teeth, leaving the door ajar. Ten more seconds dragged by. She could hear her mother *thinking!*

"So. You like this Murray from Brooklyn?"

Bobbie walked back into the room, her toothbrush dangling from her mouth. She could no longer control it. The tears began to flow. "I like him a lot, Mama. A lot."

Minnie raised an eyebrow. Her daughter had met a man she cared about. A nice boy from Brooklyn. A *soldier.* Suddenly, her eyes widened. "*Oy vey.*"

Chapter Eight

B obbie began her painstaking search for a measurable sign, some hint that this gentle, sweet soldier inching his way into her heart wasn't playing with a full deck. She likened much in her life to the challenge of a good game of gin rummy. She thought she found it two days later when Murray took her to visit his friend Sadie.

Sadie lived with her two daughters in a tiny apartment near Lincoln Road, and when Bobbie and Murray arrived with a couple loaves of challah and a bottle of sweet wine, all three women were at the door to greet them. Again, Bobbie noticed their makeup. A little too much rouge and unusually dressy attire for a simple visit.

"Come in! Come in!"

"You look beautiful, Sadie!"

"Beautiful, I'll never see again."

"You remember Bobbie from the beach?"

Bobbie fidgeted as she saw Sadie examining her. It had been a windy evening. Her hair was probably a mess.

"A face like this, you don't forget!"

Fern and Sophie stood behind their mother, nodding.

Bobbie's mouth pursed into a smile, unsure exactly

how to react. She was grateful as the evening wore on that all eyes were on him and off her. It was the first time she had observed him in the company of others, and she found herself captivated by his vitality and humor as he entertained them with stories about army life. Of course, he couldn't complain too much about his living conditions. The Sea Isle, down-sized from its original elegance, still afforded him a kind of luxury most soldiers could only dream of – especially, considering that his lodgings came with a full pool behind the hotel and close to the beach area where he worked as a physical instructor.

"Murray, darling," Sadie urged. "Tell Bobbie the one about your mama and those nice Italian boys from South Brooklyn."

"Nothing much to tell, Sadie."

"Come on, *bubala*. Don't be shy. It's a good story."

"Okie, dokie." he began, soothing her request. "I'd done about forty-three exhibition fights in small dumps around town. I came home one night. Ma saw my bloody nose and put her foot down. That was it. So, I went back to the gym. I told them. Look guys. You can't put me back in the ring any more for all the money in the world. And Guido, one of the promoters says, 'Oh yeah! Everybody's got their price. Name yours!' I said, you better talk to my ma. They looked at me like they'd just been hit by a truck. 'Your mama won't let you box?' So, I said, did you ever meet my mother? All of a sudden, these three tough guys get all quiet and depressed. 'Yeah, we met her.' And that was the end of the conversation…and my boxing career. Next case!"

Sadie smiled. "You were some kid in that ring, Murray."

Bobbie cringed. *Grown men going at each other like savages.* "Did you get to box anybody big?" she asked.

Sadie let out a belly laugh. "Did our Moishe box anybody big! Tell her, *bubala.*"

"Sure. Well, let's see. I boxed oranges, fought Jefferson, fought Lincoln—" He stopped, holding back a smile, waiting for her to get his little joke.

"Fort...Jefferson, Fort Lincoln— Oh!" Bobbie said, hitting her forehead with her fist. "You got me there, Murray!" *Larger than life,* thought Bobbie. *The way he seems to enjoy himself. He's his own good time.*

The spread Sadie laid out for her guests included a massive array of beautiful cakes, cold cuts and cheeses. "Eat. Eat!" she urged. "A pound here or there – you'll never notice, believe me."

Of course, Bobbie never had a problem with her weight, and the food was enticing. Maybe it was nerves because, even without Sadie's insistence, she seemed to be consuming much more than she would normally eat.

Murray noticed her healthy appetite. He liked that.

The highlight of the evening was the sweet wine. It had helped take the edge off her immediate discomfort. Usually, half a glass would be her limit, but this night, she helped herself to two full glasses. So she was being positively scandalous now!

Sadie and the girls seemed friendly enough. There was just...*something* about them she couldn't pinpoint. Their small apartment looked comfortable and clean, although red appeared to be the predominant color scheme. Red couch. Red and beige curtains. She didn't remember ever seeing red curtains before. Not exactly how *she* might decorate, but then to each his own. Maybe it was a Brooklyn thing.

She excused herself to use the bathroom. As she stood and walked toward the hall, she saw the women watching her.

"First door on the right." said Sadie. "We don't want you to get lost."

As she entered the bathroom, something caught her eye — a strange outline. At first, she jumped, thinking it might be an animal of some kind. Maybe a skinned rat. But that was ridiculous. She crept closer, flicking on the light over the sink. She took a breath and smiled. *Some rat!* Two rather large douche bags were innocently hanging from the bar over the bathtub. She had some imagination. *Douche bags?* She stole another look and felt an uncomfortable tightening in her chest. When she returned to the living room, she pretended calm but menacing thoughts were now toying with her ability to enjoy what was left of the visit.

—◊◊◊—

It was after nine and Murray had to return to his barracks.

As they were leaving, Sadie grabbed Bobbie's hand. "Don't be a stranger, sweetheart. Come visit anytime."

The anxiety attack that started in her chest had now

moved into her stomach. "Thank you, Sadie. I certainly will. It was a lovely evening, and you've been very kind."

"Murray, this is some piece of merchandise you got here!"

"Sadie," he replied, "I don't mean to insult you, but whoever you are, you're the only one of its kind!"

Sadie let out a powerful belly laugh. Her two girls, quiet as church mice all evening, now joined in.

—⁓—

They walked together back to the Wellington. The night air was especially invigorating. A soothing breeze was coming off the ocean. Bobbie was unusually quiet. Certainly, she was tired. It had been a long evening but haunted by what she had seen in Sadie's bathroom, she was consumed with finding the right way to broach the subject.

Murray's sturdy arm went around her shoulder, and as he leaned over to give her a tender kiss, she backed away. She felt herself choking under the burden of her thoughts. Maybe she was being absurd but she had to know.

"Murray. Those girls. Fern and Sophie. Are they—? I mean—what do they do?"

"They're in show business, Bob. Worked at the Roxy in New York."

"Oh." She looked puzzled. "As singers?"

"Ushers."

Ushers? She tried to stay calm. She fought the impulse to blurt it out, but she suddenly felt manipulated. "They're

prostitutes, aren't they? You took me to visit prostitutes."
She couldn't believe she'd said it, actually uttered those
words.

Murray lowered his eyes. Her outburst had taken him by
complete surprise. How could she possibly think he would
take her to visit whores? He took a moment to measure his
words. "When I was thirteen, my father had a stroke. He
never really recovered. I had to quit school. Sadie helped
us out, gave my mother and me work in her commission
bakery. It saved our lives. Now, she's got some hard times
of her own. I'm just trying to help a little and introduce
her girls to some of the guys I know." He paused, his eyes
probing. "You didn't like them? Were they rude or mean
to you?"

"Well. No. They were really very nice, but—"

"Good. So. There you are."

She was waiting for him to continue. However, that
appeared to be the end of it. That's all he was going to
say. He hadn't offered any excuse. *Help them out? Introduce
them to some guys?* Why suddenly, did she feel so ridiculous? Perhaps, she had misconstrued— No. She was sure
of what she had seen. She was small-town, but she wasn't
dumb. The girls may have been selling their personal
wares. Murray didn't exactly deny it. Yet, his simple, unan-
ticipated response had taken her breath away. She'd never
met anyone like him. His honesty about his family's situation. Asking if Sadie and her girls were rude or mean to
her, as if *that* was all that really mattered. Maybe, that **was**
all that mattered. He had challenged her reasoning, and

now, strangely, her perspective had changed. *Oh God. What he must think of me! Speaking that way about his friends.* An arrogant, judgmental fool, that's what she was! After that outburst, he wouldn't want to be around her anymore. *Petty. Cruel. Tactless.* She wouldn't want to be around someone like herself.

They walked along Collins Avenue in silence. The sky was unusually light with an assortment of stars forming clusters of patterns in the sky. When they reached the Wellington, he turned and looked intently into her eyes. She braced herself. *That darn tongue of hers. A big mouth and an overactive imagination. It's goodnight and goodbye!*

"So, Bob, when do I get to meet your mother?"

She took a deep breath. "You...want to meet my mother?"

"Yeah. What's the matter? You afraid she won't like me?"

She threw him a wistful look. "No, Murray. I'm afraid she will."

—〰—

Under the cover of darkness, Murray and Joe darted across the front lawn of another small hotel just north of Lincoln Road. With the routine down pat, this time they covered their faces with straw hats they had found during a walk on the beach. It was Joe's idea in case someone recognized them. They hadn't considered that the silly looking sombreros might impair their vision until Joe lost his footing and fell into an open ditch near the front stairs of the hotel.

"Shit!"

"Oh boy!" Murray laughed. "Can't take you anywhere!"

"How am I supposed to see in the friggin dark?"

"Stay there. I'll get it." Murray ran over to the restricted sign and grabbed at it, pulling hard. This one wouldn't budge. "You better get over here, Joe. Going to need some help."

Joe extricated himself from the ditch, and together they pushed and pulled with the full force of both their bodies, but the sign remained anchored.

A porch light flashed on — then off. From inside the hotel came a thunderous cry. "What the hell are you doing out there!"

"Great! Now we're gonna get caught," Joe yelled. "Why did I let you talk me into this?"

"Stop bellyaching and help me. One last pull."

They yanked again. The sign had just begun to loosen when they saw a middle-aged man staring at them from the steps of the porch.

"Let's beat it!" Murray yelled.

Suddenly, a flashlight was shining in their faces, momentarily blinding them. The man moved quickly off the porch.

Murray went to grab the sign that had now fallen over and inadvertently knocked the man to the ground. For a moment, he hesitated, then offered his hand.

The man appeared thrown by the gesture. "Give me back my sign!"

Murray regarded him with deep resolve. "We're fighting a war so people can live free. What about that don't you get?" He pointed to the piece of wood with "Gentile Clientele Only" written on it. "**That** is a bunch of crap! "

Cowering behind a bush, Joe was struck by Murray's boldness. *Why the shit is he having a conversation with the guy!* "Quit with the damn lecture, and let's get out of here!"

"You'll be sorry for this!" shouted the man, beating his fists.

"Yeah. Yeah. Go, tell it to the Marines." Murray scooped up the sign, cradling it in his arms. He signaled to Joe and together they ran across the street and down Ocean Drive. This was too close a call. He'd have to reconsider his options. Next time, he would probably go it alone. Joe was too nervous for this kind of work. He wouldn't want to get his friend in trouble.

Chapter Nine

S he felt as if a noose had been tied around her neck, the force of it dragging her down into some deep abyss of mislaid intentions. Her father's heralded warning was pulling the noose even tighter. There would be only one way out. *The Minnie Test.* She had put it off too long. Her business acumen and fierce pride were traits inherited from her father, but when it came to affairs of the heart, it was her mother whom she looked to for sustenance. Minnie had an uncanny ability to see through people — to gauge their behavior and cut through the artifice. Her dad was more circumspect, more politic.

The plan was in motion. Bobbie would ask Murray to join them for dinner. The Air Corps wasn't at all accommodating; the day and time had to be twice modified due to military demands. Finally, a date was agreed upon. Minnie suggested a somewhat fancy supper club on Lincoln Road, thinking it might have the right kind of ambiance for such an occasion, although she wasn't at all sure *what* the occasion was. Bobbie had conveniently forgotten to mention what was expected of her, but Minnie had an idea.

—〰—

With its dark mahogany walls, elegant white-clothed tables and old-world chandeliers, the supper club was a charming holdout from the restaurants of the thirties, well suited to intimate gatherings, private without being confining. A group of six musicians played a potpourri of Benny Goodman hits as patrons gracefully moved about the small dance floor.

Bobbie sat, carefully observing her mother and Murray. The introduction had gone well. Minnie was appropriately subdued yet gracious. She wouldn't be taken in by any smooth-talking New Yorker. Not on a bet. This little woman could spot a phony a mile away!

Murray was anxiously perusing the menu. He had never seen such prices. Five dollars for a steak! On his salary, he'd be washing dishes every day for a month.

Minnie noticed his contorted expression. "Don't worry, Murray. It's my treat. Have anything you want."

How could he ever repay her? This was very embarrassing.

"Look. It's the least I can do for my country," she said, hoping to ease his concern. "Besides, it wouldn't hurt you should gain a pound."

Bobbie's face went sullen. *Here only twenty minutes and Mama's already cuddling up to him.*

Murray was profoundly taken by her generosity, but it didn't feel right. He had never taken or asked for anything that wasn't coming to him. The man of the family at fourteen, he wasn't beholden to anyone. It was a lesson he learned early in life. Now, he sat in this extravagant eating joint, and he didn't have the bucks. "I'll tell you what. I've got money in ten banks, Mrs. Feinman. So, if I come back, I'm going to take you to the best restaurant in New York. What do you say?"

There was an awkward silence. *If he came back? How could Mama respond to that?*

Minnie laughed. "Ten banks. Very nice. I accept."

Bobbie couldn't erase his remark from her mind. It seemed to fall out of him as naturally as if he was telling her about his workday.

Murray was appeased for the moment, but he would try to find a way to pay Bobbie's mother back *before* he went overseas. He happened to glance over at the next table and instantly felt a flicker of agitation. A familiar face was glaring at him. He quickly turned to Minnie. "I understand you're from Poland, Mrs. Feinman."

Minnie picked up her glass and took a sip of wine. "Kikol. A little shtetl, you wouldn't know it. So, how about you?"

Bobbie gave her a look. *Since when does Mama drink wine, except on holidays?*

"Lomza," replied Murray.

"Lomza? You knew Samuel and Bella Finkleman?"

"Never heard of them."

"*Nisht gerferlach.* They left their families in Kikol. Ran off and got married. We never heard either. They should live and be well."

"They lived in Lomza?"

"No. But it's a small world. You never know."

The band let loose with "Minnie the Moocher", and the three shared a warm laugh.

Murray stole another glance at the next table; the man that he recognized was walking over to two MPs stationed near the door. He felt a rush of adrenaline and reached into his jacket, producing a package of cigarettes. He had gotten them for Joe as a thank you for helping him out. He grabbed one and took a match from the book on the table. He lit up and took a long puff.

Bobbie was watching him, aware that his demeanor had suddenly changed. It was the first she noticed him holding a cigarette. Perhaps, he was feeling a little nervous with her mother and wanted to make a good impression. She had given herself a strict warning. *Keep that outrageous imagination in check. Don't make assumptions.*

"So. How about it, Mrs. Feinman. Shall we kick up our heels?"

"Oh, no. I couldn't! I haven't danced since...who can remember?"

"That's no excuse." He put out the cigarette, stood up and beckoned her with a little dance step.

Bobbie gave her a quick wink. "Go on, Mama. Take a chance."

Her face flushed and she giggled like a schoolgirl as Murray extended his hand. Minnie rose demurely and followed him onto the dance floor.

Bobbie shook her head. *Mama is such a pushover!*

The pace of the music had suddenly picked up. She watched as Minnie began to—*jitterbug? When did Mama learn to jitterbug?* Yet, there she was on the dance floor, full of exuberance and following perfectly. She couldn't remember ever seeing her mother dance like that with her husband. Of course, Bobbie's father, Morris, rarely danced except at weddings but never— the jitterbug! This called for a toast. She eyed a glass of wine on the table and remembered a second promise she made to herself. No drinking. She wasn't exactly a lush. She had imbibed on only three occasions in her young life. Graduation. Her sister Teen's wedding and a couple of days before in Sadie's apartment to ease the tension of the visit— the night she accused Fern and Sophie of being prostitutes when they were probably no more than typical V girls. She shuddered, imagining what she might have said if Sadie hadn't forced all that food down her. Murray's friend had saved her from making a complete fool of herself, although what she said was bad enough.

She brought the dangerous liquid to her lips and started to sip a little at a time, savoring the deep aroma of the burgundy. It was as if she had never indulged. She was a woman of twenty-six. Tonight, she learned her mother jitterbugged and that drinking fine wine without the benefit of food could be a very pleasurable experience. Had she finally matured? Gotten the hay out of her hair?

She perused the room, delighted by this awakening. Suddenly, she noticed two MPs standing a few feet away. They seemed to be observing Murray. *No. Just her stupid imagination!* They were looking in his direction, but there were many people they might be watching. Besides, Murray was a wonderful dancer. Why wouldn't they notice? It was her overly analytical mind jumping to conclusions again. She allowed herself another large sip of wine and watched fascinated as Murray swirled Minnie around the dance floor. *How young Mama looks. So animated. So alive!* Obviously, he had worked his charm on her as well. If Bobbie expected another outcome to the evening, there would be no surprises now. The joy on her mother's face had irrevocably clinched it.

The music ended and Murray escorted a flushed and ecstatic Minnie back to the table.

"You are **some** dancer!" she exclaimed.

"I had **some** partner."

Minnie smiled and pointed to Bobbie. "So, now dance with her."

"Mama!"

Murray laughed and offered his hand. "What do you say, Bob? How about a—"

"Sure!" She wondered if she sounded too eager, but what did it matter? The musicians were playing "For All We Know" her favorite song. How could she pretend calm? She had needed to be fully objective this evening. Mama was no longer able to judge. Yet, she couldn't help herself. That song! The darn music was sweeping her away. It was the second time they had been out dancing together. She prayed she would be able to follow him without tripping over his feet. She had been so self-conscious that night in Flamingo Park. He had turned to her during a fox-trot and very sweetly asked if she would mind if *he* led. Her face had gone all red. She hadn't realized how hard she was working at trying to impress him. Now, as she lay her head on his solid shoulders, she could feel his breath on her neck and hear the steady beat of his heart. They hadn't danced this close, then. She wondered who had held back. She remembered thinking maybe it was him.

Murray was feeling transported; the music taking him to wonderful places, and for a moment, there was no sentry duty, no marching, no maneuvers, no war. It was just the two of them, that wonderful music and the night.

The MPs were standing just behind Minnie. He could see them out of the corner of his eye, and he felt pressed. "When are you leaving, Bob?"

"Hmm?"

"Going home."

She looked up, surprised. "You're going home?"

"No. I think *you* are."

"Oh, right. Well, yes…yes I am."

"When?"

"In five days." She lay her head back on his shoulder. She felt his body embrace hers, even tighter than before. It was as if they were suspended in time. She felt amazingly calm and carefree. Not one negative thought entered her logical head.

The music ended. They remained in the middle of the floor, dancing to a silent song.

Finally, he broke the embrace and led her back to the table, quietly signaling the MPs to meet him by the door. "Oh my God! I just realized," he shrieked, hitting his forehead with the palm of his hand. "I promised my buddy, Joe, I'd fill in for him tonight. He wanted to see his girl before he went out on maneuvers."

"You just remembered this?" she asked, stunned.

"Yes. I'm so sorry. I feel like an idiot, but I have to go." Gently, he turned to Minnie. "We'll do this again, Mrs. Feinman. Next time, my treat."

"Minnie. And you shouldn't forget." She had no reason not to believe him.

"We've got a date!" He glanced over at Bobbie. It was difficult to look her in the eye. "I hope you understand, Bob. Can't let Joe down."

"No. Of course not." She tried not to appear disappointed. She had her pride.

"So. I guess I'll see you soon?"

"Sure," she smiled.

He stood staring at her, trying to lock the moment in his memory before turning and walking toward the door.

Bobbie's eyes widened in panic as she observed the MPs fall in behind him. As she watched them leave, she realized she had found her sign. The sign she no longer wanted to find. Her soldier had done something wrong. *Nothing is ever what it appears.* Why was she so surprised that this time might be different? Who was *she* to expect—*Thank God, Mama didn't see it! Why should **she** be disillusioned, too?* She reproached herself for not trusting her intuition. She hadn't done anything to be ashamed of. She wasn't Eunice. She was stronger than that.

"Too bad he had to leave so soon," sighed Minnie. "Such a nice boy."

Bobbie cringed. Her rational side was trying to placate her hurt. *She'd get over it. It wasn't the end of the world. No one had died. No one had even made any promises.*

For the rest of the evening, she quietly picked at her roast beef and listened to her mother rhapsodize about him. Even with her best acting face, her strength was receding. She had fretted about a dangerous yearning, but she had hoped this night would be a marvelous experience and that her mother would love him. It was for a time, and Minnie did. But now...

Minnie thought she saw tears in her daughter's eyes, but she didn't say a word.

—ɱ—

Captain Crenshaw, a balding man with round, wire rimmed glasses of World War I vintage, had been assigned to Officers Candidate School at the beginning of 1942 and immediately found himself dealing with an epidemic of anti-Semitism. Before the war, the section of the beach where soldiers were now housed had been home to a number of older Jews, the only place on the beach they were allowed to live. Seeing them in the area of their makeshift barracks, many soldiers openly resented their presence. Crenshaw found himself in the strange position of having to explain that Christians lived further north, beyond Lincoln Road. Though he considered this present problem little more than a nuisance, he was intrigued enough to want to deal with it himself.

The contentious looking man sat stiff and stern in Crenshaw's office when the door opened. The two MPs escorted a somber Murray into the room. He saluted his commanding officer.

"At ease, PFC Pickarowitz."

Murray recognized the menacing look on the face of the man sitting by the window.

"This is Mr. Wilby. He claims you destroyed a piece of his property a few days ago."

The man's mouth tightened into a menacing smirk as hate filled his eyes. How often Murray had seen that look.

"He's right about that, sir."

Captain Crenshaw had expected a denial. Now, he felt a marked irritation with the ease of the soldier's confession. "Have you anything to say in your defense, private?"

"I removed a restricted sign, sir. Under the circumstances, I saw no reason for it being there."

Crenshaw saw the restricted signs that dotted Ocean Drive and Collins Avenue north of the Rony Plaza as an embarrassment, but the Army had quietly tolerated them. "Is this true, Mr. Wilby?"

"It's my property! I can turn away anyone I wish. It's a free country, and I got my rights!"

The captain stared hard at him. "Mr. Wilby, the Army Air Corps will take care of this matter. Thank you for coming in."

Suddenly, Wilby jumped up, shaking his fist. "You better take care of it! I can call the police!"

Crenshaw rarely lost his temper even in the most tense of times, but the man's arrogant outburst was totally out of line. "How would you like to be put off limits?"

Taken aback, Wilby stood silent.

"Good day, Mr. Wilby."

Wilby gave Murray another scornful look. Then, he turned and exited the office.

The soldier stood at attention, waiting. He'd probably be severely punished, but he was happy he had pulled up those signs: sorry he hadn't gotten them all. That was the plan, and now, he'd have to find another way. He felt himself go weak against the power of the captain's penetrating gaze.

The officer paced back and forth, his eyes locked on his wayward charge.

"PFC Pickarowitz, the Air Corps is a guest in this town. I'm sure you are aware of that. You are not going to change attitudes overnight, and it doesn't help matters to take things into your own hands."

How many times Murray had heard those words. As a child, his knuckles ached for days, his teacher scolding him for fighting back when kids called him names and made fun of his accent and clothes. He hadn't regretted any of those scuffles. "Whose hands then, sir?"

The question stunned the seasoned Crenshaw. He found it curiously unsettling. "I don't need a lesson in morality from **you,** Pickarowitz! Confined to barracks until further notice. A few days of house arrest might be all you need to solve the world's problems!"

"Yes, sir."

Crenshaw called the MPs to escort Murray out. But he couldn't get the soldier's words out of his head. *Under the circumstances, I saw no reason*—That impertinent young know-it-all had touched a nerve.

As Murray left the office under guard, he felt a burden lift from his shoulders. He assumed he would be put in the stockade for his crime, expecting no less from a military that seemed to condone and promote bigots and bullies. *A few days of house arrest?* Maybe, just maybe, he would be able to see Bobbie one more time.

Chapter Ten

R ed and orange hues dotted the sky as dusk moved in to envelop the last of their quiet day on the white sand. Minnie had tried several times to question her daughter about Murray, but she was reluctant to talk about him, dismissing the subject with a casual, "I don't know, Mama. It's not important." It was Bobbie's way of handling disappointment. It had been three days since the incident in the supper club, and still no word. In a couple of days, they would be going home.

Bobbie hadn't the courage to tell her mother, but she knew exactly what happened. Murray was being court-martialed for some heinous crime. Why else would he leave so quickly with a military police escort and not even call? She couldn't reconcile such passionate feelings for someone who hadn't been honest with her. She always tried to be sensible. But now, she was no different than Eunice. *A romantic fool!* Quick to rush in. Of course, it wasn't entirely her fault. You can never really know someone. Especially, in so short a time. Yet, how could she, cool-headed Bobbie Feinman, have been **so** wrong?

Two soldiers walked past with their guard dogs, the

animals obediently sniffing the sand. An older couple, well into their eighties, strolled hand in hand. Bobbie observed their mutual affection as they laughed together and whispered into each other's ear. She hadn't recalled ever seeing her parents holding hands. Certainly, they loved each other. A peck on the cheek once in a while to be sure. Thirty years and four daughters might have had something to do with it.

Minnie and Morris were second cousins from opposite sides of the family. Although the marriage was solid, the element of *passion* in their relationship was not something Bobbie ever considered. Minnie's coquettish behavior in the supper club had taken her by complete surprise. She'd never seen her mother act that way around her father, at least not during the years she had been on this earth. It intrigued her to consider what their courtship might have been like. She wouldn't dare ask. Partly, she didn't care to know. The virginal aspect of her parents' love was easier to contemplate.

Minnie let go a plaintive sigh, observing the amorous carousing of a young couple in the water only twenty feet away. *Youth! So wasted!* If she had only known how wonderful it was to be young.

Bobbie closed her eyes, lost in a fanciful daydream. A figure was running towards her, looking curiously like Murray. Soon, they were in each other's arms, their bodies lost in the wildness of their embrace as some schmaltzy forties music appropriately climaxes in the background. Suddenly, she heard an unfamiliar voice.

"Bobbie?"

She opened her eyes, disappointed at having to say goodbye to her fantasy. A soldier was standing ill at ease in front of her. She had never seen him before. A thin, small man with a nervous twitch, he reminded her of Harry Sweet, the sad young captain she met with Eunice.

"Excuse me. Are you Bobbie?"

"Pardon? Oh. Yes, but, how did you—"

"I'm Murray's buddy, Joe. He said I might find you here. Wanted me to tell you he had to go— Orders. Had to go on maneuvers. That's the reason he hasn't called."

Her eyes narrowed and her chin went into her chest. *Wait a minute!* She wasn't going to be dragged into this again. And, the poor soldier seemed so awkward, he had to be lying.

"Maneuvers? Where does he…maneuver?"

"Ah…the Everglades."

"Ah hah. The Everglades. I see. Well, thank you for the information."

"Sure." He wavered a moment as if wanting to say something more. Then, he started to walk away.

Minnie gave her a nudge. *No. Mama. Leave it alone!*

Minnie raised her eyebrow and threw her a look. *All right! All right!* She'd do it for Mama. "Excuse, me, Joe?"

Joe turned and walked back toward her. "Yes, ma'am?"

"Maybe, you could get word to him? I'm supposed to be going back home in a couple of days and I thought—"

"Couple of days? No kidding?"

"Yes. I mean, it's not so important, but—"

"Sure. I'll get word to him. We… have ways. I'll let him know. See ya."

"Bye Joe."

They watched silently as the soldier walked up the beach and out of sight. Suddenly, Minnie let out a mournful sigh. Bobbie jumped. "What's the matter, Mama?"

"What?"

"You just sighed. Are you all right?"

"What? I'm not allowed to sigh?"

"Of course, you can sigh. I just thought—Oh, forget it."

Bobbie watched the turbulent waves hit the shore, bidding farewell to the retreating sun. She was confused by a new tempest brewing inside her. She had just begun to accept it all. She was going home. What was she supposed to make of this?

"It would be nice…" began Minnie, her face resting forlornly on her chin.

"What Mama?"

"Never mind."

"Mama! WHAT!" She suddenly turned and saw a wistful longing on her mother's face.

"It's good…to be young."

"You're not old, Mama."

"I'm not young."

"You're as young as you feel."

Minnie rolled her eyes at the absurdity of her daughter's timeworn cliche. Suddenly, she cocked her head back. "Okay, so I'm young. Tell **him** that." She pointed to the shadow of Murray's buddy in the distance.

Bobbie remembered how her mother looked on the dance floor of the supper club, her face radiant with callow hope. She tried to picture her life before a husband and four children weighed her down with duty and obligation, slowly robbing her of her dreams. *We grow older, but we never grow up.* She turned and kissed her on the forehead. *Mama still has so much life in her!* She didn't know how to reply to her mother's sad footnote on the tyranny of age. At least, she would let her know she understood.

—⁓—

Murray sat peeling a few onions in the basement kitchen of the Sea Isle Hotel. His eyes were tearing, but he was feeling like the luckiest guy in the world. Almost six months before, he had requested a furlough. This past year of training, whipping clumsy eighteen-year-olds into shape, had been more arduous than any boxing match he ever fought. On his first day of house arrest, the papers finally arrived. Thank God the top brass didn't know about his present confinement. One more day, and he'd be out of there! Confident he was alone after a cursory check of the door, he pulled an old radio from under the sink. He had smuggled it into the kitchen that morning. He plugged it into a nearby socket and searched for a music station. Glen Miller. Terrific! Clutching a mop that was resting by the side of the sink, he started dipping his agile partner at strategic places in the music, then dramatically flinging it into the air. In a moment, he was back at Roseland with Woody Herman or at the Manhattan Room in the Hotel Pennsylvania with Benny Goodman, jitterbugging to a new and wonderful beat. Swing. It was 1935, and he had just turned twenty-two. This new sound was taking him to wonderful places. He had found in it a joy unlike any other. Different than escaping into the world of movies and Broadway shows. This was something *he* could participate in, and he was damned good at it.

The door of the kitchen swept open. Joe stood before him, staring dumbly. "Wow! Just like Fred Astaire! Can you do that with a real woman?"

Murray tossed him a glance. "Don't know. Never tried." Of course, he had —many times, but his dance partners at Roseland were a little more spirited, more resistant to being tossed over his head. "Did you find her?" he asked, without missing a beat of the music.

"Yep. And, she had the carnation in her hair, just like you said. I knew right away it was her. She's leaving in two days."

"Good!"

"Good? I thought you liked her?"

"I'm crazy about her."

"Then, what—"

Murray threw the mop over his shoulder again. The pace of the music suddenly slowed. "You want to learn, Joe?"

"Now?"

"Sure. Come on. I'll be the girl."

Joe walked over to Murray and stood stiffly, waiting for his orders.

"Now, first thing is – you've got to relax. Come on, limber up."

Joe started flailing his arms, almost hitting Murray in the face.

"Okay. Okay. That's enough! You don't want to KO your partner before the dance starts. Now, you've got to assume the standard fox-trot position." He took Joe's left hand, placing it carefully around his waist. "Ready?"

"Which leg do I start with?"

"Which leg? How about the first one that moves." *Oh boy!* Teaching this klutz to dance might be too big an undertaking for a mere mortal. Of course, Murray didn't feel like a mere mortal. He could do anything. And all Joe needed was a little confidence, and **he** could do anything, too. "One. two. three. One. two. three. Take your time. Feel the beat."

Joe's leaden feet had no idea of 'beat' but Murray was undaunted. "Look Joe, here's how it works. As my leg goes back, yours is supposed to come forward. Get it?"

Slowly, Joe began moving to the rhythm of the music.

"That's it. Great! You got it!" *What he wouldn't give for one more night at Roseland before...* "I'm telling you. Take it from me. The girls are gonna love ya."

Joe was beginning to relax, but his former reluctance suddenly turned to concern. "Hey, Murray, you're not planning to throw me over your shoulder, are you?"

"What? Are you nuts? This is a foxtrot."

"Yeah, but I saw what you did with that mop, and I—"

"Hold on, Joe. Here we go!" The music had just changed to the frenetic pace of a jitterbug.

"Oh, shit!" Joe struggled to keep up,

Suddenly, the kitchen door swung open. An MP stood eyeing them.

Having just completed a midair maneuver of immortal proportions, Murray turned and acknowledged him with an almost casual disregard.

Chapter Eleven

B obbie fidgeted in her chair. Max watched as she endlessly reshuffled her cards. With each of her hand maneuvers came a doleful sigh. He hadn't been privy to her personal thoughts, but he had a feeling of what they were. He had seen things like this happen to other young woman who had vacationed at the hotel over the last few months he'd been residing there. He never concerned himself. *Youth!* But, he had come to care about Bobbie – even if she did beat him in cards – and appreciated her interest in him. So did the other refugees, especially Herbert Von Frilitz, a self-described baron from Rumania whose lineage was somewhat suspect. A newly arrived boarder at the hotel, Von Frilitz would spin his tales of peril, and Bobbie would dutifully listen. The more concern she showed, the more he added to his list of remarkable adventures. Max took his stories with a grain of salt, mostly discounting them.

Bobbie stared vacantly at her cards.

Max turned to her with a gentle prompt. "Bobbie, dear. Do you expect to move…maybe today?"

"Oh, I'm sorry, Max." She proceeded to lay out her hand. "Gin."

Max's face was a mass of exasperation. He fought to regain his composure. "For someone who's depressed, my dear young woman, you certainly play very well."

Von Frilitz, joining them for today's game, moaned in agreement.

"I guess adversity agrees with me." She was surprised Max should think she was depressed. She thought she'd hidden her feelings quite well.

As Bobbie hastily recorded her win, Max's attention was drawn to the front of the lobby. In an instant, his expression turned hopeful. A familiar face had entered the hotel.

—⁓—

Like a man on assignment, Murray surveyed the room, pausing only a moment before walking over to Bobbie with an air of cheerful resolve. "Hi, Bob. What's cookin?"

Bobbie looked up. Her mouth hung open and her tongue retreated to the back of her throat. He leaned over and kissed her cheek. Her face flushed.

She licked her lips and took a labored breath. *Be calm.* "So, how were…maneuvers?"

"Fine. We didn't lose anybody."

Didn't lose anybody? Sure! She could feel her heart pounding. How annoying she had no control over it.

Discreetly, Max took it upon himself to play her hand,

drawing and discarding when appropriate while Bobbie sat staring at the phantom standing before her.

"I'm sorry I couldn't get away sooner." No need to tell her he was under house arrest and peeling onions and potatoes for a few days.

"It's all right." *All right?* Was she crazy? Why couldn't he be honest? She saw the MPs. Why can't he tell her the truth? Instead, he stands there, so casual, so unassuming, so...*sweet. Oh God!* She felt the immediate rush of indignation begin to fade. It would take all the acting talent she could summon to affect disinterest.

Murray reached into his jacket pocket and produced the coveted documents. "Look what I got? Furlough papers. Came through yesterday. I put in for them months ago."

"Very nice."

"Ten days! Terrific, huh?"

"Terrific."

"So..." Murray braced himself. His eyes met the cautious glances of Max and Von Frilitz. "Could I talk with you for a minute?"

"Well, I hate to interrupt the—"

"Go. Interrupt," pleaded Max.

She regarded Max's chide with innocent surprise as she moved away from the table, following Murray to a small alcove nearby.

Murray hesitated. He knew it would be the first and last time in his life he would ask. "So, Bob. You... want to get married?"

Bobbie felt an intense dizziness. She had to close her eyes

simply to regain her footing. Maybe, she hadn't heard right. "MARRIED?" Her shocked response resonated throughout the room. Max and Von Frilitz's card game came to an immediate halt.

"It's only ten days, but I don't know how I'll ever see you again unless—"

"You're asking me to — marry you?"

"Well… yes." He was starting to feel uneasy. Maybe, he had been mistaken about her feelings for him. Too quick to assume. Only thinking of himself. What did he have to offer her anyway?

"We hardly know each other." Her more rational side was indulging in a kind of psychological game of wills.

"Yeah. That's true, Bob."

"I mean it's a very foolhardy thing to do—wartime and all." Why, she wondered, was she saying all this? Was she trying to talk him out of it? Certainly, he would argue. She would play devil's advocate like she always does and he would disagree.

Perspiration was forming on his brow. Her words were slowly cutting a wedge through his heart. What was he thinking? Ever since getting the furlough papers, he thought only about asking her. But, suddenly, he saw it again. *The bloodied face of the half dead soldier.* "Guess you might call it… kind of crazy."

"Crazy? That's it. Yes, absolutely …crazy." Her heart was fighting her words, but she had to persist. The logical Bobbie had taken over, if only for a moment.

His features hardened into a mournful mask. He

seemed to be backing away, doubting himself, confused. "I probably won't come back."

Bobbie gasped. To think her innocent questioning had come to this! "Don't say that, Murray! Of course, you'll come back!" Impulsively, she wrapped her arms around his neck and held him firmly against her body. He felt a sudden calm in the comfort of her touch. In an instant, his concerns seemed to evaporate as they stood holding each other in a long, quiet embrace.

Max and Von Frilitz sat rooted to their seats. Their all-important card game had ceased to interest them.

Murray lifted his head. He studied her face for a moment. "So, you want to get married, then?"

She saw the glimmer of hope in his eyes, beckoning her to take the plunge. This time, nothing rational was spinning around in her sensible head. This time her heart was speaking, and there could be only one reply. "Okay."

The entire lobby of guests broke into thunderous applause.

Bobbie's face went white. *Again? Total strangers! How did they know? Who's been talking? Mama?*

Murray wasted no time responding to the ovation. He took her in his arms and planted a passionate kiss on her trembling lips.

Suddenly, she was no longer feeling embarrassed by the spirited clapping of Max and the others. She no longer heard them.

—Ⱳ—

Minnie received the news of Bobbie's engagement with equal amounts of joy and relief. It was about time her daughter found a mate. Her third born, Fay, was already engaged. So how would it look to have Fay married first? But, now, there was so much to do! So many people to contact!

—⟋⟍—

With Minnie's blessing secured, a formidable obstacle loomed ahead. *Dad!* All night, she lay awake fretting about what she would say to him. Hadn't he warned her about just this kind of situation? She looked over at her mother, peacefully sleeping in the next bed. Suddenly, it came to her. *Of course!* Putting herself through endless hours of torture, worrying needlessly. She would simply let her brilliant mother be her emissary while she would stand on the sidelines, offer support and—pray.

—⟋⟍—

The following morning at a phone booth on the corner of Fourth and Ocean, Bobbie stood by nervously while Minnie braced herself for battle and rang up her husband. If anyone could handle his excitable nature, *it was Mama.* The key to her mother's success lay somewhere between pacification and obfuscation. As a child, she doted on her father — the head of the family, the honorable businessman, the self-taught scholar who made all the important decisions. But as she grew into an adult, Bobbie saw her mother's well of inner resilience. And it was from there that her father drew much of his strength. Minnie didn't have his verbal or business skills, but her calm courage and sense of humor were the ultimate anchors that held the family together. Now, she would need all that courage and humor to ride out the impending typhoon.

"It's been wonderful, Morris. We've had a wonderful time, especially Bobbie. She had such a wonderful time, you wouldn't believe. What? Okay. Just a minute." She beckoned Bobbie to the phone. "Tell your father about your wonderful time!"

Reluctantly, Bobbie took the receiver. "Hi Dad. How are you doing? Yes, it's been really…wonderful. Yeah. Weather's been great, too. So…how's the store? Business okay? That's good." *Oh God! How was she going to tell him?* She took a deep, anxious breath. "Dad, there's something I need to tell you. No, nothing's the matter. No, we're feeling fine. But see, I met this…guy, a very nice man — a soldier, actually from Brooklyn, wouldn't you know! And well, we've been seeing each other and…he's quite wonderful and—" She turned to her mother, who smiled and nodded her support.

Minnie's heart ached for her daughter's predicament, but this had to be Bobbie's call.

She gritted her teeth and took another breath. "Anyway, Dad, you're not going to believe this. Even I have a difficult time— It's so crazy really, but he asked me to, well…to marry him, Dad and I thought about it—Hello, Dad, are you there? Oh good. I thought about it, and I said…I said—" She closed her eyes, tightly. "Yes." She put her hand over her face, waiting for the tirade, but there was only silence at the other end of the line. Panic in her eyes, she silently begged Minnie for help. This time she wouldn't take no for an answer. *Mama had to say something!*

Minnie bravely seized the phone. "Morris? Isn't it marvelous? What? Oh, wait. I'll ask."

She turned to Bobbie who was now hyperventilating. "Your father wants to know how he's going to support you?"

Bobbie took a long moment. "Tell him—tell him it's okay, Mama, remember? He said he's got money in ten banks."

Of course! Minnie remembered too. "Did you hear, Morris? He's got money in ten banks." She motioned Bobbie back to the phone.

Thank God! The worst was over. Maybe her father's anger would be soothed, temporarily. "Dad, you'll love him. Mama loves him. Mama, tell Dad how much you love him." Buoyed by her tiny victory, Bobbie handed the phone back to her mother.

Minnie was starting to wither. The conversation had to end soon or she might just drop from fatigue. Then, where would they be? How could Bobbie prepare for a wedding without *her?* She took a breath, finding a small reserve of energy. "Such a good boy, *keninahora.* So? You'll meet him. Don't worry." She listened, blankly, then turned to Bobbie. There was strength maybe for one last question. "Your father wants to know when?"

If Bobbie had any more concern, she had forgotten it

in the heady afterglow of her initial disclosure. She took hold of the phone with a new confidence. "In one week, Dad. See, he's got a ten-day furlough so he's coming to Detroit. I thought maybe we could plan a small family wedding, and you could call a caterer, and we'll be home by Sunday to take care of the rest."

There was an interminably long silence. Too long. Blood was starting to drain from her cheeks. Suddenly, there it was. The wail of outrage. The song of discontent. She was shaking as she tossed the phone back to her mother. *All was lost. Only Mama could save her now.*

"So, all right, Morris. *Mazel tov*, and we'll see you Sunday. You shouldn't forget to pick us up. Goodbye!" She hung up and looked over at Bobbie.

They both stood, silently trying to comprehend what they had just experienced. Two survivors. After a moment, Bobbie fell into her mother's arms as Minnie fell against the phone booth.

—⟁—

Murray escorted Bobbie and Minnie to the train station. He had insisted on carrying all the bags. She had urged him to let her help, reminding him that her mother traveled heavy. *Not a chance.* Listing to the right and breathing heavily, he persisted as they rushed past tourists and soldiers, arriving within minutes of departure.

Murray lifted the bags onto the train. He turned to Minnie and embraced her.

She giggled, gracing him with her most endearing smile. "So, you'll bring my stepmother back with you? God forbid she should miss a wedding."

"Only if she's as pretty as you!"

She smiled and blew him a kiss as the conductor helped her onto the train.

Murray and Bobbie regarded each other. Her right eye started to twitch. She tried frantically to control it. "Well, Murray, I guess we'll see you soon."

"Can't wait. I hope your Dad will like me."

"Oh, don't worry about that. He'll love you...when he gets to know you." She had spared him her father's outburst; didn't want to start everything off on the wrong foot. Besides, he'd have enough to worry about with his own family.

Murray noticed Bobbie's twitch. "You okay, Bob?"

"Sure. Just got some soot in my eye, that's all."

Soon, his arms were around her and he was bestowing gentle kisses all over her face. She responded with a pleased reserve, slightly overwhelmed by his very public display of affection.

The whistle blew and she boarded the train, turning back to wave one last goodbye. It was a gesture she had seen in countless movies, and now here she was – waving to *her* soldier. How handsome he looked! How confident and strong! She was getting married in a week. She couldn't believe it.

He watched as she disappeared inside the car. Suddenly, he felt it happening again. It appeared more often now,

no matter what he did to push it away. That flash of another time. *People running and screaming. The harsh sound of
shells meeting their targets. An eerie quiet and then—that final
deafening blast!* He closed his eyes, took a gulp of air and
prayed he had done the right thing.

Bobbie rushed to take the seat by the window, offering a hurried thank you to the uniformed officer who had
helped lift Minnie's bag into the overhead compartment.
Of course, by now her twitch had completely stopped.
Now, that she was safely on the train! Her eyes scanned
the crowd, hoping for one last wave. Suddenly, Minnie's
bag came loose and fell within inches of her head.

"Oy!" cried Minnie. "This is going to be some trip."

"What did you say, Mama?" she said, unaware of how
close she had come to sustaining a major blow.

"Nothing important, *bubala.*" Minnie rolled her eyes as
the soldier quietly reset the luggage.

The train creaked away from the station. Bobbie lay
her head back, exhausted by the events of the last few
hours. She took one last look out the window. A solitary
figure was running along the outside of their car. Her eyes
widened in disbelief. *Oh my God. He's going to get himself
killed!* Everyone in the railway car watched as Bobbie attempted to wave him away.

Murray was determined, stopping within inches of losing his footing—and blew her one last kiss.

She shook her head, admonishing him and blew a kiss
back. *What a crazy guy!* Secretly, she felt a sense of relief as
if his actions somehow secured his intentions.

She noticed the officer watching her.

"Boyfriend?" he asked.

"Yes."

"She'll see him in a week," Minnie offered. "They're getting married."

"Oh. Congratulations."

"Thanks."

"They only met three weeks ago."

"Mama, really, you don't—"

"Need to talk about it? Believe me, I need to talk about it. I got to practice before I see your father." She glanced over at the officer with a worried look on her face. "He unfortunately is not so happy."

"Mama!"

"What's true is true."

"I don't think this gentleman really cares what—"

The officer looked at her with surprise. "You're marrying a man you met three weeks ago?"

Bobbie thought she saw contempt in his eyes. *Who asked for his opinion anyway!* She was hoping her mother might tell him a thing or two, but Minnie shrugged her shoulders and gave her a "forget about it" look. So, she turned and stared out the window, trying to calm her rage. *Why had a stranger's rude observation caused her such stress?*

—◈—

Babies screamed as their mothers tried in vain to calm their terror. The weary old train was taking every bump on the tracks. It had been twelve hours since they left Miami. Bobbie hadn't been able to shut her eyes, not for a moment. Trembling from the cold, she looked with envy at her mother who managed to escape the rumbling torture chamber and take a little snooze. Too nervous to eat before they left, she consumed the last piece of fruit in her bag. There would be no more stopping until Detroit. She looked out the window at a slow passing train. Suddenly, her eyes were drawn to something in the back of one of the cars. For a split second, she thought she saw a man and woman—*making love in full view of everyone!* The others in the car seemed to be averting their eyes to give them privacy. In an instant, the train had moved on, and Bobbie wondered if she had dreamt the whole thing. Maybe, she was starting to hallucinate. She was certainly tired enough. She looked around, hoping to find someone who might have seen it. But most of the passengers were either sleeping or reading. She squirmed in her seat, struggling with the image of what she had witnessed. *Could passion do all that? Destroy all sense of decency and propriety?* She noticed the officer, a captain in the Air Corps, watching her, again. She had learned to identify rank. Not so difficult since every other person in Miami was in the military. *Doesn't he ever sleep?* She knew what he was thinking. That *she* was an Allotment Annie, one of those unscrupulous girls who marry lots of men for their fifty-dollar a month allotment check. She'd heard about a young woman in Detroit who married three or four combat pilots. The soldiers happened to compare wedding pictures in some officers' club before leaving for Europe, and her scheme was exposed. Bobbie cringed. Imagine this jerk thinking she was capable of something so cruel!

A conductor came by. "Excuse me. Can I get something to eat?"

"The dining car is closed. Sorry, miss."

"**You're** sorry! And will you tell me why it's so cold?"

The conductor's back arched. "Our trains don't get cold."

Their trains don't get cold! She was probably imagining that, too. Another baby wailed in protest. If only she could scream out. That's the problem with being an adult. Always have to be appropriate. Socialized! What a frustrating word. And, of course, she was the most socialized person she knew. *There should be an insurrection! Everyone on the train should demand that*—what was she going on about, like some spoiled child! She looked over at her mother, comfortably sleeping in the warm woolen coat Morris had given her on her fifty-second birthday. Bobbie marveled at her fortitude. *No one hated trains more than Mama!* She was expecting to hear Minnie's woeful complaining all the way back to Detroit. Now, here **she** was, doing just that! She pulled her fur jacket tight over her head. The constant replaying of Murray's proposal had given her a major migraine. Yet her agitation only served to camouflage the real problem. The trip had offered too many hours to think, dangerous hours for someone with Bobbie's fertile mind. Suddenly, she felt herself abruptly pulled from her private hell by a surprisingly gentle voice.

"You want to talk about it?"

Taken aback, she slowly emerged from under her jacket. The captain's callous remark hadn't made her trip any easier. Now, he seemed to be trying to make amends. She decided to challenge him. What did she have to lose? Besides, there was no hope of ever getting any sleep unless the train came to a sudden stop, like against a mountain.

"I'd like to ask you a question," she began.

"Sure. Whatever you want to know."

Whatever I want to know! "I'd like to know" she began with a measure of irritation in her voice, "what's so shocking about a girl marrying a soldier she's just—she hasn't known long. It's happening all the time these days."

The captain turned his head away a moment. Bobbie had him now, *the righteous know it all!*

"You love him?"

"Of course!" She lowered her voice. "I think so."

"Oh. You think so. Well, if you love him, why are you rushing into this?"

Had she no shame? Why was she even talking about this to a complete stranger? Probably never even had a girlfriend or a wife. Where was her pride? Yet something was forcing her to press on. That innate curiosity that made her question herself in all too many situations. "Well, he's probably going to be sent overseas soon and—"

"So. You feel sorry for him. Is that it?"

"Well, no, not exactly—"

"Think you're doing your duty to your country?"

"Well, I—"

"That's a very noble gesture. You could end up a widow."

A widow! Oh God. She felt more confused than ever. Had she said yes out of pity? She felt very attracted to Murray. He was handsome and charming and full of life. And he seemed to earnestly care for her. It was wartime. He'd probably never see her again unless—*but they **could** have seen each other. Made plans.* She would have come to visit him. But in that moment seeing him so vulnerable, she hadn't been able to think straight. Two of her high school friends married their sweethearts right after Pearl Harbor. Both men enlisted in the army. The girls now had babies, and their husbands were missing in action somewhere in the Pacific. Bobbie closed her eyes. *That darn captain opened up a can of worms!* She was defensive because she was tired. That was it. Her perspective was blurred. That's all. She'd think so much more clearly after she got some rest.

She slept fitfully. By the time they pulled into Detroit, she had made a decision. Her excuse was an obvious one. She had been too hasty. Knowing how her father felt, this change of heart would be completely understood, and canceling the wedding would be a cinch.

Chapter Twelve

*B*obbie was craving solitude as the frozen wasteland of a train slumped into the Detroit station. Minnie had survived the journey with much less anxiety. She had used part of the long trip to busily make notes for the caterer. Then, there was the business of flowers. Rabbi Adler. Guests. Where would Murray's family sleep?

They were met at the station by Bobbie's two sisters, Fay and Arleen, screaming with delight. Bobbie tried her best to *act* happy, but all she wanted was to go home and sleep for days.

Arleen, the youngest of the Feinman girls, couldn't stop giggling as she wrapped her arms around her big sister. In September, she would be going off to college. Morris had finally recovered enough from the depression, and Arleen was the next in line. Bobbie envied her sister's opportunity. When *she* graduated high school, the depression was in full swing. Money was tight, and she was afraid to broach the subject out of concern for her father's financial condition. He had just finished paying for his oldest daughter Teen's college education. It was only his excellent credit that made it possible for him to continue running his clothing business. Bobbie attended Detroit Business Institute and dreamt about someday getting a university degree.

Fay, a pert, strawberry blonde with freckles belying her twenty-two years, was especially happy her big sister would be preceding her to the alter. "Let's see the ring," she cried, tugging at Bobbie's arm.

Bobbie gave her a look. *A ring? Fay could be a problem.*

Minnie noticed the agitation on Bobbie's face. "You'll see the ring at the wedding. You shouldn't worry."

"How's Dad?" Bobbie asked, quickly changing the subject.

"Well," Fay said, "he's been kind of depressed since his letters to Aunt Esther came back unopened. Letters he wrote six months ago."

She was beginning to piece together her father's vulnerable state of mind during that fateful phone call. It wasn't simply the shock of a wedding. He had been distraught over the whereabouts of his sister in Warsaw. It had been a constant source of concern. "Why didn't he say something?"

"Guess he didn't want to bother you in all the excitement," Fay offered.

Bobbie felt a deep sadness thinking about her aunt lost somewhere in Europe. She had been hoping the family had found refuge in Switzerland. Although, Max had told her Jews were not welcome in Switzerland either. The Swiss government had insisted that a big "J" be marked on their passports. Suddenly, the horror stories she had heard at the Wellington took on even more urgency. *Poor dad, how he must be suffering.*

Together, Fay and Arleen grabbed Minnie's suitcase.

"Mama, for heaven's sake, what have you got in here?" Fay asked, dragging the bag along the rugged pavement.

"Well, a little this. A little that."

Bobbie smiled. A small pleasure, not having to carry her mother's case.

—⁓—

When the family Chevrolet pulled into the quiet, residential street on Detroit's westside, the women noticed a big black, official looking limousine drive past and stop at the Nathan home about three doors away. David Nathan's son, Robert, a first-year medical student, had proudly joined the Marines and gone overseas four months earlier. They watched in horror as two officers in dress uniform emerged from the vehicle and walked slowly up to the house. Mr. Nathan, pain etched on his face, stood stoically in the doorway. The dreaded war telegram had come to that neighborhood before, during the winter of 1942. Morris's close friend had lost his only son in the battle of Anzio and, now this. Bobbie closed her eyes. *Don't get involved with a*—She was beginning to piece together the real fears behind her father's reaction to her impending marriage. It was a dredging up of the evil eye, but that nosey captain had forced her to consider it. Dad was trying to protect her from possible sorrow.

She had decided not to mention anything to her mother and sisters, at least not right away. She had to find the right time. Of course, they were certainly not making this any easier. Within minutes of their arrival, Minnie was on the phone to every friend she had ever known, and Fay and Arleen started arguing about details — like flower arrangements and where everyone would be housed. It was getting ridiculous. She knew she had to talk to her father, soon. But when? He was probably despondent and would certainly be tired after the long commute from his clothing business in Holly. No. Not tonight. She was certain of one thing. Unlike her mother and sisters, Dad would embrace her decision.

—⚉—

Bobbie stood over the sink, trying to concentrate on the immediate task of preparing the salad for dinner. Minnie had been banned to the bedroom for a much-needed rest. Of course, Minnie felt fine. It was Bobbie who could have used the sleep, but there was too much to think about. Rest for her would come only after speaking to her father. And the sooner the better! She continued washing and rewashing the lettuce, doing her best to ignore the silly chatter behind her.

"Mama says Murray's really cute and a great dancer," teased Arleen. "But I don't know. We're going to have to check him over. Make sure he's a good kisser too!"

"Yeah," continued Fay. "Can't have our sister marrying a guy who can't keep up his end of the bargain." Both girls broke into gales of laughter as Bobbie's eyes went back into her head.

Minnie strolled into the kitchen, her face finally showing the wear of the last two days.

"Mama!" Bobbie cried. "What are you doing in here? You go back upstairs and lie down. We've got it all taken care of. There's nothing—"

"So? All of a sudden, I can't make my family dinner? What am I, an invalid?"

"Of course not. We just didn't want you to strain yourself, that's all."

"Where is it written that straining is bad? The day I can't make my own dinner in my own house – *Oye*, what a day!"

She was interrupted by the sound of the front door opening. *Dad was home!* Now, it would be just a matter of time before she could unburden herself and breathe freely. She scurried out of the kitchen. When she saw him, she froze. A handsome, dignified looking man, Morris stood in the middle of the living room, looking drawn and bent over, so much older than his fifty-five years. She'd only been away a little over three weeks. How could he have changed so quickly? They had all agreed not to say anything to him about David Nathan's son.

Bobbie ran over and threw her arms around her father. "Dad! It's so great to see you."

Morris looked befuddled. "You're home safe. That's good."

"I heard about your letters, Dad. I'm so sorry. I'm sure there's a proper explanation for all this." She saw tears in his eyes. She couldn't remember ever seeing tears in her father's eyes before.

"Forty years they've lived in Warsaw. God only knows what's—" His voice trailed off.

Minnie walked over and embraced her husband. He stood mute, vacantly accepting her hug.

Since the winter of 1942, Morris had read every piece of information he could get his hands on as reports of the murder of Jews were leaking out. He read them in disbelief. Not wishing to subject his family, he kept his darkest thoughts to himself, wrote letters to government leaders and politicians, and agonized over what he could do. He tried to send for his sister and her family, but his appeals got bogged down in bureaucratic red tape. Although thousands of European refugees had tried to flee between 1938 and 1940, Morris knew that the immigration policy in his own country was steadfastly against admitting Jews. He had signed many petitions after Kristallnacht in 1938 for legislation allowing them to emigrate, but there was a powerful group of isolationists and anti-Semites who had banded together to prevent these bills from becoming law. Now, Morris had heard of new horrors. A young Polish army underground emissary by the name of Jan Karski had been smuggled into one of the camps. His eyewitness account was relayed to the State Department and major Jewish leaders. Through a small article on page ten of *The Detroit News,* Morris learned that arrivals to a place called "Auschwitz" had been stripped of their clothes and forced into gas chambers.

Given Morris's emotional state, Bobbie was hoping her

mother wouldn't make a big deal about the wedding—
that wasn't going to be. *Too much on Dad's mind right now.*

Minnie had decided that her husband needed to be
reminded there was some good news. "We have a celebra-
tion, Morris." She winked at her husband, directing his
attention toward Bobbie.

No Mama, she thought. *This isn't the time!*

Morris's somber face softened. *"Mazel Tov."*

Bobbie felt a pang of guilt. Her father's dark mood had
been broken by *her* wedding plans? She knew she better hurry
up and talk to him before the charade went any further.

Morris's hand went to his forehead. "I almost forgot.
We've got a problem. Well, it is not so much a problem.
More of an inconvenience. A problem requires a whole
other set of circumstances. This just requires a sort of…
what? Maybe a compromise."

A problem. An inconvenience? Here was her chance.
Maybe, the rabbi was too busy. Maybe she wouldn't have
to admit her hasty decision after all. Wouldn't have to fess
up to her girlish stupidity.

They all stood, suspended, as Morris drew into himself.

"Nu?" Minnie pleaded. "What already?"

"Oh. I'm sorry. Yes. It is the caterer."

Bobbie felt a surge of energy. "He can't do it?"

Morris regarded his daughter with concern. "He
doesn't have enough food stamps."

A miracle! Thank you, God! "Okay. So. Look. It's no big
deal. We'll just cancel the wedding." She was trying to sti-
fle the rush of relief that was screaming out of her when

she noticed the faces of her family, frozen like grief masks in a Japanese Noh drama. *Even Dad!* Any hope of getting out of it easily all but disappeared. "I was just joking."

"So. Who needs a caterer anyway," replied Minnie. She brushed a lock of hair from Bobbie's frazzled face. "We'll have it in the house. I'll cook up my matzo balls and chicken livers. Everything will be perfect."

Chicken livers? Matzo balls? Was Mama kidding? She felt a twinge in the pit of her stomach and looked to her sisters, but their faces gave no indication of support. Was she losing her mind? Why was she getting so upset? There wasn't going to **be** any wedding, so there wouldn't **be** any chicken livers and matzo balls.

Minnie turned to Bobbie with a wink. "So. I was just joking, too."

"Good," said Morris. "It's settled. So, let's eat."

There had been enough tension in the house for one day. Whatever had to be settled could be handled more easily after dinner. Eating had always been the key to the unlocking of any problem. Renewal through nourishment —a timeworn tradition in the Feinman house. They all hurried into the kitchen, leaving Bobbie alone in the middle of the living room to wade through the crater of her predicament, furiously considering her next move.

—⚇—

By the afternoon of the next day, she still hadn't spoken to her father. Time was running out. Murray was probably on his way to New York to get his family. That night, Minnie broke the tragic news about the neighbor's son, and Bobbie felt she shouldn't burden her father again, so soon. But pride and embarrassment were her real enemies. So, she buried her frustration in a late-night raid of the refrigerator, her appetite directly proportional to her inability to tell anyone it was all a big mistake.

—⚹—

Morris sensed that something was bothering his daughter with whom he had a particular bond. It was Bobbie who had shown an interest in the clothing business, taking up the mantle of his son-deprived life. From a young age, she had joined him in the family business, carefully absorbing his special knowledge of the garment trade. He had named a newly acquired second store, "The Helen Shoppe" after her birth name. And, when she was old enough, he had proudly taken her on buying trips to New York, seeking and trusting her opinions on the latest fashion trends. His faith in her judgment encouraged and fed her own confidence. In the field of women's clothing, according to Morris, Bobbie had no equal. Often, she would hear her father say to his cronies. "Such a smart girl and what a head for business!" That, thought Bobbie, was just the problem. Dad had too much confidence in her judgment. And how had she repaid that faith? Jumping into marriage with a total stranger.

—⚹—

It was about eleven in the evening. The others had long ago retired to their rooms. Morris had just finished listening to the late news on the radio. Another heavy raid was reported over German industrial targets. Good, he thought. Maybe the nightmare will soon be over. From the hallway, he saw that a light had been left on in the kitchen. When he looked in, he found Bobbie sitting at the table, wolfing down a loaf of bread. An assortment of fruit, gefilte fish, cold beans, and cooked chicken was spread out before her, awaiting their turn.

"Hunger pains in the middle of the night? What's the matter? Your mother doesn't feed you?"

Bobbie's mouth was so crammed with food, it would take another moment of continuous chewing before she could muster a response. "Oh...! Dad! Hi. You want to join me?"

Morris carefully weighed the proposal. "Well...why not? That's what's so wonderful about your mother's cooking. You never feel full." He pulled up a chair and stared at the goodies laid out before him.

Finally, they were alone, out of earshot of the rest of the family. It was time. And, as Morris helped himself to some fresh challah, she sat watching him.

For almost two days, she had rehearsed what she might say. She had to strike just the right tone. Now, facing the ultimate moment, she felt confused. Should she wait until he had a bite to eat? Or, should she spring it on him right away? He might choke if she told him too soon. This was a delicate issue. Timing was everything. If she waited too long, he might get indigestion from the stress, although Mama had the more sensitive stomach. *Oh God. What to do!*

Morris started to cut himself another piece of bread.

Bobbie took a deep breath. "Dad, this has to be a difficult time for you, and I want you to know I really appreciate your support. Of course, you probably think I'm a little crazy doing this so fast, and I guess…you'd be right." She waited. Maybe, he sensed what she was about to say. She'd give him a chance to reply.

Morris began devouring the last of the gefilte fish.

Okay. Dad's just thinking. He does that. Disappears into a world of his own. Daydreaming — she understood. She had often been accused of it, herself. She'd just continue talking until he breaks in and rescues her. "The point is, Dad, everybody was so worried that Fay would be married before me. I didn't want to disappoint them." She thought she detected a small, subtle change of expression. A questioning look. She took a more impatient breath. "I know you might be thinking that Murray's not good enough for me. He's not a college boy. His father had a stroke when he was fourteen and he had to leave school to support his family."

Morris inspected a pickle that Bobbie had somehow missed. He bit into it, relishing its tarty taste. It was quite satisfying, this eating late at night. Why hadn't he indulged before? He usually snacked around eight o'clock, always in bed by eleven. He might be sick in the morning, but tonight—

She was desperate to release her secret thoughts. *Maybe, she should just blurt it out! Admit she had made a terrible mistake!*

But hadn't her father prepared her to be resourceful? How could she confess she hadn't used the common sense he had taught her? She couldn't do that. Couldn't diminish herself in his eyes. It would be like admitting he had failed to do his job – or she had failed to do hers. She continued to stammer on in muddled phrases, hoping it would magically penetrate, that he might finally save her from a decision that could ruin her life.

Suddenly, Morris looked up. His eyebrows furled, his eyes intense and probing.

He understands! Her heart was pumping so fast and hard, she might die right there in the kitchen!

He cleared his throat and wiped his mouth with his napkin. "Bobbie darling," he began. "You are old enough to know what you want to do. Besides, you should forgive me. According to your mother, you are no spring chicken."

What did he say? Something about a chicken. That's it? That's all he has to say? I'm no spring chicken?

Morris noticed a pained look on his daughter's face. Perhaps, he had spoken too harshly. He'd never knowingly hurt her feelings. "Of course, **I** was no spring chicken when I married your mother. I still took **some** chance."

Bobbie felt a sudden irritation. "You and Mama knew each other as kids. It's hardly the same."

"Big deal. So, what did we know? The truth? You never know." He leaned in close, beckoning from his personal well of knowledge. "Listen Bobbie, till you live with someone, you never know."

Maybe he did understand. He seemed to be acknowledging her fears by admitting his own. Quietly encouraging her to take the step. To jump in. Still, it was difficult to imagine her father could really *know* what she was feeling. After all, he was from another world. Another time. She couldn't remember her parents ever opening up. It was always a mark of their strength. Now, she felt mystified, her head spinning with possibilities. As if she had discovered another person inside the skin of this amazing man she called 'father'. For twenty-six years, she had involuntarily assigned her parents their roles as guardians of propriety, justice, and common sense. In Miami Beach, she realized that her mother actually had a life before **her.** And now, her father had shared a confidence about his marriage. Her heart ached with the loss of a child's truth. It wasn't an easy journey. How could she have been such a simpleton? The conceit of youth hadn't required her to understand. Her parents always seemed larger than life, omnipotent even. But, here sat this endearing, vulnerable individual, chomping away on a kosher pickle — with the same needs and worries as she.

"This Murray is going to have *some* job over there, **some** job. For this alone, he has my respect."

Bobbie felt a great burden lifting. She leaned over and embraced her father.

A tiny smile radiated from his solemn face. "Thirty wonderful years. The cooking could maybe be better, but you can't have everything. Which reminds me. You need money for a dress and whatever else you might require. Will fifty dollars be enough?"

How could she have imagined? That this would be the outcome of the talk that hung like a dense, dark fog over her thoughts for the last two days. Her father would be providing her with money for a wedding dress. He had given her silent permission to marry a stranger by trusting her judgment. And *that* gave her the strength to trust as well. Somehow, it would all work out. She smiled as she watched him tackle another large piece of challah. *What a remarkable man.* How she adored him. "Thanks, Dad. Fifty dollars will be just fine."

Chapter Thirteen

S ince her return, she had only briefly spoken to Eunice. Their one phone conversation had been strained. Maybe, she was projecting her own discomfort. She hadn't wanted to say anything until after speaking to her father. Didn't want to mention the wedding until she was sure there would be one. All those protestations about not wanting to get involved with a soldier! When she finally called with the news, Eunice was surprised, but genuinely happy for her. Yet, Bobbie sensed a sadness in her tone and deliberated over whether to invite her to help search for a dress, dismissing the idea a number of times before finally asking. Eunice eagerly accepted.

—⁓—

In Siegel's department store, Eunice watched Bobbie fumble with the zipper on a lovely light blue suit. "Why aren't you looking for a fancy gown?"

"It's hardly appropriate, Eunice. Besides, we can't afford it!" Wartime excesses weren't the custom anywhere, especially in the Feinman home. But Bobbie knew there was more to it than that. "I'm sorry. I didn't mean to jump on you. Guess I'm a little nervous."

"What have you got to be nervous about. You've got a great guy."

A great guy. Of course, he was. She hated herself for having such feelings. She debated whether she should say something to Eunice. What would she think if she knew? Her father had given her the courage to marry, but the doubts still lingered — with no opportunity to express them. Not to her mother. Not to her sisters. Especially, not to her father. Suddenly, she couldn't control them anymore. They started flooding out of her, and she exploded in tears.

"What am I doing, Eunice? We hardly know each other! I keep thinking he's giving everything for his country. The least I can do is make it happy for him, here. I don't know. Is that a reason to get married?"

"I...I thought you loved him?"

"I don't know what I feel. It's all happening too fast."

"Why didn't you just... sleep with him?"

Bobbie's face went ashen.

Sex was no big deal to Eunice, just an expression of her feelings for the man of her dreams. After the humiliation of being left at the altar, those prissy ideals about waiting for Mr. Right didn't seem to matter much anymore.

"Sorry, Bobbie, I didn't mean—"

"It's okay. You just caught me off guard for a minute."

"Have you talked about this with your family?"

Bobbie took a tissue from her purse and started to

wipe away her tears. "Well, I gave Dad a chance to get me out of it. Instead, he tells me—he says I'm not a spring chicken, anymore."

"Oh, really?" Eunice's lips pursed as she fought off a chuckle.

Bobbie felt a small cackle of her own coming on. *This is ridiculous!* The more she thought about it, the funnier it became. *No spring chicken!* Suddenly, she was standing in the dressing room laughing, uncontrollably. When she finished, she felt immensely better and thanked Eunice over and over for letting her purge her fears. "Everybody really wants this for me, and I know it's too late to turn back. I'm going through with it, but—" She lowered her head. "I feel like a fool."

"At least you have someone who wants you." Eunice hesitated. "I'm…late, Bobbie."

Bobbie looked at her, blankly. *Late?* Slowly, her eyes widened. "Oh God, Eunice. Frank? You think it was—"

Eunice nodded.

"Didn't he.. you know. Didn't he…" Bobbie certainly understood about birth control and condoms and that the man took responsibility for protection. She wasn't stupid. It was one of those useless bits of information a virgin picks up.

"What did he care. He wasn't planning on seeing me again."

"No. You mustn't think that. Maybe, you're getting all upset over nothing. Maybe, you're just…*late.* Sometimes, it happens. It doesn't have to mean that—"

"My life will be over."

The ordeal that lay ahead, if Eunice *was* pregnant, was not something Bobbie wanted to contemplate, at least not now. "Why didn't you tell me about this, sooner?"

"I guess I was afraid you'd hate me."

"Hate you? I could never hate you, Eunice. How could you even say such a thing?" She always assumed she had Eunice's confidence. Miami Beach had been the only exception. Sure. There were times her friend's behavior was outright exasperating, and Eunice probably felt the same about her. Still, she tried to be fair-minded, her thoughts more of concern than of judgment. Obviously, she hadn't done as good a job as she had hoped.

"I'm sorry, Bobbie. Guess I haven't been thinking too straight. The crazy thing is — I wouldn't mind having a baby. I'd probably have to go away to some…secretarial school for nine months like my cousin, Pearl."

Bobbie felt her throat go dry. Eunice's distant cousin wasn't exactly a loose woman. Eunice never referred to her that way, although the woman did have an unfortunate propensity for getting herself pregnant. She had married and divorced quite young. Bobbie had only met her on one occasion in between boyfriends when she had complained she could get pregnant without even having intercourse. Something about sperm crawling into the womb. Bobbie had raised an eyebrow on that one, but then, what did *she* know? Pearl would disappear for months at a time; then show up with her *adopted* baby. She now had two children. Once, she disappeared for a few days. When she returned, she had to go into the hospital and nearly died from massive internal bleeding. Eunice and Bobbie suspected she had a botched abortion but they never asked. Pearl's world was a hazy one, a bit outside Bobbie's and even Eunice's realm —until now. This was very serious business. Of course, Eunice could be wrong. Probably just a scare. But what if it was true? What would she do?

Suddenly, Bobbie felt ashamed. Here she was, selfishly going on as if hers was the only problem in the world, and Eunice – poor Eunice! Her mother and father – both gone. No close family. Facing a life-shattering predicament practically alone. *No. Not alone!* "Don't worry, Eunice. Whatever you decide, I'll be there for you."

Eunice managed a smile. "Thanks Bobbie. I knew I could count on you. I'm thinking of getting out of town for a while. Maybe stay with an old high school chum in Toledo."

"Whatever you think best." The world, she thought, was not only in a terrible mess. It was hopelessly unfair.

That night she lay in her bed, her pillow wrapped tightly around her arms, trying to convince herself she should feel grateful. How lucky she was that someone loved her and wanted to marry her. *Bobbie Pickarowitz, Helen Pickarowitz, Helen Bobbie Pickarowitz.* Maybe, if she kept repeating it, the name might sound more comfortable. She wondered if Murray was having doubts. Maybe, he was sitting up at night thinking he'd made a mistake, even agonizing over it. Why not? Was she such a bargain?

Suddenly, the door opened, and Arleen rushed in.

"Come quick. It's Murray!"

Murray? He wasn't supposed to be arriving for another two days! She felt her pulse racing. "He's here already?"

"On the phone, silly! And he sounds super!"

Bobbie felt an irritation with her sister's eighteen-year-old exuberance. "Super," she repeated as she slowly picked her body up off the bed. Arleen gave her a swift kick and booted her out the door. As she walked down the staircase, she had a vision of herself on her wedding day — Murray, at the bottom of the stairs looking up at her and wondering what the hell they were doing!

She heard her mother's voice in the living room, and it brought a much-needed smile to her face.

"That's wonderful, Murray! We can't wait! Now, don't worry about Morris. He's going to love you. Of course, **when** this will take place, God only knows, but you shouldn't worry about anything and God forbid there should be any trouble."

Minnie's eyes were drawn to Bobbie, now standing in front of her. With a playful grin, she relinquished the phone.

Bobbie took the receiver with reluctance. "Hi, Murray."

From a phone booth near the BMT subway line on Pitkin Avenue in Brooklyn, Murray had called to firm up the time of his arrival. He felt a surge of joy. It was the first time in almost a week he had heard her voice. "Hi there, Bob. How's everything going?"

"Super," she replied, flatly. She felt stifled, almost afraid that her words might be misinterpreted or that she might telegraph her fears to her mother and sister.

He detected something in her voice. Maybe she was tired or even nervous. Why not? He had a few nerves of his own. "Great. I'm picking up your grandmother, and we'll be taking the 12:15. Should be in Detroit sometime Wednesday morning."

"That'll be fine." *Here's your chance, Murray,* she thought. *It's all up to you.* "So I guess we're really going through with this, huh?"

"You betcha, Bob. Wouldn't miss it for the world!"

There was such exuberance in the tone of his voice. It was contagious, and it was pulling her back into the deep chasm of unguarded emotions. She was stirred, her former feelings of tenderness toward him, renewed. Her voice dropped to a whisper. "Me too," she heard herself say. "I mean— I feel the same. Have a safe trip."

"I will. Love ya!"

"Yes, and I—"

She heard a click. Feeling a vague disappointment, especially with her own behavior, she returned the phone to the cradle. *Me, too!* Some voice, not her own, had spoken those words. What happened to the doubting woman who had almost analyzed herself right out of the marriage?

Minnie and Arleen were standing inches away with big smiles on their faces. She tossed them a brave grin. "Yup. I guess he's coming."

—⁓—

Murray walked out of the phone booth with a renewed sense of purpose. Except for a moment when he thought her voice sounded strained, he hadn't considered she might be having second thoughts. He hadn't much time to think about anything except the logistics of getting first to New York and then to Detroit with his family. As he headed up Pitkin Avenue toward his mother's third-flight walk-up on Douglas Street, the wind had picked up with a vengeance. He pulled his jacket flap over his face. He suddenly heard a shrill, furious ring coming from the phone booth, now almost a block away. He hesitated. He could walk on. Just forget it. *No one would know.* Instead, he turned around, ran back to the booth, picked up the receiver and proceeded to speak in a heavy Polish accent.

"Hallo? Who's dis? Vat? How much?" Just as he feared, it was the operator wanting more money for the long-distance call. Murray took a deep breath. "I tink you vont the oder man. He just left." He pushed open the door and yelled out into the deserted, cold Brooklyn night. "Hey mister, come back!" He waited a moment. "Sorry, too late! Give me address in case I find him. Brooklyn is not so big." He took a pen and piece of paper from his pocket and obediently wrote down the information. "Tanks, operator." He hung up the phone, folded the paper, and meticulously placed it inside his wallet. He walked out of the booth — past memories of stickball and marbles, egg creams, long pretzels, and kosher corned beef. He stopped in front of the majestic Pitkin Theater that once propelled him into an extravagantly wonderful world of make believe. Suddenly, he was resolved. Brooklyn hadn't been so bad a place to grow up, but the old life was over. He also made a mental note. Someday, before he shipped out, he would have to send the money to the phone company. For now, they would just have to wait.

Chapter Fourteen

S he wanted the wedding to be a small family affair. She hoped her mother would see it that way, too. But Minnie had invited just about everyone they had ever known — except Meyer Zemansky. Meyer was a prune-faced bore with an enormous superiority complex. His father had been Morris's good friend, so for her father's sake, Bobbie tried to be nice to him. An amateur astronomer, he made a comfortable living as a shoe salesman, and on the rare occasion when she ran out of excuses and felt obliged to join him for a movie or dinner, he would start expounding on some dull scientific theory about the planets and then rhapsodize about the benefits of good feet. She never considered the ordeal of being in his company anything close to a date —more like an opportunity to hone her acting skills. He had no idea what a pathetic human being he was, she'd argue. Otherwise, he would do something about it. This logic was entirely lost on her mother.

Minnie was on her knees hemming Bobbie's two-piece suit from Siegel's. It was the first time she had been able to get the bride to stand still long enough to make the necessary alterations. The doorbell started ringing. Bobbie turned and looked out the front window. *Meyer!* She walked to the door and opened it. There he stood with that typically boorish look on his sun-drained face, his thin lips tightened in a perpetual smirk. Her uneasiness settled into disdain.

"Oh, hello, Meyer." She'd be damned if she was going to invite him in.

"Hello. When did you get back?"

"About a week ago."

"A week ago? One would have thought you'd have called."

Bobbie raised an eyebrow. "Really? Why would one have thought *that?* "

"No reason. You want to go to a movie tomorrow night?"

"I can't. I'm…" She grappled with the words. "getting married."

Cynicism brushed his face. "That's a joke, right?"

A flush of irritation settled on hers. "No joke."

Meyer's eyes narrowed. "You've only been away three weeks. That's a little hard to believe."

Bobbie winced. What was he thinking in that judgmental brain?

"Four o'clock, Sunday," offered Minnie as she walked toward him, her arms outstretched. "You'll come by for a little nourishment and a beautiful wedding, Meyer darling. Then you'll believe. Goodbye." Minnie waved him out and closed the door.

Mama had invited everyone and now, Meyer, too! Oh well.

He would be a tiny cockroach on the wall — insignificant, until someone noticed and swatted it. Suddenly, her face went white. What if petty little Meyer spread the rumor that she was marrying because she —God forbid – had to?

Minnie recognized the pained expression on her daughter's face. "Let them talk, *bubala,* As long as **you** know the truth."

It's that crazy mind of hers! Too concerned about what *other people* think. "Thanks, Mama. You are always so right."

"So. It makes me an Eastern Star. What do I know?"

"A lot."

Minnie smiled, shrugged her shoulders and resumed hemming. It was never that important to be so right.

—⟞⟝—

Murray tried to ignore the noise and discomfort of the crowded train as it pressed and churned its way to Detroit. His mother, Sarah, a tiny red-haired woman with deep-blue, determined eyes sat eyeing Bobbie's grandmother, Edith Rosenthal, equally small and equally determined. It had been a hectic few days since the engagement. He had called his mother, taken the train back to Brooklyn, and hurriedly arranged for the trip to Detroit with Sarah, his younger brother, Benny and Edith. Make sure everything's organized and everyone's comfortable! That was his first concern. This was the first time since the proposal he had time to *think* about the wedding. Mostly, he felt upbeat and positive. But, once in a while, grim thoughts struggled to push through. He'd quickly try to dismiss them, turning his attention to more important things. Where, for example, would they honeymoon? With only three days before he'd have to get back to base, Chicago might be nice. He'd never been to Chicago, and it wouldn't be as expensive as New York — an important consideration for a guy on an army allowance. Suddenly, his face twisted in panic. He turned to his brother. "Benny, you got the ring?"

Benny stared at him before carefully examining his pockets. Nothing. He nervously reached up and grabbed an overnight bag from the top rack as Murray, Sarah, and Edith watched; their faces frozen in horror as Benny produced everything but the ring. It had belonged to Sarah. Murray's father had given it to her when they married. Not worth much, it had sentimental value. Since Sarah was now remarried, she wanted her son to pass it on to his bride. And now, it appeared to be misplaced.

Benny let out a huge sigh. "What's the matter with you? You almost made me crazy! Don't you remember? I gave it back to you."

"You sure?"

"Yeah. You didn't trust me with it, so you took it back."

"So. Where is it?" asked Edith.

"You shouldn't worry!" Sarah shot back. "My boy takes care of everything." She turned to her son with the order. "Murray, find the ring!"

Murray reached into his inner jacket pocket, felt the ring's presence and smiled.

Sarah, Edith, and Benny let go a huge communal sigh.

"What did I tell you," beamed Sarah. "This is some boy your granddaughter's getting!"

"And you should know," countered Edith, "my Bobbie is so sweet and such a wonderful human being, you could *plotz!*"

Benny and Murray exchanged looks. The women had been silently studying one another ever since the train left the New York station. At last, they had something to talk about.

—⁓—

It was one in the morning. Sarah and Edith had been chattering away for hours, and Murray's head was spinning. Their endless prattle made sleep a luxury only Benny seemed able to enjoy.

"He left school when his father got sick so he could help me in the bakery. Such a blessing I have, you should only know!"

"My Bobbie worked for her father in the store since she was a baby. Such a head on her shoulders, *keninahora!*"

"Your son-in-law made her work as a baby?"

"She wasn't *such* a baby."

"My Murray used to—"

"Ma!" cried Murray, "Go to sleep!"

"Who can sleep? Edith, you want to sleep?"

"I'm too excited to sleep!"

Sarah turned back to her son. "So, you hear? We can't sleep. **You** sleep."

"I can't sleep, Ma. You're keeping me up."

"So? You couldn't maybe say something before?" Sarah leaned over to him in a calm, reassuring manner. "Our tongues should fall off if we speak another word."

Edith agreed. "Does a chicken live a hundred years?"

Does a chicken live a hundred years? What the hell does that mean? Fearing another round of animated dialogue, Murray decided it would be infinitely safer to smile and nod his thanks.

The women waited, patiently watching his eyelids go heavy. Then, like two naughty school girls, they let go triumphant giggles, placing their fingers over their mouths to shush each other. Now, at last, they could continue comparing notes, uninterrupted, deep into the night.

—∿—

Bobbie lay awake in the quiet of her bedroom. More questions swirled around inside her head, destroying any hope of a good night's sleep. How would she feel seeing Murray again? What would his family be like? What if her father didn't like him? Would his mother like **her?** She finally dozed off around five in the morning, and if it hadn't been for her sisters dragging her limp body out of bed, she'd have easily slept through his arrival.

She and Arleen climbed into the red Chevrolet her father bought her months earlier, the car's color – compliments of mobilization in the wartime economy. With gas rationing, it was difficult to drive all the way to Holly on just one gas ration book. Now, with her own car, they could take turns and still be able to have enough stamps to last the month.

Arleen noticed a tension in her sister's demeanor. A normally good driver, Bobbie was traveling very slowly, even stopping at green lights. Arleen wondered if she was feeling ill. They might never get to the station at this speed. Bobbie reassured her. She was simply *thinking*. Driving sometimes got in the way.

—⁓—

She watched nervously as the train limped into the station. They had made it within ten minutes of Murray's arrival. As the passengers disembarked, her eyes jutted from uniform to uniform. She tried to picture what he might look like after that long, uncomfortable ride. *Probably exhausted and out of sorts. Not as nice as she remembered.* She prepared herself.

Her heart took a sudden leap. There he was! His clean, sparkling uniform stunning against the gray, cold sky. His delicately handsome face—*luminous? How dare he look so good?* She remembered *her* train ride back to Detroit. A silent wind had wrapped itself around her body, tearing mercilessly at her clothes, turning her hair into a mangled mess of fuzz. She watched fascinated as he assisted a little woman in a long black coat off the train. *Could this be his mother?* Somehow, the image didn't fit. Here was a lady, probably her mother's age, looking like a newly arrived immigrant from the shtetles of Europe. Murray had spoken of Sarah with such admiration, Bobbie had come to think of her as quite modern. And, **he** was so assimilated with his Brooklyn accent and his love of American music and baseball. She expected his mother would be more Americanized, like her own parents.

Murray glanced around the platform, caught sight of Bobbie, and tossed her a warm wave. She met his glance with a well-rehearsed smile. Suddenly, she recognized her grandmother slowly emerging from the cramped car. Uncomfortable about facing the ultimate introduction, she nudged Arleen, and they both ran to Edith and embraced her. It had been over a year since they'd seen their mother's stepmother of whom the girls had the deepest affection. Edith had married Minnie's father after his first wife died in childbirth. Minnie was two at the time. At the young age of twenty-one, Edith was raising his five children and would eventually give birth to three more of her own. Although Minnie's heart silently ached for the love of her real mother, Bobbie had always been impressed with the inherent fortitude of the only grandmother she would ever know.

Bobbie turned to Murray. Perhaps he'd have second thoughts about seeing her. She examined his face for the signs.

He wasted no time, taking her in his arms with an energetic bear hug. Suddenly, she felt Sarah's penetrating gaze. *The woman hates me!* She could feel it.

Murray saw his mother staring but shrugged it off. "Ma, this is Bobbie."

"*Azoy dar!*" exclaimed Sarah.

"Ma!"

Bobbie felt a vague sense of relief. Yiddish had been her parents' private language. The only sister who made a point of learning it, she enjoyed the fact that people didn't know she understood. *She thinks I'm too thin. Well, it could have been worse.*

"Nice to meet you, Mrs. Pickarowitz. Murray's spoken so well of you." She could feel the sweat dripping off her face.

Murray turned to his brother. "And this is my brother, Benny."

"Hi there, Bobbie. Great to meet you!" His hand-shake was lively, making up for his mother's more somber greeting.

Sarah's stare remained steadfast. *What the hell is she staring at? Maybe, she thinks I'm not good enough. Mothers feel that way about their sons.* She was glad her father had girls —not that he had particularly adored any of **her** boyfriends.

Arleen cleared her throat. In all the excitement, Bobbie had forgotten about her. "Oh, and this is my kid sister, Arleen."

"Arleen!" exclaimed Murray. "Cute as a button. Just like you said, Bob."

Bobbie had no recollection of telling him that. *Boy, what a charmer this guy is!*

Arleen giggled as Murray and Benny each shook her hand with a similar exuberance. Through it all, Sarah stood mute, her eyes still fixed on Bobbie.

"My car's right outside." Bobbie offered, feeling her comfort level drop. "Can I help you with the luggage?"

"I got them, Bob," Murray insisted, picking up all the bags. Unburdened by the tensions of his soldierly duties and grateful to be off that train, four little suitcases posed no problem at all. "You've got your *own* car, Bob?"

Bobbie smiled. "It's the motor city, Murray. No subways here."

A car of her very own! What a girl! He used to sit on the stoop of his apartment building in Brooklyn and dream of someday owning a big expensive automobile – maybe a Cadillac. He had planned to make it a reality one day. But, with the depression and now the war, it had become a hopeless dream.

As they walked out of the station, Bobbie braced herself. Sarah had turned again to her son. Any minute another observation might be offered up.

"*A zoy—*"

"Ma!"

Chapter Fifteen

*M*urray's entire paycheck had gone toward the trip to Detroit. Sarah had to slip him ten dollars so he and Bobbie could go to a photographer. It embarrassed him. Taking money from his mother. But, Sarah knew her son was good for it. He had taken care of her for years.

—⟋⟍⟋—

Sitting for their wedding picture was one of the few times they would be alone together before the ceremony. Yet the communication that passed between them was curiously light. The careful getting to know you chatter about their families, how different Detroit was from Brooklyn, the honeymoon plans in Chicago. Shouldn't there be other things to discuss, she wondered. Where they would live? What he hoped to do, after the war? But Murray was strangely reticent about the future. It's all happening so fast, she thought, trying to reconcile her need to talk about it and his apparent need to avoid it. Perhaps, it was best not to push him. First one thing and then the other.

She took special enjoyment out of seeing him behind the wheel of her car. He had asked if he might drive, and she gratefully accepted.

Like a child with a new toy, Murray found everything about driving thrilling — even stopping for red lights. She never found downtown Detroit particularly interesting, but he did – especially since Canada was only a tunnel away.

"What do you think, Bob? You need anything in Windsor?"

His easy-going nature made it hard to turn him down, but gas rationing had limited their ability to go anywhere. "Don't worry, Murray. After the war, I'll give you a full tour."

He turned away. *After the war...*

Minnie was Murray's biggest fan, constantly laughing and joking in his presence. In this, Bobbie took comfort. Thank God her family had responded well to him. And though the doubts still lingered, there wasn't time to dwell on them. Even Sarah warmed up. Bobbie started speaking to her in Yiddish, and Sarah embraced her as a long-lost daughter returning to the tribe.

Minnie and Sarah seemed to be getting on without any major hurdles, although there seemed to be some sparring over the correct way to prepare meat loaf and matzo ball soup. Minnie did find it troubling that Sarah and Edith constantly discussed Bobbie and Murray's virtues. Secretly, their spirited discussions fascinated her. But to join in? *Never.* She might somehow incur the evil eye and she wasn't about to challenge a two-thousand-year superstition.

At first, Morris remained cordial but aloof. With thoughts of his sister's plight in Europe hanging over him, his mood was somber. Bobbie had spoken to Murray about it briefly, hoping he wouldn't misconstrue her father's detachment, and he instinctively understood. If it wasn't within his means to alleviate a problem, Murray usually put it out of his mind. That thinking helped him all his young life—from his war-torn childhood to coming of age in America, to the loss of his father and through the lean days of the depression. It was his personal coping mechanism and it served him well. His openness and humor were infectious, and Bobbie began to notice her father starting to enjoy his company. It didn't hurt that Murray's first name as it appeared on his army records was 'Morris', a coincidence not lost on the rest of the family.

—⁂—

An undefined tension filled the air as the guests sat around the dining room table quietly consuming Minnie's gefilte fish, matzo ball soup, and cooked chicken. Earlier that day, it was reported that a German submarine had sunk a fourteen-thousand-ton U.S. aircraft carrier in the North Atlantic. Troop ships were leaving American ports all the time now heading for England, and the news of the sinking quieted even the usually animated Minnie.

Morris broke the silence and turned to Murray with strained civility. "Bobbie says your outfit could go overseas anytime now."

Murray hesitated, searching for a way to ease the worried looks all around him. "I report back to Miami Beach, and then it's anybody's guess."

Morris was a rational man, but hope had become his only comfort. "Rommel is retreating with big losses in Tunisia. You think it could be over soon?"

Murray took another bite of his chicken and glanced over at Bobbie as if to find in her eyes some consolation from what he was thinking. An eerie quiet had penetrated the room. He saw the sadness etched on Morris's face. He couldn't tell him what he really felt. "You never, know, Morris. It could be over just like you said. We've got to have hope." His voice sounded upbeat, and his words seemed to allay some of their fears. He saw the looks of relief on their faces. He was grateful they had believed him or at least pretended to. It was easy for him—telling them what they needed to hear.

There was a sudden ringing of the doorbell. Minnie excused herself and went to see who could be interrupting their family gathering. Her house was open to friends, night and day. Yet, she didn't remember inviting anyone except close family to this dinner.

—⟋⟍—

Lou Weisgal was Bobbie's favorite uncle. A thin, angular man of sixty, he was married to one of Minnie's sisters. An independent spirit, an ardent Zionist, and a perpetual optimist, he had introduced her to the world of opera at the Metropolitan in New York. During the middle thirties, he'd invested in a production of *The Romance of a People* sponsored by the Jewish Agency for Palestine that his brother had helped produce. It was a biblical journey of the Jewish people with a cast of thousands, mounted at Soldier's Field in Chicago during the World's Fair. When the production played Detroit, Bobbie was able to secure a small part in the chorus. Lou's next venture was to invest in a Broadway musical drama called *The Eternal Road,* directed by Max Reinhardt. Lou's brother, Myer, had conceived the production in 1937 as a way of alerting a then unaware country of Hitler's persecution of the Jews. The show ran for 153 performances but was expensive to mount and never able to recoup its losses. Not a wealthy man, Lou had gambled his savings on the project, even trying to coax Morris into investing. But Morris, always the careful businessman, was skeptical. After all, the depression was on, and he had a family of five to feed. Eventually, Lou lost his investment and never complained. Morris, careful not to hurt his brother-in-law's feelings, never said "I told you so".

Minnie never expected any of her sisters and their husbands in New York to attend the wedding on such short notice. When the call came that Lou would be coming, everyone, especially Bobbie, was overjoyed.

"Lou!" she cried as she opened the door. "You come in a day early! You don't call? Someone would have picked you up."

"You've got plenty to do, Minnie. I took a cab. It's okay." He was always doing crazy spur of the moment things. It was part of what made him so loveable. "Everybody here?"

Minnie gave him a wink. "Come. You'll meet him."

As they entered the dining room, Minnie turned to her family with a subtle smile. "So. Guess who dropped by?"

Bobbie jumped up to embrace her uncle. His presence would help ease the pale that had settled over the dinner conversation. An avid storyteller, he was always good for some inside information that never appeared in the newspapers. Morris sometimes questioned the veracity of his tales, but at least Lou was interesting and his commentary often made for spirited discussions.

"So, Lou," said Morris, "I thought you were coming in tomorrow?"

"So, Morris, *nischt geferlach*, I lied."

After dinner, everyone sat around the dining room table listening intently as Lou spoke of the thousands of people who gathered in Madison Square Garden a few days before, urging Roosevelt to act on behalf of the European Jews. He told them about the resolution proposing their rescue through neutral agencies. He felt hopeful that the government would explore all possibilities for their resettlement.

Bobbie's thoughts went back to the refugees at the Wellington — the lucky ones who got out. Murray began thinking about his childhood friends in Lomza, the ones who may have stayed behind and were now—unable to leave.

Lou eagerly talked about an international conference scheduled for the following month in Bermuda. He was convinced it would be successful. To his hope-starved listeners, his words resonated like a beacon of light.

Morris, usually full of opinions, kept his head down. Just that morning, he had read in the back pages of the paper more demoralizing reports about Nazi slaughter of Jews at a place called "Treblinka".

A self-taught man with a fascination for history, Morris saw the old refugee policies of the twenties enforced in the forties. Thousands of people were being kept out of the U.S. He knew that Assistant-Secretary of State, Breckenridge Long, controlled the program that actually made up the meager rescue effort. Long believed that Nazi agents could come ashore with the relaxing of the visa policies and had expressed concern about "Jewish agitation" weakening the war effort. Morris had some inside knowledge of his own, but it was too distressing to repeat to the family. Through one of his oldest friends who worked for the Treasury Department, he learned that Long was a notorious anti-Semite.

No longer able to keep silent, Morris raised his head.

"Lou, since when does the world care about a few million Jews?"

"Don't be such a pessimist, Morris. Roosevelt has to listen now. He'll come to their aid, you'll see. I've got a good feeling this time."

Morris's face flushed; his breath became labored. "You've got a good feeling? Where have you been? Hundreds of thousands already murdered in Poland! Every day, we read about more atrocities. Still, they do nothing! And you say I am a pessimist? YOU ARE A FOOL!"

"Morris!" Minnie reprimanded.

A cold hush fell over the table. Bobbie covered her face with her hands. *Why had they chosen this time to have such a depressing quarrel? One day before her wedding!*

Murray sat, quietly listening to Lou's optimistic assessment. He wanted to believe it, but he understood the perplexing implications of Morris's charge and knew in the depth of his soul that Morris was probably right.

Lou stood up from the table. He knew better than to start an argument with Morris, especially one which he could never win. Emotions were too high. Besides, it was the wrong time. "If you will excuse me, I have some unpacking to do."

As he left the room, darkness again settled over the gathering. Although embarrassed by his outburst, Bobbie suffered for her father who sat sullen and despondent. His concerns touched her deeply; yet she couldn't know how prophetic his words had been. (By the end of 1943, most of the Jews of Europe would be annihilated.)

A sudden voice like that of an angel attempted to lift them out of their despair. "I hope everybody had enough to eat. The butcher said there's a problem with the beef."

All eyes turned to Minnie.

"What do you mean a problem?" Morris asked. "Is it bad?"

"Did I say it was bad?"

"You mean a shortage, Mama?" Bobbie asked.

"Yes, that's it."

"So why didn't you say that?" charged Morris.

Her eyes sent daggers to her combative husband. "*Zorg zug nischt!* I **said** – there's a problem with the beef!"

Oh, God, thought Bobbie, *what an example of our family life.* Maybe she should cut her wrists now and get it over with! Her sisters always accused her of being a drama queen, but this was heavy stuff for a young woman about to make the plunge of her life. Didn't she have enough to worry about?

Seeing the despair on Bobbie's face, Murray turned to Minnie with a twinkle in his eye. "Minnie, the matzo balls were delicious! Just like Mama makes."

Sarah raised an eyebrow.

Minnie started to giggle. Finally, he called her *Minnie.* "It's very easy. Like nothing to make. You want the recipe, maybe?"

"The recipe we got," Sarah shot back.

The women stared at each other in subtle defiance.

Oh, God, thought Bobbie. *Was there no way of rescuing this evening!*

Suddenly, Murray pulled back his chair and stood up. "There's something I've got to say."

That's it! He sees it's all a big mistake and he going to end it right now! She held her breath. The room grew silent.

"I'd like to make a toast."

Everyone clapped wildly, grateful for a reprieve. But Bobbie was suspicious, her hands poised on her chin. *Maybe Dad will find some fault with Murray's words, too.*

Murray lifted his wine glass high above his head. Unusually quiet during the ruckus, he never liked arguments. *Such a waste of time!* But, when he saw Bobbie's sweet face flush with embarrassment, he knew he had to act. "Here's to my future wife who on Sunday will make me the happiest man in the world." He leaned over and placed a gentle kiss on her cheek as everyone howled their approval.

Bobbie's eyes welled up. *Their only intimate moment since his arrival, and it happens in front of everyone!* Yet, his timing was perfect. The tension was broken and the room was animated, again. Even her father rallied. She caught him smiling.

Minnie stood and lifted her wine glass toward Murray. Two thousand years of superstition be damned. She'll risk the evil eye just this once. "In my humble opinion, Murray, you are getting the most wonderful daughter in the world, although I got two more wonderful daughters here, and there's our Teen in New Jersey. She's going to have a baby!"

Murray's face lit up. "I'll drink to that!"

"My son's the most wonderful boy in the world," Sarah offered. "You shouldn't worry."

"Am I worried?" Minnie replied. "I could see that as soon as I met him. A perfect match."

"*Keninahora!*" added Edith, "With my Bobbie, the mold they broke. I remember when she was a little girl—"

"Edith, *shah!*" reprimanded Morris. He had been observing the compliments with an air of good humor, but too much wasn't so good. He glanced over to Minnie for her support in the matter. And this time, she agreed. They had all become much too vulnerable. The evil eye was beckoning. She backed up her often-exasperating husband with a quick '*tzu tzu tzu*', then batted her eye lashes and bestowed upon Murray her most endearing smile.

Mama was flirting! Bobbie could feel herself go red, again.

—⁓—

That night in the quiet of her room, she lay restless, replaying the captain's menacing words, *You could be a widow. A widow!* She winced. What, after all, did she really know about Murray? Enough to base a marriage? Sure. It was the times. Everyone was doing it. So what? Was she supposed to feel comforted by that? And what about her father's original warning? He must have known something. Why hadn't he tried to talk her out of it? It must be the right thing to do. *Oh God. Leave it alone, already!* Sleep. She needed sleep. She could feel the bags under her eyes pushing into her nose. She readjusted her pillow, pulled the covers tightly over her head and started counting sheep. It had miraculously worked its magic on her as a child. And now, she needed all the help she could get.

—⁓—

Arleen and Fay had gone to stay with friends to accommodate the Pickarowitz family. In the small bedroom he now shared with his brother on the second floor, Murray stared at the branches of the maple tree rustling outside the window and listened to the stirring of the wind against the sill. A normally good sleeper, he wasn't a bit tired. He thought of knocking on Bobbie's door, but it was way after midnight, and she was probably fast asleep. He felt an undefined agitation. Something had been troubling him — something he hadn't shared with anyone. He looked over at Benny snoring in the next bed. He took his pillow and threw it at him, brushing his face. Benny fidgeted, and the snoring stopped. The silence only encouraged Murray's apprehension. Suddenly, relief swept over his face. He retrieved his pillow and lay back on his bed. *What a jerk he'd been. Of course!* He didn't need to feel guilty about asking Bobbie to marry him. He wasn't being completely selfish, after all. As the beneficiary of his ten-thousand-dollar G.I. life insurance policy, she would be taken care of — at least for a while.

Chapter Sixteen

T he front doorbell was ringing erratically. *Now what?* thought Minnie, as she rushed to answer. Already frustrated by the seemingly endless details, she worried there wouldn't be enough food, or the flowers wouldn't come in time, or Rabbi Adler, their dear family friend, would somehow forget or go to the wrong house. None of it made much sense but Minnie wanted the wedding to be perfect and things always had a way of going wrong at the last minute. Suddenly, she realized – *Did Fay remember to tell Bobbie when exactly to come down the staircase?* She made a mental note to ask as she opened the front door.

Boshie Cohen, a thin, light-haired boy of twenty, stood before her, upheaval etched on his face. The only son of Minnie's best friend from her childhood town of Kikol, Boshie had spent some of his summers with the Feinmans, and Minnie once nurtured a wish that he and Fay might someday marry. Then, the families would be united. The problem was that Fay could never abide this spoiled mama's boy, and Boshie had never shown the least bit of interest in the opposite sex.

"Boshie, darling, come in! So, how was the trip?"

"Don't ask, but my mama said I shouldn't miss this wedding for the world."

"That's very sweet, Boshie. We're happy you came. So, how is your mama?"

"That woman will be the death of me, but she sends her love."

The only member of the family who tolerated his constant whining, even *she* was feeling a lapse of patience. "You want maybe something to eat?"

"Ugh! No food. The train ride took care of that. That railway company should rot in hell! But, I would kill for a bath."

"You don't have to kill, *bubala*. Upstairs, you remember? First door on the left. You should knock twice, just in case."

Boshie tossed her a quick nod, picked up his small case, and flew upstairs. Minnie rolled her eyes and heaved a deep sigh.

—⁓—

Like a caged animal, Murray paced back and forth in his room. That morning, he had awakened early, managed about one hundred pushups, then took a long walk around the neighborhood. He found pleasure in the lush, well-manicured lawns in this quiet residential area of Detroit, so different from the stoops and tenements of Brownsville. The beautiful old maple and oak trees buzzed with crooning birds. He could actually hear their melodies. *How come they never sing like that in Brownsville?* Even with the few trees scattered throughout the borough, Brownsville's birds didn't have the energy to compete with the noisy street life around them. Their sounds were more muted, more of a hacking than singing. He closed his eyes and listened to the gentle sway of the trees, relishing the chance to be away from the commotion of the last two days. *Too many people! Too much going on in this house! Poor Bobbie! Stuck in her bedroom. If only she could have come along.* Fay and Arleen had been guarding the door of her room with hawkish determination. He hadn't yet figured out a scheme to get them out of the way, but he was working on it.

He stopped at a small restaurant a few blocks from the house, ordered a cup of black coffee and started to read a newspaper. Suddenly, he felt sick to his stomach. He lay his head on the table and waited. He knew the feeling well. Like an old, trusted friend, it had returned. The disturbing dream that interrupted his sleep more often now. It was still stalking him, rudely cutting into his thoughts, challenging his sanguine nature. After a moment, it passed, but he resented the intrusion.

Benny had finished polishing his well-worn shoes when he noticed Murray's pacing. *Probably just wedding day nerves.* He idolized his older brother. When their father died, Benny was ten. Murray became a surrogate father, always taking care to shield him from any problem he might face. Benny didn't have the same fighter instinct. Born in America, never knowing war, he had a somewhat easier childhood.

"Hey, Murray, you okay?"

"Yeah. Yeah. Fine. But, maybe, I'll see what Bobbie's doing."

"What? Are you crazy? Don't you know? It's bad luck on your wedding day."

"You, too? What is this? A conspiracy? That's a lot of crap, Benny."

"Okay, big brother, be my guest. Go, if you dare."

Murray headed for the door. He had to find a way to get her out of that bedroom. He couldn't exactly bribe her sisters. With what? No. He'd have to create a diversion. Then, the two of them could take that walk together and listen to the birds sing.

Suddenly, they heard a powerful knock followed closely by another. The door flew open, and Boshie stood before them, gazing at the two specimens of male splendor.

"Well, hello! I'm Boshie from Chicago, and who might you be?"

Benny cleared his throat. "I'm the groom's brother, Benny."

Murray shuffled his feet uncomfortably and offered up a careful smile. "I guess that would make me the groom."

"Oh. It's the one!" He ran over, embraced him and placed a sloppy kiss on his cheek. "Just had the most horrible train ride! Thought this was the bathroom. Guess not." He leaned in to Murray. "We'll see **you,** later!" Then, like a bolt of lightning, he was gone.

Murray stared at the door, taking a deep breath and reconsidering his options. Perhaps, he'd been too hasty.

Maybe he wouldn't venture out of the room right away. *Don't want to tempt the fates,* although he had never been the least bit superstitious before. Finally, he looked over at his brother with resolve. "Come on, Benny, let's play some cards."

—⁓—

Minnie was ecstatic. The fireplace was draped in some of the most beautiful white and red roses she had ever seen, compliments of a Holly florist who had received a large last-minute shipment and insisted on bringing them all to the wedding. Morris had done a great many kindnesses for the man's family in the years they had lived in Holly. And, now, he could repay him in a small way.

Two soldiers — Herman Sperling, a tall, swarthy Feinman cousin, and Louis Cook, a close family friend — were helping assemble the purple velvet chuppah. Lou was trying his best to supervise, but neither soldier was intent on listening to his suggestions.

Sarah and Edith were seated in the living room, exchanging more vital information. And, Minnie was discussing last-minute music arrangements with Doris Abrams, a rotund little woman nervously holding two worn pages of sheet music and looking confused. Everything was in place —except Rabbi Adler had yet to arrive.

A concerned Morris looked anxiously at his watch and walked over to his wife. The guests had now moved to their chairs and were regarding *their* watches.

"*Nu?* Where is he?" he asked.

Minnie wouldn't let him see her concern. "I told him four. He's coming. You shouldn't worry."

"He's coming? So's the messiah."

Minnie turned to Doris. "Doris, sing something."

"I only know one song."

"So?"

"So, I was saving it for when Bobbie walks down the stairs."

"So, you'll sing it again. Nobody will notice."

Doris stared at her music, cleared her throat and sang "Oh Promise Me" off pitch.

—⚹—

Bobbie lay in bed longer than usual this morning. To keep herself from getting too agitated, she read the telegrams —like the one from her older sister, Teen, in New Jersey. Teen had married three years earlier and was expecting her first baby any day. Since she had once suffered a miscarriage, it was decided she shouldn't make the long trip. Fine with Bobbie. She certainly didn't need another sister policing her every move. She had hoped to find a few moments alone with Murray. Perhaps if she knew what **he** was thinking about this day, she might feel a bit more comforted, but Fay and Arleen insisted she stay out of sight. *A virtual prisoner in her own house! Locked up in this stifling little bedroom! The whole situation is absolutely absurd!* She hated people fussing over her, telling her what she was supposed to do. All she wanted was to be left alone, but Eunice had insisted on coming over early to help her dress. *Why did she need someone to help her get into a suit?* Afraid of hurting Eunice's feelings, she relented. Mustn't act ungrateful, especially since the man of Eunice's dreams was probably somewhere in England unaware that he might be a papa. Mustn't look too happy, either. Eunice might get depressed.

Her friend was guarding the door as Bobbie stood before the mirror combing her long, black tresses. At Eunice's insistence, she had dressed way too early, and now she couldn't sit down or she'd wrinkle her suit. *Why is she looking at me like that? Probably waiting for me to explode.* Bobbie would show *her*. She'd be the very essence of calm. After all, she was a master at the art of pretending.

"You comb your hair anymore, and it's going to fall out."

"Good, Eunice. I've got enough of it. If I go bald, so be it!"

It was the only thing that kept her hands from trembling, and she wasn't about to stop. *She might comb her hair right up to the moment she had to go down those stairs! She might—*

There was a knock. Eunice opened the door a crack. Fay slid in, shutting the door quickly behind her.

Bobbie felt her heart beat with a little more urgency. "So?"

"Rabbi Adler hasn't come yet."

"Wonderful. I'll just stand here till I drop. Did you get it?"

"Yeah, but it wasn't easy." Fay reached inside her bosom and produced a thinly wrapped corned beef sandwich.

"Perfect! Thanks." She grabbed the sandwich from Fay's hands, tore away the foil paper and bit into it with frenzied zeal.

"This woman is remarkable," mused Eunice. "Getting married any minute and she eats a corned beef sandwich!"

"That's my big sis," remarked Fay. I wish I felt as calm. I'm just a bundle of nerves!"

Bobbie smiled to herself. *What an actress! Why, she should be heading for Hollywood or Broadway with such talent!* And, what's the big deal about wanting a corned beef sandwich, anyway? She hadn't eaten all day and she was starving. Of course, she'd be damned if she was going to tell that to them.

The door swung open and Arleen dashed in. "He's here!"

Her mouth full of food and her eyes flashing terror, Bobbie dropped her sandwich and stared at her kid sister. Suddenly, the hot corned beef she had already chewed felt like a constriction in her throat. All those fears – the doubts she had so cleverly concealed from everyone except Eunice that day in Siegel's department store – no longer hung like an albatross around her neck. She ran into the bathroom throwing them all up.

—◊◊◊—

They sat on the steps at the top of the staircase apart from the others. Lou had just finished serenading the guests with a medley of Yiddish songs; now, he was relentless in an attempt to engage them in another songfest around the well-provided food table. The wedding had been delayed about two hours and the only activity the guests wished to pursue was stuffing food into their hungry mouths. Bobbie felt grateful that no chicken livers and matzo balls were present. And, although her mother and sisters had pitched in and provided a feast of cold cuts, fruits, breads and desserts, she wasn't able to eat any of it.

Boshie and Arleen sat together on the feather-down divan in the living room listening to Meyer Zemansky, who had arrived just in time for the cold cuts, declare that according to the alignment of the planets, the war would definitely be over in six months. He had it on good authority.

Minnie and Morris stood a few feet away. "Boshie and Arleen look good together, no?" whispered Minnie.

"What? You're still trying to make a match?"

"So, what's wrong? I can't dream?"

"Dream? More like a nightmare."

On the other side of the room, Benny sat crouched uncomfortably on a straight-backed chair with a vacant look in his eyes as Eunice hovered over him.

"You know, Benny, I was there at the beginning, and I told Bobbie right away. 'That guy would be perfect for you!' I only wish it could happen for me. It almost did. They say there's a right person for everyone, and I am ready! I'm telling you, kiddo, I'm sick and tired of the single life. How about you? You ever think of settling down?"

Benny had just turned twenty-one. Unlike his oldest brother who married quite young, he was in no rush. He was hoping to follow Murray into the Air Corps, but a bad hip kept him out of the Army. "I guess it's harder on women, Eunice."

"You said a mouthful, Ben. Let me ask you something." She moved closer, slowly maneuvering her arm around his shoulder. "Now, be honest, okay? Don't be afraid to say what you feel. Do you think you could ever be attracted… to an older woman?"

"No."

Sarah and Edith sat together at the kitchen table, oblivious to everyone around them and diligently comparing notes.

"He could have been a doctor. My brother, the doctor, wanted him to come to Cleveland. He stayed with his mother. Such a good son."

"You think you got such a deal? My Bobbie could run a company, but she would rather work with her father in the store."

"So? Better she should run a company."

—◦◦◦—

Bobbie was grateful for a few moments of quiet from the endless toasts. A few solemn words from the rabbi may have turned them into a married couple, but they weren't exactly soul mates—not yet. They hadn't shared the kind of intimacy of that first day on the beach when he had opened up to her and, inadvertently given her a glimpse of the vulnerable child within. Since his arrival, she had ardently wished for something to happen, something maybe more personal, but most of their talks had been upbeat and vague. Like well-rehearsed actors in some strange comedy of manners, they were each faithfully speaking the lines, the audience responding appropriately with cheers and claps. Now, the play was over — the rabbi, having decreed them husband and wife. Strangely, she felt closer to him than she ever thought possible. And, the way it happened, she never could have guessed. She had panicked and almost ruined the entire wedding. Nearly humiliated her family and brought shame on herself!

It started before Doris began singing "Oh Promise Me". That was supposed to be her cue to walk out of her bedroom and down the stairs. Instead, she was in the bathroom whooping up the corned beef, and neither Fay nor Arleen could get word to Doris to stop singing. Doris wasn't only tone deaf, she was heavily nearsighted.

Horrified by her sudden sickness, Bobbie wept before the bathroom mirror. Nothing was right. Her hair was a mess! The hair she spent hours combing. Her suit was wrinkled and water stained—the suit she stood in for more than two hours to avoid wrinkling. She tried so hard to do the right thing. To be appropriately thankful, confident, and glad, but now she couldn't help herself. The tears wouldn't stop.

Murray was waiting alongside his brother. After the second chorus of Doris's song, he turned toward the stairwell. Bobbie was nowhere in sight. He bolted up the stairs to the gasps of the impatient guests. Fay pointed him toward the closed bathroom door, and he knocked lightly. "Bobbie?" Hearing a click from within, he tried the door. It opened easily. He entered and walked over to her, offering his handkerchief. His eyes were warm and reassuring. He took her in his arms. To her surprise, they felt strong and safe, and he held her firm until her tears dried and she was ready. He gave her a wink, and they walked out of the bathroom and down the staircase together as Doris, cued by Minnie, sang "Oh Promise Me" in still another key.

He had been there at certainly the most embarrassing moment of her life. He had allowed her to cry on his shoulders until the last tear of apprehension and regret had been cried out. He hadn't judged her, hadn't shown any irritation at all. It was his quiet strength that gave her the courage to go down those stairs.

Now, as she sat on the landing, gazing at this stranger who in a few short moments had become her husband, she found herself thinking about his lean, muscular body and feeling an urgent desire to be alone with him in that other way. Could it be that all along, she had been a sex fiend masquerading as a virgin?

Murray turned toward her. His own amorous thoughts were dizzying his senses. He didn't want to rush things, but he wondered whether to mention that they should start thinking about going to their hotel so that they could... get a good night's sleep before their morning train trip to Chicago. "This was a wonderful wedding, Bob."

"Yes. It certainly was. Your mother seemed to really enjoy herself." *God, she hated small talk!*

"She loves a good party. She's just like me."

There was a momentary silence, both struggling to find something interesting to offer to the other.

"You've got a great family," he droned on.

"So do you. I mean your brother, Benny...very sweet."

"Yeah. He's a great guy." *Just say it, jerk!* "So, Bob, you want to get out of here?"

"God, Yes!"

Her quick response surprised him. He pretended to lose his footing on the staircase, offering both of them a much-needed laugh.

—⋙—

It was more than an hour before they could finally escape. A quiet exit had been impossible with the many new rounds of toasting to their happiness.

Morris started talking about the challenges of marriage, all the time affectionately nudging Minnie who stood by his side, beaming. When he spoke about Bobbie, it was her integrity that he admired most. She was so moved she had to excuse herself and leave the room. She'd never heard such loving words from her father's lips. She didn't feel worthy.

Minnie giggled her way through a charming chronicle of Bobbie's childhood; how she used to lie on the railroad tracks as a little girl if she couldn't get her way. Bobbie hadn't done that since she was ten. *Did Mama think she might try it again?*

Eunice provided them all with an unsolicited and raucous history of the last three weeks, complete with Bobbie's screaming episode on the beach. The guests were uncomfortably silent while Bobbie stood cowering with each detail. There had been something cruel in Eunice's need to humiliate her. Perhaps she had too much to drink, but Bobbie showed no anger.

Just after midnight, Fay and Arleen whisked them out the back door, and a Feinman cousin drove them to the Cadillac Hotel in downtown Detroit.

Chapter Seventeen

*T*he curt, humorless desk clerk eyed them with suspicion as he asked their names.

"Mr. and Mrs. Murray Pickarowitz," exclaimed Murray.

Bobbie quickly produced the ring. It was common in wartime for soldiers and their girls to say they were married. The ring would be important proof.

He gazed back at her with a calculated arrogance. "I believe you, madam!"

At least, he could be civil, she thought.

"Newlyweds?" he asked.

How did he know that? Had she appeared too eager? Maybe, she had misjudged him. Perhaps, he wanted to offer his congratulations.

They each nodded, smiling affectionately at one other.

"In that case, please try to keep the noise down. Most of our guests are already sleeping."

What a rude, condescending old fart, she thought. She would tell her friends to boycott this pretentious hotel in the future.

At least the old buzzard hadn't asked for their religious

affiliation. Murray could laugh at impertinence, but a bigot—that was something else.

—⚋⚋—

The honeymoon suite was a modest, scantily decorated space looking out to a tiny courtyard. Bobbie hadn't taken much notice since she retreated into the bathroom as soon as they arrived.

Murray sat on the side of the creaky double bed, waiting for her to emerge. He was feeling exhausted, and the bed suddenly looked very inviting. He struggled to keep his eyes from closing. How would it look if she came out of the bathroom and found him snoring away? Some macho guy *he* was! He needed an activity, something to keep him alert. He picked up the silk pajamas that he had already taken from his suitcase and started untying the knots. He didn't wear pajamas but had promised his brother who had gone to great expense to obtain them, that he would wear them on his wedding night for luck. At first, Murray balked, but Benny was adamant. Now, he understood why. Every opening had been stitched up. *Very funny!* He looked over toward the bathroom and wondered if he should check on her. He had knocked earlier. She said she was fine. That she'd be right out. That was over a half hour ago. Between her bathroom duties and his efforts to get his pajamas unstitched, he seriously wondered if they had time to make love before their 10:00 a.m. train to Chicago.

Bobbie gazed at her reflection in the bathroom mirror.

She felt uneasy in the sexy white negligee her sisters had given her as a wedding gift. Perhaps, it was too daring. After all, what was she trying to prove? And why was she acting like such a child? Why couldn't she open the door and walk out into the arms of her loving husband? Millions of women had done it before her, and no one had died— at least no one she ever heard of. So, what was the *problem?* She never thought to ask her own married sister about what to expect. Certainly, she wouldn't presume to question Eunice. It all seemed so personal. Instead, she had to be satisfied with those great works of literature, the ones that didn't make it to the best seller lists. *All this knowledge makes her an Eastern Star?* It was her mother's favorite phrase. Now, it had become hers. She read everything, and she knew nothing. A twenty-six-year-old virgin standing in the john shaking with fear. *A country bumpkin!* She closed her eyes. Maybe, she should pretend she was in a Hollywood movie. She had seen all the great screen romances, hoping at least one might offer some insight. Just when it appeared she might learn something, the scene would always fade out. Hollywood's morality code was a big laugh, even to virgins. Where were her witty lines? Where was the swell of music ushering in the appropriate response? Who could she be? *Lana Turner? No. Not clever enough. Maybe, Mae West in those thirties flicks. That's it!* She would be Mae West and slink out into the awaiting arms of her paramour—if she could only keep a straight face.

When she finally emerged from the bathroom, Murray was sitting on the bed in his underwear, fumbling with his pajamas and looking so forlorn that it gave her strength. At least, he wasn't lying there naked with wild expectations! It might have been too overwhelming. Her heart might not have been able to handle it.

Murray looked up. *Finally! How radiant she looked! Whatever she did in there for almost a half hour couldn't have made her more beautiful.* "You look terrific!"

"Thanks."

He watched as she carefully made her way toward the bed. "I got to tell you. For a while, Bob, I thought you fell in."

His humor helped temper her apprehension and put a much-needed smile on her face. She sat down next to him and noticed the pajamas. "I see you've got a little problem."

"Yeah. Benny's idea of a joke. I don't wear—"

"Here, let me try." She took the nightwear in her hands, hunting for the magical string that would loosen the knots. "I bet my sisters had something to do with this, too." She remembered how they had been giggling in a corner of the kitchen with Benny right before Murray and she left for the hotel. Their comic effort had actually brightened her mood. She would remember to thank them. It was exactly what she needed. A job. It was as if her entire relationship with her new husband depended on it.

Murray watched as she worked her fingers over the thread locked sleep wear. "Well, Bob. Here we are."

"Yup. Here we are." *What a wonderful release. Taking out these knots!* "So, Murray, you think it'll last?"

204

"Can't say for sure, but I love your mother, so I don't see why it shouldn't."

She laughed. "**Your** mother hated me at first. That could be a problem."

"Nah – She loved you. It's just her way." *How long is she going to be fiddling with those pajamas?*

"She thinks I'm too thin."

Murray looked puzzled. "So what? Is that a crime?"

"In some circles." She glanced at him, seductively. *Something had to happen soon. What was he waiting for?*

The clock on the bed stand ticked away. It was almost 1:00 a.m. Another few minutes and he might fall over from exhaustion. She'd think him a wimp or worse. His ardor was fighting against his need to sleep. Suddenly, he grabbed the pajamas, threw them over a chair next to the bed and turned back to her with a wink.

This was it! She could feel it. He slowly leaned in. She felt the warmth of his lips on her mouth, his muscular body wrapping around hers. She couldn't catch her breath. She was drowning in some strange and wonderful prehistoric ritual. Soon, they had fallen back on the bed, locked in a passionate embrace. *No turning back, now! The anticipated moment had arrived! What she had been waiting for all her young life! What the great poets had written about! Now, she would finally understand!*

—⁀⁀—

She lay on her pillow gazing at the cracks in the ceiling. She glanced over and saw the look of contentment on

Murray's face and wondered why he had fallen asleep so quickly. Maybe, he was tired from the hectic schedule of the last two days. Had he been a good lover? How would **she** know? To whom could she compare him? Their love-making was sweet and a bit painful. She never read about *that* part of it. She couldn't tell him. Couldn't hurt his feelings. He had been so gentle, so loving. Yet something had been missing. Lust? The stuff of those steamy penny novels? The ones she read as a girl and still perused away from the discerning eyes of those who might misinterpret and think she was needy. It must have been *her* fault that he fell asleep. She was hardly the reckless heroine of those romances. A part of her held back, a part she hesitated to show. Why couldn't she be freer like Eunice? Certainly, she had the same needs, same yearnings. Poor Eunice. Look where her freedom got *her*.

She lay beside him, hoping he might wake up and take her again in his arms. She needed to be assured—of what? That they were right together? That their hasty marriage would last forever? *Till death do us—the war! This damn war!* She realized it, now. She had been afraid to get too close. He would leave her and maybe never come back. She needed to protect herself. She felt consumed by a strange loneliness. Impulsively, she called out his name. But her voice was weak, and her soft pleading fell on deaf ears. Perhaps, she was being selfish and immature. She was much too tired. Tired and confused. She shouldn't bother him. He looked so peaceful, so content, lying next to her with that sweet smile etched on his face. At least, she hoped she had lived up to his expectations. *Oh, stop thinking so much!* Everything would look better in the light of morning. What is it about the night that shades her thoughts and turns things so ominous? She looked over at the small clock perched on the bed table and listened to the hours tick away.

For the first time since he left New York, PFC Pickarowitz was getting a good night's sleep.

—ᴡ—

It was 8 a.m. The ringing of the telephone brought Bobbie out of a fitful slumber. For a moment, she felt disoriented as she surveyed the room and regarded the stranger sleeping comfortably next to her. The subtle curve of a smile was still on his face. She reached over to pick up the receiver. Her voice cracked. "Hello?" She mustered more strength. "Oh hi, Mama. Fine. And how are you? Yes, I slept just fine, Mama. How's everything there? All the commotion died down?" She heard Sarah's booming voice in the background, "Don't ask her if she slept well. Ask her if she stayed up well!"

Minnie was giggling through her words. It was difficult for Bobbie to understand her.

"What, Mama? Murray? Oh, he's…" She glanced over at her dozing husband. "Actually, I think I killed him."

She heard Minnie gasp.

"Just kidding, Mama. No, really, he's just fine. Yes, it'll be wonderful. We can't wait. So, I guess I'll see you in three days. Did Uncle Lou leave yet? He's what? No... of course, I don't mind. That'll be fine. Sure." She bristled at her choice of the words. *Life is fine. Everything is fine. Fine, fine, fine with the former Bobbie Feinman.* "Dad feeling okay? Good. Give him my love. Tell Arleen and Fay thanks for all their good work! They'll understand, Mama. Just tell them. Oh, and Murray sends his love, too. Bye." She replaced the receiver and turned to find him staring at her.

"Good morning, Bob!" he beamed. "Sleep well?"

"Great," she lied. "How about you?"

"I gotta tell ya. Like a baby."

Lucky him! "That was Mama on the phone. They all wish us a good trip. And...Uncle Lou will be going with us to Chicago."

"He's going with us on the honeymoon?"

"No. Just on the train. He'll stay with family." Her behavior prior to the ceremony hadn't exactly instilled in the family an abiding faith in her ability to cope. She thought her uncle probably wanted to accompany them in case there were any problems. She could have declined, but he might feel hurt. She hadn't given much thought to how Murray might react. Too soon to gauge that kind of thing.

The prospect of having to share his bride even for a few hours didn't feel right. They only had three days before he'd have to go back to Florida. Bobbie's uncle was an interesting story-teller and a bright man, and Murray was an easy-going kind of guy. Besides, it was a six-hour trip to Chicago. How bad could it be? Suddenly, a look of panic enveloped his face. He remembered Lou trying to force the guests to sing around the dining room table. Of course, Murray loved music as much as anyone, but the noise had become a strain on his ear drums. Certain gradations of sound always affected him adversely from the time he was a child with the explosion of bombs in Lomza, "Let me ask you something, Bob. He's not going to…sing?"

"No. Of course not. Don't be silly. Uncle Lou has better things to do with his time. He'll probably just talk about his life. Maybe, ask a few questions about yours."

—◊◊◊—

On the train ride to Chicago, they both sat courteous and trance-like as Lou serenaded them with some of the Yiddish songs he didn't get to croon at the wedding. Mercifully, his voice gave out two hours into the trip.

Chapter Eighteen

T hanks to the Army Air Corps, their three-day honey-moon included the opulent Drake Hotel where soldiers got special rates. With its expansive Victorian lobby, the lodging proved warm and welcoming against the gray March sky and the cold wind coming off Lake Michigan. And, with the one hundred dollars they had collected in gift money, they could eat in some of the more interesting night spots, including the basement of the hotel with its charming little bar/restaurant. Not as crowded as the usual tourist spots, it was dark and intimate and — Bobbie thought, very romantic. However, Murray found it way too quiet. She noticed that he seemed uncomfortable in such a setting, preferring the spark of a nightclub where he could dance away the night without having to engage in too much conversation or answer any of her questions. Maybe, she was being too analytical. After all, dancing with Murray was an electrifying experience, and she had become quite adept at keeping up with him, especially during the jitterbug.

—◊◊—

To her delight, Murray suggested they see some theater. He told her how he loved going to shows on Broadway. He didn't tell her that he second-acted most of them, the only way he could see anything during the depression. These days, soldiers got in half-price or even free. He hadn't any opportunity to take advantage of this luxury until now, and he was looking forward to seeing a play or musical from the beginning.

To their chagrin, the Chicago theaters were all booked, so Murray thought they might find a lot of drama at a boxing match. *A boxing match?* Bobbie wanted to be accommodating. She had never seen a competitive fight, and she wanted to keep an open mind. But, as she observed round after round of long-in-the-tooth boxers beating each other's brains out, she cringed. *No wonder Sarah put her foot down!* Thank God she didn't have to see Murray in the ring. This sport was no better than those barbaric bull fights she'd heard about in Mexico. *Poor, sweet animals, mercilessly taunted by their cowardly tormentors before the fiery, blood thirsty crowds! Ugh!* It would take all her acting ability to pretend amusement. More of a skill than a sport, Murray told her — to elude your opponent. *That makes perfect sense,* she thought. *Who in their right mind would **want** to get smashed in the head?*

Murray followed the action with short energetic jabs, occasionally reaching over to give her a peck on the cheek. She tried to avert her eyes from the ring as much as possible. She saw how he seemed to be enjoying himself, and she couldn't be rude. She would glance down at her watch and tell him she was having a wonderful time.

Not anywhere as exciting as the fight he witnessed at Yankee stadium in 1938, when his hero, Joe Louis, KO'd Max Schmeling in the first two minutes of their famous rematch – still, Murray was having a good time. It didn't matter that the boxers were all over the hill for pugilists and didn't seem to be taking any risks. He started thinking about his own missed opportunities – the Golden Glove preliminaries in 1930 – when he was landing all the punches except one, the fatal one that broke his nose and led to his mother urging him to quit. If he had only stayed with it a little longer, maybe, he might have made something of himself. He understood the sport could have perilous consequences if he hadn't been good enough. And, he was so young. *Maybe, Ma knew something.*

—ɯ—

It was raining on the last day of their honeymoon. Bobbie sat on the comfortable featherbed in the warmth of their well-appointed room, listening to the news on the radio and waiting for Murray to return. The allies it seemed had suffered a lot of casualties in North Africa, and her comfort level was beginning to drop. *Where has he gone?* He mentioned he had a "surprise" and would be right back. That was about an hour ago. She was starting to get concerned. Certainly, he had been loving and attentive these last two days. She couldn't complain about that. And, with his happy go lucky nature, nothing seemed to bother him. The temperature had fallen to below zero and snow was falling almost constantly, but Murray seemed to find joy in everything—even the bad weather. She would have liked to understand more about his childhood or his thoughts about what was happening in Europe, hoping it would bring them closer. "That's not important, now," he would tell her. *Oh well, it's a honeymoon. Can't solve the world's problems or bond in two days!* That's the excuse she gave herself before the wedding, and nothing had really changed.

She listened to Edward R. Murrow reporting from North Africa. ***"No one seems to doubt that we will throw the Germans out of here. They aren't going to cut and run. The other day, I saw a long line of tank carriers moving over narrow mountain roads…"***

His prognosis gave her some momentary relief. The Red Army was pushing the Germans back. In the South Pacific, American bombers had heavily attacked five Japanese bases. Churchill was telling the House of Commons that all was in preparation for the "grand assault" and Roosevelt had spoken of slowly winning the U-boat War. Suddenly, Bobbie shuddered. *All those troop ships going across the Atlantic! All those menacing German subs waiting to pounce!* She attempted talking to Murray about that as well, but he would simply smile and change the subject. Nothing was going to deter him from having a good time on his honeymoon. *Nothing wrong with that.* Except, she was beginning to wonder if that was all he cared about.

Suddenly, she sat up, remembering. *Oh my God, Gracie!* Her cousin Grace was lingering in a Chicago hospital with gallbladder problems and couldn't come to the wedding.

Bobbie had promised they would visit her when they came to town. But, in the confusion and excitement of the last few days, she had forgotten all about it.

The door flew open and Murray raced into the room like an excited schoolboy. "Bobbie, you're going to love this! Benny Goodman's playing tonight. Right in the hotel! And guess what? Just got the last two tickets! Terrific, huh?"

"That's great...but we've got a little problem. I told my cousin, Grace, we'd visit her in the hospital."

Murray's face rippled in a wave of disappointment. "Our last night in Chicago?"

She felt a tension in him she hadn't noticed before. Both had been on their best behaviors, proper and cordial, careful not to appear too needy or demanding. "Well," she began, searching for the right words. "She just had a gallbladder operation and we can't just leave without seeing her. She'd be heartbroken."

Murray's brow furrowed. He loved Benny Goodman and now, he'd just spent the last of their wedding money on the tickets. This was asking too much. "Why don't **you** go, Bob? You can meet me back here afterwards and catch the rest of the show."

Her lips quivered as she sat, bursting with silent irritation. *What would Gracie think of her? Was he really asking her to go alone?* "But, she's anxious to meet you. What am I supposed to tell her?"

Murray's face brightened. "I got it. Tell her...Tell her I'll come visit when her bladder heals."

When her bladder heals? Bobbie eyes narrowed. She tossed her head back, defiantly, her voice treading nails. "It's a *gall*-bladder, Murray. It doesn't heal so fast. Besides, we're leaving tomorrow."

The air became thick with resolve. They had reached their first impasse. She'd witnessed a stubborn streak in her new husband but failed to recognize it in herself. Certainly, she wasn't being unreasonable. She had promised her cousin. Given her word. *Why couldn't he understand that?*

Murray walked over and sat on the side of the bed, his head exploding with gloomy images. He hated the inside of hospitals. They made him ill with the smell of sickness and death. He had known some of the soldiers from Anzio, amputees who lay forgotten in a makeshift hospital on Collins Avenue in Miami Beach. They would watch from their windows—the life going on in spite of them; the music that played till two in the morning that wouldn't let them sleep. Two of the boys had been his buddies from Brooklyn, and they begged him to speak on their behalf, to make the music stop. He wondered what they thought he could accomplish? He was only a Pfc. But these battle-worn veterans trusted the streetwise kid from Brownsville and knew he wouldn't let them down. So, he asked the owners of the hotel if they would please curtail the noise. The answer was "no". Undaunted, he went to his superior officers. The music did stop, but only for a week, and Murray was in anguish. He had failed the boys from the neighborhood and it bothered him still.

Then, there was that other memory. The harder one. The pathetic face of his father lying mute in a hospital bed, lingering for weeks until death finally freed him from the bondage of his useless body. *How could he tell her all this?* He didn't want to burden her, but mostly he felt embarrassed by his weakness.

He turned toward her and noticed the disappointment burrowed on her lovely face. It made no sense. He loved Benny Goodman. He must be crazy! *Okay, he'd go with her, but he wouldn't like it. Nope. He wouldn't like it at all.* "You think Uncle Lou might be able to use the tickets?"

"Why, I bet he would!" She reached over and gently kissed his cheek. "Thanks so much, Murray. It's a mitzvah. You won't be sorry."

"Yeah. Sure, Bob."

———

Grace Feinman, a zoftig woman of thirty-six, struggled to raise two children after her husband dropped dead at the age of twenty-five. When Bobbie and Murray entered her room at Augustana Hospital, she was asleep and snoring loudly. Her legs were suspended above the foot of the bed in traction.

Poor Gracie! All she's had to bear and now, this! They sat down and waited.

After almost three quarters of an hour, she was still snoring, and Bobbie was noticing Murray's growing agitation.

Overcome by the suffocating smell of disinfectant, he

was feeling sick to his stomach. He knew he had to get out of there and decided to make a quiet exit, inadvertently knocking over a chair.

Grace opened her eyes, looked around the room, recognized Bobbie and tried to smile, but her face twisted in pain.

"Hi, Gracie, dear. How are you doing?"

"Oh, Bobbie! Good. I'm really good."

"That's swell. I brought you a visitor just like—"

Suddenly, Grace let out a blood curdling scream, and Murray's face went ashen.

"Sorry about that, Bobbie. I got a few pains."

"I know, Gracie. I'm so sorry. How is your gallbladder?"

Grace took a labored breath. "It came out."

"Yes, yes, we heard that it did. But you're looking just… great."

"Yeah. Well, in case you're wondering, I slipped in the bathroom yesterday, and my back went out, too." Her eyes darted to the back of the room where Murray stood with clenched teeth.

"So. This is Murray." Her eyes examined every inch of his body. "Very nice—OH MY GOD!"

Bobbie saw the torment on Grace's face. It seemed to mirror the look in Murray's eyes. "Do you want us to get the nurse, Gracie?"

"NO NURSES! I don't want them to touch me! NO!"

"Maybe we should go, then. You probably need your rest."

"That's probably best. Take care, and thanks for coming."

"Bye, Gracie," Murray offered. He grabbed Bobbie's hand and started to rush her out of the room.

"MURRAY!" screamed Grace.

He took a deep breath and walked back a few feet. Bobbie watched from the door.

"I just want to say *Mazel tov* darling. Take care of yourself. You should have a good life together."

Murray inched his way toward her bed, praying his stomach would hold out. "Thanks, Gracie. Next time we'll go dancing. What do you say?"

"OH MY GOD!" she wailed, her pain now beyond endurance. "Go. Please just GO!"

Nothing could keep him on that death ward any longer! Bobbie had a choice. Go with him, now — or he'll have to leave without her. She followed him down the hall, struggling to keep up.

—⊶—

Outside, the moon was radiant, lighting up the night sky. They each took deep gulps of cold air. *What a fool she was. Making him give up Benny Goodman.* But, how could she know? She had promised Grace. "I'm so sorry. I thought it was the right thing to do. I didn't realize—"

"Don't worry about it, Bob. I never liked—" He checked himself, then looked down at his watch. "You want to see if we can still catch the show?"

Bobbie's eyes widened. "You think we can? You gave the tickets—"

He smiled. "They don't call me the second-act kid for nothing."

"The second-act kid?"

"Yeah. Let's try it. I bet we can get in."

He grabbed her hand and they ran to the nearest bus stop. Within a few minutes, a bus arrived and took them to within a block of the Drake. The snow was coming down heavily, but neither took notice. Their faces full of anticipation, they rushed down the block, into the hotel, and up the stairs. They could hear the sounds of Goodman's orchestra spilling into the lobby. *This is going to be great,* thought Bobbie, feeling the rush of Murray's excitement.

When they reached the top of the staircase, hundreds of people were lingering outside the Grand ballroom. The crowd was pushing and pulling in an effort to get in, but the doors were closed tightly.

Murray's face dropped as he looked around. What could he do? How could he get in?

They stood together, motionless.

"I'm so sorry about this, Murray. I should have—"

"Never mind, Bob. No big deal. Would have been a lot of fun, though." He looked past her, hoping she wouldn't notice his disappointment. "You would have loved it."

They walked arm in arm down Michigan Avenue. The snow had tapered off. but the sounds of the brisk Chicago street life filled only some of the silence. He kept assuring her he wasn't upset, but she wasn't convinced. Desperate to understand what he was thinking, she realized she might never know. As guarded as **she** was, **he** never opened up.

That night in the warmth of their room, they made love. She wasn't the only one holding back.

"Murray. You're sure you're not angry about—"

"No. Of course not, Bob. Forget it. Next case!" He leaned over and kissed her gently on the mouth. Then, he turned around and closed his eyes.

She was enveloped by another strange loneliness. Like on their wedding night. He was going to sleep, leaving her alone to fend off the dark thoughts. Suddenly, she needed to ask him. He had casually changed the subject, before. Maybe, it wasn't the time but she needed to know.

"Murray." Her voice was gentle, but firm.

"Hmm?"

"You got any idea what you'd like to do after the war?"

"After the war…"

"Yes. I was thinking. Dad could help you find a job. I don't know exactly what kind of work you want to get into, but I'm sure he could—"

"Don't worry about that, Bob. So far away."

"Yes, but it's important to make *some* plans. If you have any ideas, it might be good to talk about them. I wondered if you might like to live in Michigan. I know it's not like the excitement of New York, but it's really a very gentle kind of life and—" She looked over. Too late. He was fast asleep. She turned on her side, her heart heavy with the burden of a new truth. Maybe, she knew it all along. There wasn't going to be any "after the war". Murray had married her for *now*, not *after*. No need to talk of plans. Of jobs. A home. A family. There would be no tomorrow for them.

Murray awoke feeling energized. The disappointment of the last evening had long faded. The honeymoon was over, and there was a job to do. In order to get back to base on time, he would have to take a train directly to Florida. He was grateful Bobbie's uncle would be accompanying her on the trip back to Michigan. She had seemed unusually reticent during breakfast. Maybe, she was upset with him. Had he embarrassed her at the hospital? He asked if something was wrong. She told him everything was fine. She was simply tired.

Lou met them at the hotel and thanked Murray for a wonderful evening. Benny Goodman and his orchestra had been fabulous.

At the train station, Murray tried to brush off a strange melancholy. Bobbie was too consumed with her own sadness to notice.

Lou extended his hand to his new nephew. "Good luck, my boy. And God bless you."

"Thanks, Uncle Lou," he said, giving him a firm hug. "You be well and have a safe trip."

Lou smiled and boarded the train.

They stood, awkwardly staring at one another.

"I'll write you every day, Bob."

"Yes. I'll write you, too."

"Had a terrific time. Chicago's a great town."

"Not so terrific, Murray. Could have been better if I had—"

"No. Really. It was great! You take care of yourself, now."

"Yes. You too. I hope that—" She checked herself. "I'll look forward to hearing from you."

"I don't know what's going to happen when I get back, Bob." He was hoping they could spend some time together before he went overseas, but he had no idea when he'd be going. It was more than just a problem of finances. They had put him in the Army Air Corps and sent him to paradise. He belonged to *them*. Now, it was payback time.

He held her face in his hands, then pulled her toward him. He took her in his arms, his body tight against hers. She felt a heavy reluctance as she let him kiss her on the mouth — a generous, tender kiss. She appreciated the warmth of his touch but felt herself holding back. She needed to be strong, but for a moment, she thought she might pass out. She was consumed with such a yearning. He seemed so loving now that they were leaving one another. Why hadn't he been there to comfort her last night when she lay next to him in bed, longing for a gentle hug and a whisper that everything would work out? She had disappointed him. He was being kind not to tell her so, but she could see it in his eyes. How different these three days might have been if he wasn't a soldier going off to fight in that terrible war. It was the reason they were together. And that not so subtle reality was now tearing them apart. No time to *get acquainted*. A lifetime of living crowded into a few days, a few months. She may never know the man he might have been. She wanted to shake him and tell him he wouldn't die in Europe. He would come home, and they would have a wonderful life together. But she needed to protect herself. It would be easier in the end.

She broke the embrace and boarded the train. She was desperate to look back, but her eyes were welling up, and she didn't dare.

Murray watched until she disappeared inside the train. He thought about calling out to her. He hung out on the platform eyeing each window, hoping she might see him on the platform and wave one last time. But there was no sign of her. Finally, he turned and walked away.

—⟁—

Bobbie sat staring ahead as the train chugged its way out of the Chicago station. She had spent three days with her new husband. She still didn't know him at all.

Lou noticed the turmoil on his niece's face. "That Benny Goodman is some musician. Thoughtful of Murray to give me his tickets. My cousin, Molly, who never goes anywhere, was in such heaven. A very good-natured fellow."

Bobbie looked distracted. "Benny Goodman?"

"No. Murray."

"I married a stranger, Uncle Lou."

"After the war, it'll be better, you'll see."

"He doesn't think he's coming back. That's why he asked me to marry him."

"No! He told you that?"

"Not in so many words. It took me a while to see it. I need to plan things. I've been that way all my life. He just lives for the moment. A good-time Charlie. I should be depressed about leaving him. Instead, I almost feel relieved."

Lou's eyes filled with sympathy. Certainly, Bobbie couldn't mean what she was saying. She was confused, scared and obviously upset. His face suddenly contorted with the image of another place. "Bobbie, terrible things are happening in Europe. Unspeakable horrors. We get reports, but we can't believe them. Murray must hear the same news. Let him have his good time while he can. Maybe, you shouldn't expect too much right now. As for after—" He stopped, trying to purge from his mind the horrible knowledge that hundreds of thousands of boys might die before the war was over. He cleared his throat. "As for after, either you'll grow to love and value each other or you won't."

After the war. Her uncle was a wise and understanding man. She wanted to believe him, but what did she and Murray really have in common? She rushed to marry a nice guy who looked great in a uniform. Why? Because her family was concerned her younger sister would marry first. But, no one forced this on her. It wasn't *their* idea. This was **her** decision, hers alone. Love? What did she know about love? *After the war.* Could Murray be trying to protect himself, too?

Lou started humming "Oyfn Pripetchik", a Yiddish song her mother had tenderly sung to her as a child — a song full of love and hope. Tears suddenly rolled down her cheeks. She felt grateful she had a home to go back to. She was one of the lucky ones. Many wives had nowhere to go. She had read about them, following their husbands from town to town, never knowing if they'll ever see them again. She, too, was sitting in that big waiting room with everything on hold. She had a family who loved her, a roof over her head and a job in her father's dress shop. Yet, she couldn't calm that desperate longing. The hollow, lingering pain of not knowing. *Oh God!* Here she was, again — on another long train ride with too much time to think.

Chapter Nineteen

*T*hat summer, Bobbie continued working in her father's clothing store in Holly. She and Murray exchanged safe, newsy letters with no talk of tomorrow. He wrote about training some of the most inept recruits he had ever seen; and about having a chance to meet Clark Gable on the rifle range and talk to him about the movies. Once in a while, they would speak on the phone, but their conversations seemed stilted to her. Letter writing was easier.

She tried to find juicy bits of gossip to keep him entertained. She created a running commentary on Ethel Johnson, the town prostitute. Like the time Ethel came into the Helen Shoppe after a particularly healthy night of work, insisting Morris wait on her for bras and girdles. Bobbie always opted for humor. And, if she couldn't find anything interesting to write about, she would invent it. She hadn't cared much for socializing, preferring instead the comfort of her home and her family. Once in a while, she would join Morris at one of the special box socials at the local high school to raise money for the war effort. The women of the town packed lunches, and the men bid on them. Morris usually outbid all the other men, pay for the lunches, then announce that he couldn't possibly eat all of them, himself. Consequently, he'd give them back to be resold. The ladies always made a bundle for Uncle Sam.

Although she read the papers every day, Bobbie didn't mention anything about the war in her letters. The less said, the better. That's what her dad had told her. *Murray had enough to deal with.* More distressing information was coming out about the whereabouts of the Jews, and this hadn't helped to encourage any sense of hope that the war would be ending any time soon.

—⁓—

In June, Murray worked out a plan for her to join him in Miami, again. But right before her departure, he called and cancelled. He never explained why. Just said it was orders. *All too frustrating!*

Her sister, Teen, came to visit the family for about a month and brought her new baby. The child's presence gave Bobbie a much-needed boost. It also introduced a new longing, which she tried desperately to ignore. Generally, she went about her life mechanically, without any particular joy. She seemed to be living in a prism of deep gloom all the time. Minnie could see her daughter's malaise, but Bobbie never wanted to upset her parents about personal things. So, she usually blamed it on the general state of the world.

Occasionally, she would join Eunice for a movie. Eunice's prediction about being pregnant was right, and Bobbie supported her decision to keep the baby. Eunice stayed around Detroit until she could no longer hide her protruding stomach as simple weight gain. Since the baby was due in December, she decided to move to Toledo where she had a friend willing to take her in. As far as anyone knew, she'd be going there for a year of business school. The girls had discussed it, and Eunice felt she had no other choice. It would be best, considering the circumstances, for her to have the baby elsewhere. Too many people knew her in Detroit.

On the night before Eunice's departure, the girls had an early dinner at Eunice's small apartment near downtown. Eunice was looking especially radiant, and Bobbie was grateful the pregnancy seemed to be going well.

"You heard from Murray, lately?"

"Of course. You know we correspond all the time."

"You haven't really talked about him much, and I was just wondering…"

"Don't worry about it. Everything's fine."

"Well, I don't want to pry but—"

"Just ask, Eunice. I'll let you know if I think you're prying."

"It's just that Evelyn Randolph just got back from visiting her husband in North Carolina, and I know you haven't seen Murray since the honeymoon."

Bobbie's back arched. She was getting tired of hearing about Evelyn Randolph. She knew she was being defensive, but Murray hadn't asked her to come down, again.

It would be her obligation to go if he did. *Her obligation.* But he hadn't. At first, she thought it strange, but as the months went by, she hoped he wouldn't. It pained her to admit it to herself. How could she tell that to Eunice or her family? "Don't you remember? He made arrangements for me to come back down in June, but somehow, it didn't work out."

"Oh yeah. I remember you mentioning that."

"I guess he got too busy." She was probably offering more than she needed to, but she couldn't stop herself. She felt guilty. "Besides, I've heard horror stories. Evelyn was just lucky. Did you hear about what happened to Alice Fisher?"

"What about her?"

"Well, she went to visit her husband somewhere in Louisiana and ended up paying sixty bucks a month living in some old chicken coop, and she hardly ever saw him."

"Right. I remember. Some devotion, huh?"

"I guess so."*Devotion.* Bobbie looked away. *Darn Eunice. She has a way of piling it on.* Yet, it was true. The papers were full with tales of women trying to keep up with their husbands, moving from camp to camp, some forced to pay exorbitant rents in sub-standard housing. She hadn't been willing to do the same, and it bothered her.

"Don't get me wrong, Bobbie. I'm not judging you. It's just that, here I am about to have a kid, and I'd do anything to have someone in my life."

"I know. It seems all wrong, somehow. I almost wish—" She couldn't tell her the truth. That her marriage was

basically a sham. She had convinced herself months ago,
not long after the honeymoon. It was her secret. She
could never tell the family. What would they think of
her? No. She would feign contentment. Easy to do. She
could hide out in the store and play the supporting little wife. She once thought about opening up to Eunice,
but it seemed wrong to burden her. Eunice had broken
down a number of times in the last few months, even
threatening to abort the baby. She hadn't reconciled
her anger toward Frank. She had pleaded for Bobbie
to help her locate him. Against her better judgment,
Bobbie asked one of her father's officer friends if he
might know how to go about finding a soldier. It ended
up that the Army Air Corps gave her a telephone number in New Jersey. Bobbie gave it to Eunice. She begged
Bobbie to make a call, but Bobbie was adamantly against
it. Eunice carried on so much, she finally relented, took
a deep breath, and placed the call to New Jersey. When
a woman picked up the phone, Bobbie pretended to be
a journalist seeking information on some of the hometown boys. The woman said she was Frank's wife and
that he was stationed in the north of England. Bobbie
thanked her and hung up. She hesitated to tell Eunice,
thinking she might do something crazy, but Eunice's response was unusually calm. She suddenly seemed reconciled. Frank's actions, though reprehensible, somehow
appeared easier to understand. From that day on, she
began to enjoy her pregnancy. *No.* Eunice doesn't need
to hear *her* sob story.

"Look, kiddo. Don't worry about Murray and me. We're just fine. What's important here is **you,** and I'm going to do everything I can to help. As soon as I can get away, I'll come visit and we can make plans, okay?"

"Thanks, Bobbie. That would be swell."

Eunice's questions had bothered her. It was easier not to think about her marriage. When she did, she not only felt guilt, but a deep sense of failure.

That night, she sat at her desk composing another letter. She had written to Murray two days earlier. But she couldn't stop thinking about Alice Fisher's *devotion*. There was something else on her mind, and she wanted to unburden herself. It had to do with the events of the past summer. She started to write. Her hand was shaking. She calmed herself and continued.

It began after Roosevelt signed an executive order banning discrimination in defense industries. The ban caused resentment among Southern white workers who had recently come North, carrying with them, according to Morris, "two hundred years of prejudice". About 60,000 blacks had also migrated in search of work in Detroit's lucrative war industry, and violent race riots had broken out at Belle Isle in the Detroit River. *The Detroit News* carried word of the spreading race war. Before federal troops moved in, many people – mostly blacks – had been killed.

Bobbie was sickened by the events. Her area of the country seemed so prone to fanaticism. There was Father Coughlin's constant barrage of hate over the airwaves during the thirties, the German-American Bund and their fascist mass rallies – and now, the white masks of the KKK whose popularity was enjoying a renaissance in small-town America.

She had been writing feverishly for about an hour when she stopped, tore up the letter and threw it into the waste paper basket. What could Murray do about it? Would he even care? He had too much on his mind, already. *Don't burden him.* Everyone had told her that. *Nothing negative.* She began again, searching for the banal. It was getting more difficult. She was looking through a screen of deep pessimism, her heart heavy with immeasurable sadness.

—ᴍ—

One fall afternoon, Morris stood checking the day's grosses at the front register of the store. Bobbie was on the phone with Eunice, who was thriving with a new job and new life in Toledo. The girls were quietly discussing plans for Bobbie's visit.

"I'm so glad you called, Eunice. Yeah. I can't wait to see you, too. Until next week, then. Bye." She hung up the phone.

Morris looked over. "Eunice finished with her secretarial courses, yet?"

"Not yet. You don't mind if I get away and spend some time with her, do you dad? Just a couple of days?" She had broken the news to her mother, swearing her to secrecy, but she continued the charade with her father. She never lied to him about anything, and she hated having to conceal the truth, now. Inherently, she knew he'd be supportive. He was such a fair, respectful man. But, Eunice had asked her not say a word to anyone.

"Of course, Bobbie. Go. It'll be nice for both of you." He may have sensed what was going on, but true to his character — he wouldn't say a word.

Suddenly, Fay ran into the shop agitated and out of breath. "There's another fire out at the Turners!"

Bobbie and Morris regarded one another, a look of fear blanched their faces.

"This is the third in a week. I'm going out there, Dad."

"Wait. I'll go with you."

Morris was concerned for his friend, Ed Turner. He had encouraged him to fight for his job at a local defense plant. Told him that the ban against segregated industry wouldn't do much good if it couldn't be enforced. Ed took Morris's advice and tried to stand up to the picketers. Now, the KKK had tried to run him and other black families out of town.

Ed, his wife and young son were standing outside their house as Morris, Bobbie, and Fay arrived. A large, white cross stood burning on the front lawn.

Here it was, thought Bobbie, that other enemy—not thousands of miles away but in their own back yards.

"Sorry about this, Ed. I should have realized—"

"Now, don't you go blaming yourself, Morris. I knew the score. And you were right. We didn't come all this way to back down, now. Just a few bad eggs, that's what it is."

A few? thought Bobbie. Thank God the Turners still had their home. A week before, another family saw theirs go up in smoke. The fire department stood by. Bobbie was incensed. Her father had gone to the town mayor and complained. The mayor said he'd look into it. That was all he could promise. Nothing happened and Bobbie castigated herself for not doing more. But what could **she** do? She felt helpless. Disgusted with the hypocrisy that allowed this kind of injustice to fester, she didn't feel free to talk about her feelings except to her father. Perhaps, people would think she wasn't being patriotic. After all, this wasn't the time to tear down your country. There was enough of that going on among the fanatics who spoke as if they had special rights — those "true Americans" as they liked to call themselves. It seemed you only needed to scratch the surface to find the face of hatred, nowadays. Her father's special place in the community made it that much more difficult. The only Jews in a small-town business — she didn't want to rock the boat. It was hard enough. Some of their customers might be part of all this ugliness. She hoped not. She tried to look into their faces, to gauge their thoughts and feelings, but it was impossible to know. People were unwilling to believe the truth about their own neighbors. The bigotry in the Midwest was different than in the South. Less obvious. Here, it was all God and country. The white robes were hidden deep in their closets. How, she wondered, did these people explain their hypocrisy? She came to realize that the only sense of real community was in the total commitment they all had toward the war effort.

—⁓—

A few days after the Turner fire, the family was sitting around the radio in the front parlor of their Detroit home listening to Edward R. Murrow reporting from England:

"I listened to the accents of boys who come from the West Coast, from the deep South and from the flat lands of the Middle West. They were Negroes, Indians, Swedes, Poles, and Italians. My British friend remarked, This is a grand advertisement for your country."

Bobbie shook her head. "Some advertisement."

"Roosevelt did the right thing," said Morris, putting aside his paper. "But ignorance and hatred— that doesn't go away so fast."

As Bobbie turned to another channel on the radio, there was a loud crash of breaking glass. The family gasped, a look of terror on their faces. A rock had been hurled through their front window. Morris walked over and picked it up. A note was attached. It wasn't the first time he'd been involved in this kind of incident. For the first few years after moving his family to the small community that would eventually embrace them, there were some who didn't want them there. "Kill the Jews" or "Jews go home". Those were the usual invectives. Bobbie used to wonder what *home* they were talking about. "Everyone came from somewhere else, didn't they, Papa?" she'd ask with a child's curiosity. Eventually, Morris grew to adore his life in this tiny, rustic village, so unlike the squalor of New York's sweatshops. Although he moved his family to Detroit right after Bobbie finished high school, each day he'd return, traveling fifty miles to the small clothing business that he had established there. And, he had been generous to his adopted town, donating time and money toward a number of projects. Never one to speak of his deeds, he would quietly gather up clothing and shoes and distribute it to the needy at Christmas. And, while he became a beloved figure to many, there were still those who never bothered to know him or to see.

The note that was thrown through the front window of their Detroit home that evening had a hauntingly familiar message. *Nigger lovers.* Not wishing to upset the family, Morris quickly tore it up.

The telephone began ringing. Morris let it ring three more times before moving across the hall to answer. As he gingerly lifted the receiver, Bobbie saw her father's hands shaking. After a moment, his reluctance eased as he turned toward her with a smile. "It's Murray."

Her immediate feelings of relief were soon replaced by another anxiety. Their correspondence had continued to be simple and uncomplicated. Murray had been sent to another training facility. Their long-distance marriage was free of frustration and responsibility. Nothing more said about the future. They were coasting along on the quicksand of their hurried vows.

—◁w▷—

From a phone booth in Fort Bragg, North Carolina, Murray stood shivering. The temperature had suddenly fallen to below freezing. After trying for hours, he had finally gotten through. He was so pleased to hear her voice that the nagging wind had ceased to affect him.

Bobbie took the receiver. "Hi there, Murray. How's North Carolina?"

"Cold," He laughed. "But, I've got a terrific plan to warm it up."

Here it was! Finally, he would be expecting her to visit. She hesitated. "Just what would that plan be?"

"Got a three-day pass starting Sunday. How about meeting me in Raleigh?"

She felt heartened. He wasn't asking her to come and stay indefinitely in some old chicken coop of a room. Just three days. Three days were better than six weeks. But, what about her father? She couldn't just leave him alone in the store. Of course, she knew she was rationalizing. Dad would want her to go. They had been separated for so long. She had prepared for this day, hoping she could be strong and invent some excuse. But hearing his voice again weakened her resolve. "It's really a busy time in the store."

There was a silence at the other end of the line. When he finally spoke, his tone was somber, his words – discreet. As she listened, she closed her eyes. A feeling of raw anxiety saturated her lungs, and she labored for a breath. She hadn't allowed herself to think about *that*, not since their honeymoon when she cried herself to sleep and decided she never wanted to feel that lonely, again.

"Okay, Murray. Of course, I'll come."

"That's swell! Send me a wire from the train, and I'll pick you up."

She was still breathless and weighed her words. "That'll be great. So, guess I'll be seeing you soon."

"Okey dokey! And don't worry about a thing. We'll have a terrific time. I'm so glad you're coming. Regards to your folks. Love ya."

"Love you, too," she whispered. Her eyes started to well up. As she carefully replaced the receiver, she wondered if Murray had sensed her hesitation. She turned toward her family and saw her sadness reflected in their eyes. "I have to go to North Carolina," she said, softly. "He'll be going over, soon."

—⟁—

Murray felt reborn as he walked out of the phone booth. It had been a long wait – almost eight months since they were together. He remembered how detached she was when he had taken her to the train in Chicago. If he had done something wrong, certainly she would have mentioned it in one of her many letters. But they had revealed nothing negative about their time together. They were always up-beat. Yet, he knew the honeymoon hadn't gone well and he blamed himself. He had been holding back. He had been reconciled – until Chicago. Then it all hit him – how much more he wanted from this life – how impossible it would be. He had expected to go overseas within a couple months of his marriage. How could he know that orders would be reversed three times? His life was a roller coaster of misplaced hopes and futile longings. He had lived his young life by a code that kept him relatively sane. Never look back. Never analyze or wonder what could be. He had come to accept his fate once he became a soldier. He knew what was in store. But in Chicago, he seemed to lose all strength of will and purpose. With his new wife beside him, he sampled a world he never knew. The missed Benny Goodman concert and the visit to Bobbie's cousin in the hospital served as grim reminders – as metaphors for his life. The first – what he hoped for. The second – what he expected to receive.

When he returned to base after the honeymoon, he started saving money to bring Bobbie back to Miami Beach in style. No crummy cold-water flat for *his* girl. In June, he had enough to pay for a tiny room in a small building not far from his barracks. He worried that it wasn't nice enough, but it was all he could afford. He telephoned her with the good news, but then he was called out on bivouac again and came back swollen and full of mosquito bites. He developed a fever and spent more than two weeks in the infirmary. He never mentioned it in his letters. Not a particularly *manly* thing to admit. By the time he was well enough, he had lost his deposit on the room and within a few weeks, received new orders. He would be moving to Fort Bragg, North Carolina where his unit would prepare for its relocation somewhere in England. Fort Bragg was no Miami Beach. The drabness of camp life and the expectation of shipping out weighed heavily. This definitely wasn't a place for Bobbie. Besides, even if she came, he wouldn't have any time to spend with her. So, he put himself into his work and found comfort in her humorous letters. When time permitted, he would organize boxing matches for the soldiers. He was good at that, and it was a way to deal with the nerves, the tedious waiting and a strange melancholy he had to constantly fight.

Chapter Twenty

*U*ncomfortably crouched on her one piece of luggage in the aisle of another train resurrected from the First World War, Bobbie noticed the old chandelier that dangled threateningly above her head. Once a sign of class and elegance, it now appeared drab and dirty, certainly ready to retire at any moment from its weary thirty-year position of dignity. With military personnel on the move between training camps and the constant flow of civilian traffic, the railroad transported at least two million people a month now. The railway companies had begged people not to travel. The day before she left, she saw an ad in *The Detroit News* for the Atlantic Coast Line Railroad that read "You'll be more Comfortable at Home." *What an understatement!*

She sat in the middle of the aisle – her fur jacket pulled tight around her body. What she wouldn't give for one of those cramped coach seats! The cold was a common problem everywhere these days. Because of fuel shortages, the temperature in their home had barely reached fifty-five degrees Fahrenheit. But, at least at home, she could put a log in the fireplace. But here she was, on another clunky old train traveling to North Carolina to visit her husband. She wondered if Eunice might think better of her now. She fervently hoped so. But, why should it matter what *she* thought, anyway? She certainly wasn't doing this for Eunice or for her family. She was doing it for Murray. She *wanted* to be there for him. It was clearly her responsibility. He was a soldier going off to war. What if Eunice thought she was a selfish, cold fish? As long as **she** knew the truth, as Mama had told her so many times. Why couldn't she simply believe that? Not enough self-worth, maybe. Whatever the reasons—growing up in a small town, being one of four sisters — they were all excuses, anyway. No one had made her feel particularly unattractive or untalented or unimportant. Certainly, not her parents. Although she would have appreciated a little more show of affection. Didn't her dad trust and respect her business abilities? *So, I have a head for business. Big deal! That makes me an Eastern Star.*

The train came to an unexpected halt, and Bobbie fell over onto the lap of a somber looking woman sitting in a more comfortable seat. "I'm terribly sorry," she said, as she quickly moved back into the aisle. The lady nodded blankly and continued to stare ahead.

"I'm meeting my husband in Raleigh." Bobbie offered, hoping conversation might ease her boredom. "He's supposed to ship out soon."

"Oh."

"What about you?"

There was a moment of silence.

"I'm on my way to Raleigh…to see my son."

Bobbie felt an immediate empathy. Bad enough to see a husband off — but to have to send a son. "Will he be shipping out soon?"

The woman hesitated, her eyes full of anguish. "No. He's coming home." Tears began streaming down her face.

Oh, God! That stupid mouth of hers! A thoughtless comment in some misguided attempt to be cordial! "Please forgive me. I'm so sorry" She reached over, trying to comfort her.

After a few moments, the woman's tears dried. Calmly, she explained that her only child had been killed in the Pacific campaign. She was on her way to Raleigh to retrieve his body. Today was his birthday. He would have been nineteen.

As the hours passed, Bobbie sought a more tolerable space by leaning against the weight of her suitcase. Having spent a miserable hour castigating herself, she was now feeling a great deal better. The stranger she had so tactlessly upset seemed to have needed and appreciated the chance to talk about her son, finding in Bobbie a compassionate ear. Now, the distraught woman was getting some much-needed sleep, and Bobbie's thoughts turned again to Murray. A smile grazed her face as she remembered his sweet words to her on the phone. But, a new anxiety had found its way into her constantly churning mind. In a few hours she would be meeting a husband she hardly knew, and soon he'd be going off to war. Suddenly, she felt almost grateful for their estrangement. It would be easier to say goodbye.

—◦◦◦—

Carrying an overnight bag, Murray headed for the bus stop outside Fort Bragg, grateful for the three-day reprieve. Army life had become something of an anathema, challenging his independence and his sense of justice. He had finally received his corporal's rank. It was supposed to happen months before. He hadn't said anything about it to Bobbie. *Corporal. Big deal!*

His ears caught the steady rumble of a jeep as it pulled up next to him. The two sergeants inside had been watching and waiting until he was well beyond the camp grounds. He turned and regarded the men with a calm caution. His heart started to sink as he recognized the one in the passenger seat — a man notorious for his mistreatment of Negro soldiers at a nearby camp. Now that the sergeant had been assigned to Fort Bragg, Murray knew it would only be a matter of time before he would go gunning for Jewish boys. He had tried to keep a low profile.

"Hey Pikawitz, hear you made corporal. So, where do you think you're going?"

Be careful, schmuck. He's trying to rile you. You've waited too long. "I have a pass, sir."

"Must be some mistake. No passes allowed. New orders."

"I don't remember hearing that, sergeant."

"You questioning me, Corporal Kikawitz?"

He felt his body go hot with rage. He struggled to control himself. "No."

"No, what?"

In peacetime, there wouldn't be any hesitation. He would have taken him on. But, now, bullies and racists could continue their harassment under the protection of the U.S. military. Hit a superior, officer or not, and you could serve time. Unless you were surrounded by high-placed witnesses, your word meant nothing. Murray knew he wouldn't have a chance. Most of these psychopaths waited till they got you alone to rough you up and throw invectives at you. He stopped wearing a Jewish star around his neck because there had been too many incidents, but his last name still made him easy prey. He thought about the Negro soldiers relegated to separate eating and recreational facilities and how, in an ironic twist, he had envied them. Unfortunately, there would be no separation for him. He still had to eat, sleep and train with these bigots.

"Did you hear me, Kikawitz? No—**WHAT**!"

Murray could feel his stomach churning. "No, sir — and my name is Pickarowitz, sir."

"Same difference. One Jew name's like any other."

His only hope was to walk away. If he stayed, he risked an altercation. He couldn't trust himself anymore — couldn't trust the anger burning inside him. *Leave it alone. Just go. GO NOW!* He turned and looked toward the bus stop. *If he could just make it.* He started walking in quick urgent steps. Three soldiers were already there. The sergeant wouldn't dare continue his hateful rant in front of them, and he would be free. Bobbie would be waiting for him in Raleigh. They'd have a wonderful weekend. *Just a few hundred more feet.*

"Come back here, Goddamn Jew boy, you hear me? I didn't release you yet!"

The other sergeant turned to his friend. "Dick, it's enough already. Leave it—"

"You hear me, you chicken-livered bastard!"

Don't look back. Just keep walking. A few more yards. He could hear the taunting – the mocking – the piercing insults. Language he hadn't heard since his childhood. Abusive. Disgusting. He stopped and turned back, staring intently at this vile excuse of a human being who, through the irony of fate, only slightly outranked him.

"What's the matter? You got a problem, Kikawitz?"

That was it! There were more important things than three-day passes. He ran back to the jeep and seized the sergeant by the neck. It took a moment for the startled man to get his bearings. He came at Murray with a series of bad punches. At first, Murray's agile foot work eluded him — until miscalculating, Murray caught a hard blow to his left eye. Still, the sergeant was no match for the street-smart Brooklyn slugger. That punch was all he needed. Instantly, the new corporal served up a perfect right jab that sent the hate-filled bully reeling to the ground.

It had been snowing heavily, and Bobbie had to send another telegram. Her arrival time would be delayed. When the train pulled into Raleigh station five hours late, she searched the platform and the sea of faces. Everywhere she looked, soldiers were embracing their girls. She felt consumed with longing, but Murray was nowhere in sight.

Perhaps he had been detained by the weather. Maybe, he hadn't received her second wire. After lingering for a few minutes inside the waiting area, she finally left word with an MP and went to the ladies' room to freshen up.

—⚹—

Lying on a cot in the cold drab cell, he felt an intense pain rippling through every inch of his body. His left eye was swollen and pounding. *How did he end up like this?* In solitary. He could expect a court-martial. No less. Army regulation was clear. It was his fault. He reproached himself for messing up. He had received Bobbie's first telegram. She'd be waiting for him at the station and wondering why he hadn't met her. She'd be alone in a strange town. She'd call the base and find out that he was in the stockade. It was humiliating. He had screwed up. He always sensed that his life would be short. It was in the genes. To make every day count — that was the challenge. He was proud to be a naturalized citizen, to help support the country that had given him a new beginning. Though he knew what was in store, he couldn't wait to get over there and fight the murderers. But around him loomed the menacing faces of hypocrisy and intolerance. The captain at MP headquarters in Miami Beach told him he wasn't going to change attitudes overnight. *Overnight?* All his life, he had been a one-man crusade, and now he had gone too far. His chance to fight the Nazis in jeopardy and his marriage probably over. *Impulsive! Hot headed!* Bobbie has come all that way to see him, and he let her down. What would she think of him now? Their last chance for a little happiness ruined because of his stupid temper. He closed his eyes and pictured her beside him. Her hair smelled of roses, her skin soft and comforting against his bruised, stinging face. He needed to sleep. It was his only escape, but his constantly throbbing eye made it almost impossible.

—m—

Bobbie emerged from the rest-room with a worried look on her face. She kept reassuring herself he'd probably be coming any minute. It had to be the weather. The blizzard was still raging. Otherwise, he'd certainly be there. She noticed a very young girl with long blond Shirley Temple curls sitting on her luggage, quietly sobbing. "Did you lose your mommy?"

The girl looked up with a strange expression on her face. "No ma'am," she replied in a deep southern drawl. "I lost my husband."

"Your…husband?"

"Yes. ma'am. He's stationed at Fort Bragg. I was supposed to meet him here, and now I don't know what to do. I'll probably never see him again." She buried her head in her arms and continued crying.

Bobbie's brow wrinkled. She wasn't going to leave the child here alone, married or not. "Look, I'm supposed to meet *my* husband, too. They must have been held up on account of the storm. It's a mess out there. Not fit for man or beast."

A glimmer of hope filled the girl's red swollen eyes.

Bobbie felt sorry for her. She couldn't be more than fifteen. "What's your name?"

"Caroline."

"Well, Caroline, don't you worry. I'm going to call the base and find out what happened. What's your husband's name?"

"Jimmy Joe Slawson."

"Okay, good. Now you wait here, and I'll be right back."

Tackling her assignment with dogged determination, Bobbie walked to a pay phone, called the operator and secured the number of the camp. She dialed quickly trying not to forget. She felt calmer now. She had a task — a direction. There was a simple explanation— somewhere, and she would definitely get to the bottom of it.

After waiting an excessively long time, she was told by a camp operator that both Murray and Caroline's husband were listed as out on three-day passes and neither of them had left any messages. She felt an intense dread, but prepared herself. *Be strong.* When she returned, the girl was still sitting on her luggage, fear in her eyes. Bobbie knew she had to come up with something.

"There weren't any messages, but I'm sure it's because of the weather." The strain of the past twelve hours was beginning to wear heavily. The Raleigh station was hardly a comfortable place to wait. The few areas to sit were taken up by soldiers and civilians bedded down for the night. "I have an idea. Let's leave word with the MPs and go to a hotel. I'm sure they'll find us."

Caroline jumped up and hugged her benefactor. Bobbie almost fell over from fatigue. She asked an attending MP for the name of a reasonable hotel and gave him and the clerk at the information desk the names of their husbands. Then, she took Caroline by the arm and led her out to a taxi stand.

Within fifteen minutes, they were in the comfort of a warm hotel room. Bobbie felt grateful for the company. This needy child gave her strength and kept her from dwelling too much on her own predicament *Why hadn't Murray left word? What if something has happened?* She felt confused by the magnitude of her concern. At least, he hadn't shipped out. That had been her first worry. The call to the base had relieved that anxiety. *There has to be some explanation.* Whatever occurred, she wouldn't deal with it now. Tonight, she had a weeping child on her hands — and after hours on that cramped, freezing train, she couldn't wait to get into a bed.

Chapter Twenty-One

A gain, he saw it. The hideous image of that other place. Buried for years in a child's memory. *Destruction. Devastation. The piercing sounds of bombs falling. Those shrill, paralyzing blasts that burst his young eardrums. The anguished cries of people running for cover. The repugnant smell of burning flesh. Then, that same faceless, bloodied soldier crying out for water—*

The cell door opened. Murray was jolted out of an agitated sleep by the first crack of light in almost ten hours — and for a moment, it blinded him.

A crusty looking fifty-something commander entered, followed by two MPs. Murray attempted to lift himself off the cot, faltering twice before finding his balance. He stood at attention as best he could.

"At ease, corporal."

Out of his one good eye, he noticed the officer studying him — at the same time, perusing a large black notebook perched in his hand.

His eye was burning. He felt he might collapse from the throbbing pain in his head.

The commander continued to inspect his notes. "You're quite a scrapper, Pickarowitz. We've got paper on you all the way back to basic. Seems you have a fondness for getting yourself into trouble."

A record of everything! All those scuffles! Right there in front of him! "Yes, sir. Sorry, sir." He shuffled his feet. Any minute, his legs might give out.

"I also have reports—" He stopped, examining the papers with a probing intensity. "Reports saying you're helpful to your fellow GIs, not afraid of taking on some of the toughest assignments."

It was some vague compliment before the kill. A cruel joke. Murray's one good eye was closing; the officer was going in and out of focus. *Hold on. Keep it together.*

"Seems you have a fairy godmother."

His whole world had fallen apart *and this guy's talking fairy tales?*

The crevices in the commander's face started to relax, and a strange glint appeared in his eye. "The other sergeant corroborated your story."

What? The other sergeant corroborated? Unbelievable. No matter what his punishment, Murray felt a sense of redemption. Maybe, just maybe, there was some justice after all, some measure of a morality code.

The man's expression sobered. He was no longer looking at Murray, but sifting again through the papers in his notebook. "However, I need to inform you, corporal, you'll be losing your stripe."

Losing his stripe. He'd worked so hard—*never mind, jerk. You won't be needing it where you're going. Next case!*

"You're free to leave. Keep your nose clean."

Free to leave? The officer was right. He did have a fairy godmother. What else could explain it? He raised his arm in a weak salute. "Yes, sir. Thank you, sir."

The commander threw the soldier an impassive glance, masking deep thoughts. He felt pleased. Most GIs in a situation like this wouldn't be as lucky. It had been a trade-off. At least, he'd gotten the kid off. That's the best he could do. It wasn't easy, but it was a beginning. He hesitated, then turned and walked out.

Murray's legs felt like jelly. He fell back against the wall of the cell. The MPs helped him to his feet and waited until he found his balance.

"Excuse me—."

"Yes, corporal?" replied one of the MPs, addressing him by his now former rank.

"Who was that officer?"

"That's Captain Cohen. Just came on base two days ago."

Captain Cohen. A subtle smile crossed Murray's bruised but grateful face.

—॥॥—

From the warmth of her hotel room, Bobbie stood, grim faced, watching the blizzard howling outside her window. She felt crazed from lack of sleep, and Caroline had been crying for three straight hours. Bobbie called the base again. Murray's leave had been suspended. *First, he's out on a pass. Now, his leave is suspended?* Something was definitely wrong. Something they weren't telling her. Could he be preparing to ship out? Certainly, she would have been told *something*. Tomorrow, she would go to Fort Bragg and demand an answer. Tonight, she had another problem. Caroline. Maybe if the girl could communicate with her parents, at least her constant wailing might end. Bobbie asked for the number and placed a call to the girl's father in Georgia. She gave the phone to Caroline, then listened, hoping for some reprieve. The crying slowly abated as the child kept repeating "Yes, sir. Yes, sir." to whatever her father was telling her. *Finally. A little peace and quiet!* But, as soon as Caroline was off the phone, the tears started flowing again.

Bobbie threw herself onto the bed, covering her head with a pillow, a silent scream filling her lungs. *It was all Murray's fault!* Why did she allow him into her simple, uncomplicated life? She would tell him a thing or two when—

There was a knock at the door. Bobbie looked over. Caroline sat up.

"Who is it?" Bobbie called out.

"Private Jimmy Joe Slawson," responded a pubescent voice from behind the door. "Is my little girl in there?"

With a sprinter's speed, Caroline ran to the door, opened it and jumped into her husband's startled arms. They began kissing with such intensity that Bobbie had to avert her eyes. She envied their boldness, remembering how self-conscious she felt when Murray tried to kiss her in public.

It was soon apparent that the couple's potential for lovemaking was becoming much too real. Politely, but firmly, she cleared her throat. They looked up, as if her presence was a complete surprise as well as a minor inconvenience.

"Oh, I'm sorry, ma'am. This is my husband, Jimmy Joe?"

Bobbie was amused with the way Caroline turned every sentence into a question, but the constant reference to her as "ma'am" was beginning to play on her nerves.

"Hi, ya, ma'am. How are you doing?"

Bobbie's teeth clenched in a locked smile. "Oh, I could be doing better, thank you."

Jimmy Joe turned back to Caroline. "Sorry sweet pea, but I thought you were coming on a later train?"

"That's okay, honey-bunny, You're here now."

As they started another cycle of kisses with even greater abandon, Bobbie's eyes rolled back into her head. *Enough is enough!* "Look, why don't you two take this room. I'll just get my things and—"

Jimmy Joe extricated himself from Caroline's passionate clutches. "No ma'am, we couldn't let you do that. You've been so nice and all to my little darlin'. We'll just get another room."

Fine with her. She couldn't wait to get rid of them. *And, if they called her ma'am one more time!* "At least let me go down to the front desk with you. Make sure everything's okay." She wasn't taking any more chances. She had to get some rest.

—w—

The road to Raleigh was deserted, the air frigid, and the sky – a blanket of snow. It was coming down so heavily now that Murray's vision was almost totally obscured by the white pellets burning his eyes. Briskly, he edged his way down the road, executing some simple dance steps – hoping they might take his mind off the cold. Whatever pain he felt was tempered by his determination to get to Raleigh.

An old battered pickup truck approached. It was the only vehicle he had seen for the last three miles, and he was desperate to flag it down. His eye was throbbing again. The truck seemed his last hope of getting a ride.

The middle-aged black man behind the wheel eyed him cautiously. From a distance, it looked like some crazy soldier dancing in the snow. *Can't be too careful!* Besides, the sun wasn't up yet. In this part of the country, a white soldier was no guarantee of anything, least of all protection. He rolled his half-frozen window down a notch. "Where are you headed in this mess?"

"Supposed to meet my wife in Raleigh. Could I get a lift?"

He studied the soldier with the cunning of a fox maneuvering his way around a wolf. *Seems to have a nice enough face. Isn't condescending. Didn't demand.* "I can get you about five miles from the city. That do?"

"That'll do just fine." Murray's hands were shaking as he quickly jumped into the passenger side of the truck. "Sure appreciate this, sir!"

The man smiled with guarded surprise. He couldn't remember a white boy ever calling him "sir".

—⚊—

In a tattered bathrobe, an outsized nightcap and wearing an eye patch, the old desk clerk gazed skeptically at the woman, the child, and the young soldier standing expectantly before him. "Sorry. No more rooms."

No more rooms? It can't be! Bobbie grasped Caroline's left hand and laid it firmly on the desk, revealing a wedding band. "Look, mister. It's *very* late. They're *very* married, and I'm *very* tired! So, before I do something I might be sorry for, I suggest you find a room really quick, cause I sure as hell won't be spending the rest of the night watching them mate!" She wasn't backing down. Murray was God knows where. There was a fire in her belly, and she'd be damned if she was going to lose this one. *Rest. She needed rest!*

Her histrionics had pierced the old man's psyche. His defenses were starting to unravel. This volatile dame could cause him a lot of trouble. She might call the cops. Blow his cover. It had been a good life since those heady days in the numbers racket of the early thirties. Better not take any chances. Grudgingly, he produced a key and pointed to the elevator. "Third floor. Second room on your left."

Thank you, God! Bobbie hugged Caroline, wished them both well and ran up the one flight of stairs back to her room. She threw off her clothes, climbed into the bed and closed her eyes. She should never have come to Raleigh. It was all a big mistake. *Please God, let Murray be okay.* She felt the room spinning. Soon, she fell into a deep sleep.

—⚍—

They were driving in a heavy blizzard. For the first ten miles, the man hadn't said much to his indebted, fevered passenger and Murray didn't offer. It took all their concentration just to keep the truck on the road. At one point, they had skidded across the highway, almost colliding with an Army jeep. But, as the weather started to clear, so did their nerves.

"Air Corps?" asked the man, perusing Murray's uniform.

"That's it."

"My son is with the Ninety-Third Infantry Division stationed in Arizona."

"I heard about those guys. You must be very proud."

"Yup. Sure am."

Murray had read a great deal about the Ninety-Third. What he understood, made him more aware than ever of the injustices in the American dream. He knew that Negroes were facing a more rigid system than anything they had ever known in civilian life. The Navy made them mess hall attendants. The Marines didn't accept them at all. The Army had assigned them to segregated units and originally trained them for noncombatant positions. The Air Corps was closed to them as well — until, with the urging of Eleanor Roosevelt, they started to organize segregated combat units like the Ninety-Third Infantry and train aviators like the Ninety-Ninth Fighter Squadron. Despite their treatment, they had wanted to serve – the numbers way over their proportion in the country. *To fight and possibly die for a land that had segregated them and made them feel inferior!* Murray had an immense respect for those soldiers and felt incredibly honored to share a ride with the father of one of them.

The truck came to a stop. "Raleigh's to the right about three miles. Sorry. I can't take you all the way."

"That's okay. This was just terrific. Can't tell you what it means to me, sir."

"I enjoyed the company. Good luck to you and come back safe now, you hear?"

"Thanks so much, and the best to your son, too." Murray jumped out, gave a parting wave and watched his own special angel in the mercy vehicle drive away down the road.

He took a large, labored breath and began his trek into the city. The sun was fighting to make an appearance, dissolving the blizzard's last gasp of power. There was still a light snow falling, and he could feel its cold flakes brush hard against his bruised face. He saw only shadows now, a vague outline of the road ahead. A new anxiety suddenly hit him. *Maybe, Bobbie has given up and gone back home.* He quickly brushed the thought aside. Now, he must concentrate on one thing — finding her. He'd check at the train station. Maybe, she had left a message.

Chapter Twenty-Two

*F*our-thirty in the morning. Bobbie lay awake, shuddering. *Just a bad dream. Darn nights!* It would be better in the morning. She would go to Fort Bragg. And, she would face it, whatever had happened. She tried to overcome her fears. He was her husband for better or for worse. *Husband.* The word sounded so peculiar. She had jumped in. A rational, sensible woman, she had behaved like a smitten teenager. Taken a major step — because of love? No. Something else. She closed her eyes. *Sleep. She needed to sleep!*

—⁓—

At seven in the morning, she was awakened by a light tapping at the door. *Another dream?* She closed her eyes. There it was again — almost imperceptible but definite taps. She jumped up and ran to the door. "Yes?" she asked, breathless.

A faint voice called out. "Bobbie, it's me."

She felt a flutter in her heart. She unlocked the bolt and opened the door.

There he stood, shrouded in snow from head to foot, his body shaking uncontrollably. He attempted a smile, but his face was frozen with pain, his eye pulsating. He wished he could see more than the contours of her lovely face.

"Hi, Bob. Couldn't get here sooner. Had trouble getting a lift."

"Don't worry, Murray." she heard herself say. "You're here now."

They tried to embrace, but it was awkward. He wanted to wrap his arms around her, but he felt weak. Suddenly, his legs buckled. "Oh, boy! Better not put me on a dance floor."

She put her arm through his, assisting as he tried to lift himself up. She hid her concern, sensing he didn't want to make a big deal. She saw he was trying so hard to stay strong. She guided him into the room and helped him onto the bed. His hands were still shaking. She helped him remove his jacket and gloves. He was exhausted and suffering. This wasn't the time for hard questions. Whatever happened, he was alive and had finally come to her.

"You walked in this snowstorm?"

"Just the last mile or so."

As she helped him off with the rest of his soaked uniform, she saw the bruise on his red and swollen eye. "Your eye, Murray."

"It's nothing. Must have hit something on the road."

He was still trembling as she wrapped a blanket around him. She took a washcloth, soaked it in hot water and gently patted his eye.

He had no strength to explain. He didn't want to lie, but he was afraid she would think badly of him, think he was irresponsible. He lay on the bed in silence as she rubbed his hands in hers. Then, she put her arm around him, gently caressing his frost-burned forehead.

"You must be beat."

"Yeah. Guess I am." He hesitated. "I'm sorry, Bob. Only one more day of the pass."

"Shh. Don't talk, Murray. It's okay."

He was fighting to stay awake, but whatever reserve he had left was failing him and soon, his eyelids went heavy.

She continued stroking his forehead. "Sleep tight," she whispered. "Don't let the bed bugs bite." Her mother used to say those words to her as a child. A common expression of love, she had never repeated them to anyone.

She lay next to him, watching his chest rise and fall. He seemed so peaceful and hopefully out of his pain. How quickly he had gone to sleep their first night together. How lonely and rejected she felt then. She'd resented him for that — couldn't help herself. Especially, since *she* couldn't sleep at all. Often, in these last few months she would rehearse what she might say to him, now that she had nothing but time to reflect on their hurried decision to marry. She had blamed him. It was wrong to ask for her hand. It was wrong and selfish.

Now, as he lay in her arms, her indignation began to fade as she listened to the faintly discernable rhythm of his labored breath. *Dear God, let him be okay.* It didn't seem to matter anymore. None of it. Yet it *had* mattered, once.

It mattered a lot. She spent too much time feeling disappointed — mostly with herself. And, she was sure there were things he was still keeping from her. Yet, a distinct calm had settled over her tormented spirit, revealing an extraordinary idea that lay hidden under layers of misunderstanding. Someday, he might tell her — if it was important for her to know. Seeing him like this, so vulnerable, so exposed — made her feel special. This independent, enigmatic soldier *needed* her.

She wondered what would become of them as she lay watching him long into the morning. Everything seemed so muddled. She did know one thing. It was as evident as the deep laceration that lingered rudely over his swollen eye. Something was definitely changing — maybe for both of them.

—⟋⟍—

It was late afternoon before they emerged from their hotel room. Still somewhat shaky, he insisted they get out and see the town. They walked the streets of Raleigh, past snow drifts and half-hidden cars. The bright sky and warmer weather stood in marked contrast to the gloomy, violent former day. He was walking with a slight limp, and his eye was still hurting, but when they stopped to watch children building a happy face snowman, he suddenly became animated. Eagerly, the kids gathered around, drawn by Murray's uniform and warm smile, asking questions about where he was from and what he thought of Raleigh.

Bobbie watched in awe as he picked up a little girl and hugged her while her beaming mother took a picture. Then, he reached into his pocket and took out some coins which he freely distributed to each child. Bobbie hadn't given it any thought before. Dare she think it, now? *He might make a wonderful—*

They passed a sign reading "Boxing Matches Today" Murray started to walk on, but Bobbie suggested they might have a look. Murray was surprised, sure he had sensed her deep distaste for the sport when they were on their honeymoon. Now, she was asking to give it another try. And, this time, as she watched the old boxers tangle with each other, she wondered why everything seemed different. After all, nothing had really changed. She still couldn't understand the appeal of the sport. *Punching bags of testosterone beating up on each other with grisly force, blood spattering — the crowd screaming with perverted ecstasy.* Yet, this time as she turned away from the action, she started to watch Murray. His pantomime of boxing jabs was quite amusing, really. When she turned back to the ring, the boxers seemed more engaging than she had remembered. It was still too violent but somewhat less offensive. How was that possible? Was she simply getting used to it?

—ᴡ—

In a little diner a few blocks from their hotel, Bobbie sat with her hands on her chin watching Murray chew on a mangled looking piece of black meat that in better times might have been considered steak. With the rationing these days, it was hard to tell. You took your chances. The waiter called it a steak. That was enough for Murray. Bobbie was intrigued by the way he was holding his fork. Not like the way she had learned. He held the fork in his left hand. Then in his right, a knife lay suspended over the plate waiting for the meat, or whatever it was, to be cut. *Interesting.* Certainly more practical than her habit of constantly changing hands.

Murray caught her staring at him. "What's the matter, Bob? Something wrong with your food?"

"No. It's fine. Guess I'm not very hungry." She couldn't tell him what she really thought of her sandwich. She didn't want to complain. But, the lettuce limply lodged between two pieces of stale white bread and the green tomato wedged between some odd looking bacon made her suspicious of what the bacon might have been in its former life. She still hadn't asked him any questions. Strangely, she wasn't in a hurry to know. First, she would need to gain his trust, then maybe— She wondered how she had gotten so smart all of a sudden.

A group of eight young men dressed in work clothes entered the diner escorted by three guards. Bobbie recognized their language but couldn't believe what she was hearing.

"Who are they?" She asked.

"German POWs. Supposed to be about 200,000 of them in the country now." *Lucky bastards!* He wondered why the Army had shipped them over here.

Bobbie's face filled with revulsion. There they were. Only feet away — the enemy! She remembered the horror stories — the newspaper articles about the death camps on page ten. Yet, these were just *boys*, hardly as old as she. And they were laughing and joking with one another as if life was just dandy and people weren't dying thousands of miles away. *Grotesque,* she thought.

Her attention was suddenly drawn to the front of the restaurant. "Murray, look over there."

Murray turned and saw two black soldiers standing very still outside the diner, staring through the window.

After a moment, the soldiers opened the door, walked in and quietly sat down at the only open booth nearby.

The proprietor, a large stocky man, stood leering at them. "This table's taken."

The older of the soldiers looked up with an air of defiance. "I don't see anyone sitting here."

"I'll just say it once more. This table's taken."

A wave of disgust crossed Bobbie's face.

Murray stood and calmly walked over to their booth. "Excuse me. Would you two like to join us?"

The soldiers stared at him, taken aback.

The proprietor leaned in, pressing the full frame of his bloated body across the table. "You know we don't serve coloreds. Now, get the hell out of here!"

"Let me get this straight," Murray offered. "You're refusing to serve American soldiers?"

The proprietor turned around fast. "You got some sort of hearing problem, boy?"

"No mister. I'd say you had the problem. Seems to me you've got your priorities a little confused."

The man tossed his head back, fuming with contempt. "I don't take kindly to some Yankee boy telling me about my priorities. Seems like you got two choices here, big shot. Either you leave with your kind, or—"

"Or what?"

"You can just step outside. Unless, you ain't got the guts, soldier boy."

Bobbie was watching with mounting agitation. It was the South. Bigots abounded. What could they do? She stood and walked over to her husband. "Come on Murray. Let's get out of here."

The two soldiers regarded with reluctant appreciation this white stranger who dared to interfere. "It's okay, sir," said the older one. "We don't want any trouble. It's not your battle."

Not my battle! He saw the silent pleading in Bobbie's eyes — the soldiers, ready to retreat. They would all go. It would be easy. Just walk away. *You can't change attitudes overnight.* He stared at the corpulent, six-foot bully with hate etched like putrefied dung on his face, and suddenly he felt his whole body go hot with purpose. He couldn't help himself. It was his curse.

—⟋⟍—

She sat next to him on the bed tending to his other swollen and bruised eye. Obviously, his right hook wasn't as good as he thought. He had ended the fight after delivering a perfect blow to the proprietor's head, but not before he had opened himself up to a couple of major punches. *What a skirmish!* The professional boxing she had witnessed was downright tame next to this. It horrified her to watch him get bloodied. Yet, she felt curiously proud.

"You got some left jab," she joked. "But that right hook, I don't know."

Left jab? Right hook? He smiled at her use of boxing expressions. "Didn't do much good, did it. Can't beat brains into them."

Bobbie patted his eye with a warm solution.

"Ouch"

"Sorry. You know, Murray, I thought you might be a little certifiable back there. Now, I'm convinced of it. That brute could have killed you. We were just lucky there weren't any police around. I had visions of spending the rest of our time together talking to you behind prison bars."

Murray twitched. He considered it pure luck that no one had called the cops. For a moment, his thoughts turned to the kindly truck driver who had given him a lift in the snowstorm. "I got a ride into Raleigh with a man whose son is in the first Negro combat unit. You should have seen the look of pride on his face. And then, that bastard in the restaurant —" He stopped himself. "Sorry, Bob. I didn't mean to—"

"What are you sorry about? That you swear? That you're human? Let me tell you. I was beginning to wonder. Truth is, I was...very proud of you today."

"No kidding?"

"No kidding."

Then, it happened. Like lava freed from the confines of its ancient volcano, thoughts began pouring out of him. He'd been arrested for stealing restricted signs in Miami Beach. That's why he hadn't called her after their short evening together in the supper club. He hadn't been able to meet her at the train station in Raleigh because some idiot sergeant had called him a bastard Jew. He had lost his temper and ended up in solitary confinement for twenty-four hours; How a Jewish commander, newly on base, had taken away his corporal's stripe but given him back his freedom. How a great country like America could offer an immigrant kid like himself a chance at life and then deny it to others born here. He talked long into the morning. Each disclosure deepened her respect. And, as she listened, she reproached herself for ever judging him, for inventing answers that conformed to her perception of the truth.

Listening to him helped release her own frustrations. How her father had spent years building up a reputation only to have the Father Coughlins' of the world tear it down; How the Turner family had to fight for their jobs in the once segregated Detroit war industry; about the hate-mongers who burned crosses in their yards and threw stones through her family's window; Of her deep disappointment that she couldn't do anything to change things. It felt *so good* to be able to talk. To know he shared similar feelings. She finally felt comfortable enough to voice her concerns about the war.

"No need to talk about that now, Bob."

"Well, I just thought it would be good to—"

"Don't worry about me, he said, brushing away her anxiety. "I got myself a fairy godmother."

"What's that supposed to mean?"

"It means that everything will work out." He leaned over and placed a loving kiss on her mouth.

She broke away, trying to grasp his words. Had he said enough to address her fears? He spoke so fervently about his country and his beliefs. Yet, when she wanted to talk about tomorrow — about their future together, his voice became curiously hollow. *He did say that everything would be all right, didn't he?* Certainly, he expected they would have a life together. She was being too analytical. *After the war... but who really knows about tomorrow? Does anyone?* So much has happened between them that is good. *Leave it alone.* Today, they reached a new plateau. Made an important connection. *Trust.*

She looked into his gentle eyes and responded easily to his embrace — for the first time letting herself believe he truly loved her.

Chapter Twenty-Three

Morris was worried. Bobbie was constantly hugging him. *What happened in North Carolina?* Since the wedding, she had projected a world weariness that contradicted her nature. Now, she had a constant glint in her eye, laughed easily and appeared full of energy. *What could it all mean?* Minnie told him to stop analyzing everything. Whatever happened, it was good to see the old Bobbie again.

With a vigorous sense of purpose, she went back to work in the Helen Shoppe, started attending war bond rallies and volunteered at the local hospital. *Keep busy. Don't think about tomorrow.* She even allowed herself a couple of days with Eunice in Toledo. Never far from a telephone, she waited for his call.

"I don't know if I can be here when the baby comes, Eunice. Murray's due to be shipped out soon and—"

"You going to see him off?"

"Well, I don't know about that, but I can at least be near him. He's supposed to be leaving from New York. I hope you'll forgive me. I really wanted to be here for you."

"Don't be ridiculous. Murray's shipping out. You should be there. You know, for a while I thought—"

"What? You thought what?"

"Well, I kind of wondered about you two."

"What do you mean, Eunice?" She knew perfectly well what she meant.

"You didn't act much like a woman in love."

A woman in love. She looked away. They were never best friends. Never soul sisters. It was only since their trip to Florida together that she and Eunice seemed to get closer, mostly because of Bobbie's guilt over what happened to her. "Well, there were a lot of things going on, Eunice. And I didn't exactly know—" She hesitated. Why does she have to explain herself? Can anyone really understand what's in someone else's head? *A woman in love.*

"Bobbie?"

"Hmm?"

"Now, you're holding back. What were you going to say? You didn't exactly know what?"

"Just thinking about what you said. Love's a very complicated thing."

"Isn't that the truth!"

—⚍—

Two weeks later, the Air Corps sent Murray to Fort Dix, New Jersey. When he telephoned, Bobbie had her bags packed in ten minutes. Morris suggested she should buy stock in the railway company. She laughed and said she'd consider it. She stayed with her sister, Teen and Teen's husband, Sol, in Jersey City and waited.

Bobbie adored her little niece. Now, eight months old, the baby helped ease the strain. Teen saw the tension beginning to take its toll and urged her younger sister to get away for a while, maybe take in a couple of shows in New York. But, ever aware of the continuously departing troop ships, Bobbie took up a faithful vigil by the telephone or busied herself with cleaning every inch of Teen's already immaculate apartment. This miscalculated generosity was more than Teen could bear. So, in a fit of sisterly rebellion, Teen declared she could wash her own floors. And, after promising a million times over to take all messages, she finally succeeded in kicking Bobbie out for a few hours.

—⚒—

When she stepped off the bus on that chilly, windswept day in December of 1943, she felt a charge of electricity in the air. Broadway bellowed with the voices of servicemen grateful for a few hours on the town, wide-eyed tourists dashing from show to show, the steady but strident sounds of traffic rumbling through the streets. In the afternoon, she cried crocodile tears over Lillian Hellman's war drama, *Watch on the Rhine*, and in the evening — beamed with pride as *Winged Victory*, honoring the Army Air Corps, unfolded its inspiring themes. *If only Murray could see this!* She would insist on it. *Maybe, he might feel differently about—* Of course, she knew she was fooling herself. All the patriotic shows in the world couldn't erase the memories of what he has seen. They were offered as a morale booster, probably more for the civilians than for the soldiers.

—⟋⟋⟋—

It was just after dinner the following day. They sat in the blackout, listening to Edward R. Murrow reporting from a troop carrier. Suddenly, an alarm rang out, loud and high pitched. Bobbie clasped her sister's arm. It was her first experience with air raid sirens. To Teen and Sol, the blasts were a regular part of their nightly ritual, a small inconvenience easily tolerated. No enemy planes had dared to penetrate the military's new radar system. But, the continuous shriek sent a paralyzing chill down Bobbie's spine, bringing back memories of sitting before the radio only three years earlier, listening to a steadfast Murrow report from London as German bombers terrorized the city.

As the final all clear signal roared from some distant source, the brilliant ring of the telephone suddenly jolted them back. The sisters eyed one another. Both rushed to answer. Teen won and Bobbie hovered over her.

"Hello?" Teen's face softened. "Oh Hi, Murray! It's Teen. Yes. I've heard a lot about you, too! Uh huh. When do you expect to be shipping out? Oh. Uh huh. Uh huh. Uh huh…"

The tension was unbearable. Bobbie could hardly take a breath as she snatched the phone away from her sister. "Murray! It's me."

"Hi, there, Bob! What's cookin?"

There was something comforting in the sound of his favorite expression. "We're all just sitting here in the dark, wondering about you. How are things going?" She had promised herself she wouldn't get emotional.

"Just great, Bob. Your sister sounds like she's really something."

Bobbie turned a skeptical eye toward Teen. "Yeah, she's something, all right."

"I think I can get away tomorrow. Thought we'd go to Ma's. That okay with you?"

Bobbie's face flushed with excitement. *They would still have some time together. Maybe even take in a show!* "That's just great. They'll let you off base?"

"Sure. Nothing to it." He felt energized by the joy in her voice.

"Wonderful! Oh, Murray, I went into Manhattan yesterday, Saw a couple of terrific shows. Maybe you'd be able to meet me there one day and we'd—"

"Sure. sure, Bob. Gotta go now. Pick you up about six."

"Okay. That'll be fine." A ray of disappointment tinged her face. Certainly, she was pleased they would be together, and of course he should see his mother. *Did he say they'd be able to take in a show together?* She couldn't remember. It all seemed so rushed. Murray wasn't much into phone talk or drawn-out conversations. Their long night confessional in Raleigh was probably as big a gift of gab as she could expect from him. At least, they had that. Besides, he was preparing to go overseas. *Don't make demands.* Yet, time was running out, and there seemed so much to talk about. So much to understand. *Don't dwell on things beyond your control!* That's what her mother told her before she left home and what Teen kept reminding her, now.

—⚏—

He left his barracks with a small backpack, humming "This is the Army, Mr. Jones". He hoped the tune might help calm him in the tense moments ahead. When he arrived at the entrance to the camp, he looked around to see if he was being watched. All seemed clear. He walked up to one of the guards and cautiously presented him with a small wad of bills. He had been saving up for months — and now, he was taking some chance. The whole thing could backfire. The guard could call an MP, and he could get busted. *Bribery!* How many weeks of incarceration would that be? What difference did it make if he couldn't see Bobbie one last time. It was his only hope of getting off base. He was counting on the force of human nature.

The guard looked down, discreetly inspecting the payoff imbedded in the soldier's half opened palm. Murray took an anxious breath. As the seconds ticked away, a tiny bead of perspiration surfaced on his forehead. The guard looked up, an icy stare on his face. Murray couldn't tell if it was envy or contempt. He winced as he suddenly pictured himself back in the deep dark hole of solitary. But, just as a cloud of doom was about to sweep down and envelop him, the taciturn guard seized the cash – carefully folding it into the inside pocket of his uniform. Suddenly, Murray was a free man — until seven in the morning. Otherwise, he'd be AWOL.

Couldn't risk that! He looked toward the heavens and whispered a quick "Thank you, God," and still distrusting his good fortune, continued humming the Irving Berlin song until he was on the bus and well away from Fort Dix.

—⟪⟫—

"What a little doll!" Murray said, as he sat rocking Teen's baby back and forth in his arms.

"She doesn't go to just anyone," smiled Teen, genuinely taken with his adoration of her daughter.

The baby cooed and giggled, enjoying the attention. Bobbie thought she noticed a sadness in Murray's eyes. Perhaps, it was her imagination.

After looking through an endless supply of baby pictures and listening to Teen's extensive explanation of the exact circumstances of each shot, Bobbie started to fidget. If they had any hope of getting away, it would be up to her to make the first move.

"We're going to have to leave," she announced firmly. "Otherwise, we could miss the last bus. What would my mother-in-law think?" She held her breath and waited.

Teen looked over to her husband. Finally, she nodded. "Sorry. I didn't realize the time, but Murray didn't seem to mind and I only wanted—"

"Mind? I loved seeing those pictures!"

Oh great. Now, we'll never get away. Teen's going to bring out the rest of them.

"Really?" replied Teen. "Maybe you could stay! I've got tons—"

"Teen!" The looks Bobbie had given her for the past hour hadn't made a dent. This definitely called for some heavy acting. She braced herself. "Have you ever met Murray's mother, Sarah?"

"Of course not. How was I supposed to—"

"Well. Let me tell you. Formidable. Probably has the police out looking for us right now, right, Murray?"

"Ma can get a little upset, especially when she's made a big dinner."

The old mother-in-law ruse, and Murray handled his lines like a real pro! She wished she could have been more straightforward, but her sister hadn't responded to any of her cues, and Murray was really enjoying himself around the baby. *I'm just a selfish fool,* she thought. She couldn't help herself. Everyone wanted a piece of him, and time was so short.

—◈—

Nothing had prepared her for what she found when she arrived at Sarah's third floor walkup on Douglas Street in Brooklyn. When Murray told Minnie that he had money in ten banks, Bobbie assumed it was only said in an attempt to win her affections — that he was probably exaggerating. She had used that same line on her father. She hadn't given it much thought — until now. As she scanned the small, dingy rooms of Sarah's overcrowded apartment, she understood that, although not impoverished, they were far from well off. Bobbie had grown up in a fairly comfortable house in a small Midwestern town. The worn furniture of Sarah's apartment brought back childhood memories of her grandparents' lower eastside tenement. Even their place had a washbowl in the bathroom. Here, the only running water was in the kitchen. *How could they wash, brush their teeth, shave, do dishes and whatever else in one tiny sink?*

Suddenly Bobbie was drawn to Murray's sister, Betty, a pretty redhead trying in vain to appease her three-year-old daughter's temper tantrum. Vying for her mother's attention, the child proceeded to relieve herself on the kitchen floor. Sarah grabbed a bottle of bleach and insisted Betty clean it up immediately. The little girl's petulance was finally blunted when, exhausted by the sheer force of her screams, she fell asleep in Sarah's bedroom. Bobbie admired her sister-in-law's endurance. *Not easy bringing up a child without a father.* Betty's ex-husband, whom she married in a fit of rebellion was nothing more than a "louse" she casually told Bobbie, and she was better off without him.

Murray's older brother, Samuel, sat in a corner of the living room laughing at Murray's Army stories as his wife, Hannah, a thin-lipped, attractive young woman stood next to him, waiting for a chance to offer up her own stories.

Bobbie found Sarah's second husband, Kalman, a tender, congenial little man whose adoration of Sarah was rewarded by her constant attention to his needs. Amused at Sarah's girlish behavior around him, Bobbie wondered if there might have been less tension around the dinner table in Detroit if he had come to the wedding. With his dry wit and sense of humor, it was easy to see why the family loved him. Both Kalman and Murray had similar, optimistic natures. *How warmly Murray seems to connect with him* — the father he never really had, the man who brought a smile to his mother's timeworn face and taught her to laugh again.

Sarah seemed delighted that her daughter-in-law had more meat on her bones. And, although she hadn't gained even a pound since the wedding, Bobbie was grateful Murray's mother had finally found something worthwhile in her appearance.

Soon, Benny arrived. The brothers hugged and kissed as if they hadn't seen each other in years. Bobbie hadn't noticed it at the wedding. Now, she saw the very real affection they had for one another. She loved her sisters, too, but they weren't as demonstrative.

Dinner, served around eight thirty, proved a genuine feast. More food than Bobbie ever remembered on her mother's table. As everyone helped themselves to lavish portions, all conversation came to an abrupt halt. How, she wondered, could they consume so much food at one sitting? And, such strange kinds of dishes! Chicken and some other gray looking meat in a sauce with seltzer. And, the soup which Minnie always served first – was offered after the main course. *And, look how they all eat with their forks in their left hand! Just like Murray. Obviously, a European thing.* Her family had become so Americanized, she didn't remember even seeing her grandparents eating that way.

Somewhere after the meat and before the matzo ball soup, Bobbie started to feel a vague ache in her stomach. Already stuffed and the second course hadn't even been served! *Mama's meals were so much lighter.* She suddenly realized why her father privately grumbled of never feeling full. For a moment, she deliberated about what she should say. The dinner was certainly fit for a king. In fact, his entire kingdom could eat at this table, and there would still be leftovers. It was all very perplexing. She didn't want to appear rude. Maybe, she could sip the soup, one spoonful at a time and throw up later. She sat staring at her bowl.

Sarah gave her a look. "What? You don't like it?"

"I'm full, thanks. But it looks—great!"

"Don't be shy."

"I'm not shy, Sarah. I'm…full."

Full? All her motherly life, she had been serving her family this food, and no one had ever used that strange little word.

Murray saw Bobbie's face go pale. "Ma. If she wants more, she'll take it. Don't scare her away so soon."

"Yeah, Ma," offered Benny. "Give her a couple of years, then you can start in."

"You hear this?" quipped Sarah, glancing at Bobbie. "You treat your mama this way?"

Murray leaned over and placed a kiss on his mother's cheek. "Come on, Ma. We love ya, anyway!"

Betty and Benny followed their brother's lead, each leaning in to give their mother a loving peck. Sarah sat beaming.

How tenderly her children respond to her, Bobbie thought. *Even after a gentle reprimand.* She wished her own family could be that expressive and open with their feelings. She knew she was loved. There was no question of that. Certainly, there was always a lot of laughter in her house. Bobbie had been quite the jokester herself, especially in high school. Her friends loved to visit the Feinmans. Their house was always full of guests; yet, something indefinable had been missing in the family dynamic. Maybe, she sat on the railroad tracks as a child for attention. It had happened after her sister Arlene's birth. It was an unexpected pregnancy for Minnie. Could she have been *jealous —of a baby?* No. She loved her younger sister. She was just being a brat. She had simply gone and sat on the railroad tracks when she couldn't get her way. Since the tracks were right next to her house, it was the perfect set up for a child with a dramatic flair.

Samuel moved toward his mother to offer her a hug, when suddenly Hannah cried out, "Sammy, I got a terrible pain in my neck. Could you give it a rub!"

Murray shrugged his shoulders and returned to his matzo ball soup. But, Sarah had a look of frustration on her face.

Betty sensed that her mother was about to say something she might regret, so she cleared her throat, tapped her water glass with a spoon and began: "Okay, everybody,

I want to make a toast." As the family watched with anticipation, she reached for her glass of wine. "Bobbie and Murray should be forever happy. They should have a beautiful life together. And—" Her voice started to crack. "May God protect our dear, wonderful brother and bring him home safe. *L'chaim!*"

"*L' chaim*," everyone repeated.

Bobbie looked over at Murray. He was staring at her with an almost melancholic smile on his face. Suddenly, tears filled her eyes.

Later that evening, Murray's step brother, Phil, stopped by. Kalman's only son by his first marriage, Phil, also in uniform, was looking forward to spending some quality time with his favorite stepbrother and his new wife.

During another New York blackout, the family sat obediently listening to Hannah describe her latest battle with intestinal gas. Sarah was wistfully looking over at Kalman who sat in his favorite chair, snoring.

"I told my doctor I had stomach pains. What was he going to do for me? Everybody's a doctor. So, I said, 'Please do your job and give me something to make it go away.' I remember last year—"

"For God's sake, enough already!" demanded Betty. "For one hour, we're listening to your problems. Let somebody else talk!"

Hannah's back arched. "Maybe, we should leave!"

Suddenly, there was a hush in the room.

"Good idea," countered Betty. "You're probably very tired. I know we are."

"Come on, Sammy, let's go home!" Hannah marched toward the door.

Samuel walked over to Bobbie with an embarrassed smile. "I just want to say welcome to our family, and I hope that we'll have a chance—"

"Sammy!"

Samuel flared his nostrils and stared at his wife. The family waited for something momentous to emerge from his lips. Instead, he turned and dutifully followed after her, giving her a loving peck on the cheek on his way out.

Sighs of relief rumbled through the room.

"That woman should get the stick out of her ass," said Betty. "I think she'd feel a lot better."

Sarah started shaking her head. "My Sammy."

"Look Ma," Murray offered. "They're happy together. He must like it."

"*Feh*! He doesn't know what he likes."

Bobbie was taken aback by the honesty of their feelings — played out right in front of her. *Nothing sacred here!* If this had been her family, she would have buried her face in her hands and prayed for an opportunity to disappear. The whole episode simply rolled off Murray's back. *Not as uptight as she was with foolish concerns like pride and family issues.*

It was after midnight. Betty had taken her child and gone home. Sarah revived her snoring husband and marched him off to bed. Bobbie sat on the living room couch trying to keep her eyes fixed in a prolonged stare to avoid falling asleep, and Murray sat next to her, yawning.

"I remember when Murray boxed that Italian kid, Tony Sabatini, in the Golden Glove tournament." said Phil. "KO'd him in the third round. Boy, was that something. You remember, Murray?"

Murray turned his head mechanically, uncomfortable with the attention. *Big deal.*

"Yeah. His dad was a mob boss," Benny continued. "We were plenty scared. Thought the old man would be miffed. Instead, what do you think he goes and does? This tough guy? He offers Murray a contract. Of course, Ma put an end to that!"

"Look, guys," Murray said, fatigue enveloping him. "I'm all beat in. Got to get up at five. You entertain Bobbie." He stood up and left the room.

Bobbie stared after him, a wave of confusion and hurt on her face. *Does he expect me to follow?* She felt tired too, but it wasn't polite.

"What a great guy," said Phil. "Just like a real brother. He'd do anything for anybody."

"Yeah," Benny continued. "I remember the time he gave all his stock boy salary to help get Hymie the "mouse" out of jail. Hymie had a club foot and all the kids used to tease him. He had a knack for getting into trouble, and Murray was always sticking up for him. My brother had this sense of fair play."

A *sense of fair play.* She felt herself weakening. *If she could keep her eyes open just a little*— Suddenly, the room went out of focus, and her head lowered.

Phil and Benny carefully lifted her off the couch and helped her to the tiny bedroom off the kitchen.

"Oh, I'm so sorry. I didn't mean to—"

"Don't worry about it, Bobbie. Phil and I talk too much."

"Yeah," replied Phil. "We especially like to talk about Murray, but he gets embarrassed and can't take it." They both wished her well and said goodnight.

She lay next to him in the overstuffed double bed with smells of cooked chicken penetrating her nostrils. Suddenly, doubts were starting to creep back in. *Damn.* She thought she had reconciled them. She looked over. There he was. Sleeping soundly without an apparent care in the world. *How does he do that?* She worried enough for both of them. Her eyes started to go heavy and soon, she fell into a deep sleep.

She awoke at 5 a.m. Her eyes widened. *Horror!* He had gone! Left without her! She jumped up, opened the door, and rushed out into the kitchen — her hair in chaos, her clothes rumpled.

"Hi there, Bob! Have a good night?" He was sitting at the table drinking a cup of coffee.

She tried to calm herself. "I guess I did."

"Great! So, sit down. Can I make you some eggs or something?"

"No, thanks. I'll just have some coffee. Kind of early for me."

"We've got to be out of here in a half hour, unless you want to stay and take a later—"

"No. That's fine. I'll just go and put myself together. Probably look like something the cat dragged in."

"What are you talking about? You look beautiful!"

She blushed. "Yeah, right — like an Eastern Star."

She rushed back into the bedroom and jumped out of her now wrinkled dress, grateful she had remembered to bring a change. She wondered why he suggested they leave separately. Why would he think she'd want to stay and take a later train? She dismissed the thought and hurriedly put on a warm slack outfit.

It was difficult, the goodbyes. Murray held his mother tight in his arms for a long time as Sarah softly cried. Neither of them seemed to want to let go. Bobbie struggled to keep from breaking down, herself. *To send a son...*

He held her hand during the subway ride to Pennsylvania Station but appeared deep in thought. She considered whether she should interrupt him. The rumble of the train had made conversation almost impossible. Still, she needed to talk.

"I'm glad I had a chance to meet the whole family,"

"What? Oh, sorry, Bob. Yeah. They all loved you."

"You really think so?"

"Absolutely. One hundred percent."

She thought of asking him why he left her so abruptly and went to bed, but in the freshness of a new day, she wavered. Again, she was too quick to assume, and he had been so sweet at breakfast, even promising to take her to see *Something for the Boys* with Ethel Merman. Phil had seen it and said it was terrific, not to be missed. Tickets wouldn't be expensive for soldiers.

As the train roared toward the station, Murray wondered how he was going to get off base again, especially after the last bribe. He had given much of his last paycheck to his mother. Bobbie refused his money, saying that she was working and had her own. This bothered him, but he felt satisfied knowing she'd be getting the fifty dollars a month allotment check from Uncle Sam. Even if he could get off base, what would he use for money? He might not be able to keep his promise about going to see the musical, and he hated to disappoint her. He looked down. There, resting on his wrist, was the answer. His grandfather's watch. It was the last link to his past, given to him when he left for America. Maybe, he'd be able to get a few bucks for it. What good would a watch do — where he was going? He suddenly felt a sense of relief.

They continued to hold hands in silence. At Penn Station, he kissed her and put her on the bus to Jersey City saying he would call soon.

—⁓—

Bobbie was unusually quiet when she returned to Teen's apartment. She knew Murray's departure was imminent. When he telephoned two days later, he apologized and said their Broadway plans would have to wait. He couldn't get away early enough in the evening. He would try to get off base the following night after ten. They made plans to go to a small hotel a few blocks away.

—◦◦◦—

Teen watched with mounting concern as Bobbie began packing, then unpacking the same nightgown. "Is something wrong, Bobbie?"

She hesitated. Rarely, did anyone in the family engage in any emotional bloodletting. Teen might castigate her, say she was being weak and expecting too much — tell her she should look around — that she wasn't the only one whose husband was going off to war.

A deeper need was suddenly driving her. "Do you and Sol talk a lot?"

"Talk? I guess. We talk about the baby. About the war."

"I mean, about your feelings. Do you talk about your feelings?"

"I don't know. Sometimes. Why?"

Bobbie felt herself tighten up. Her mother had a nervous breakdown right before her menopause. The family had nursed her back to health and now, five years later, she appeared totally recovered. No discussion, no questioning, and no one had spoken of it since. As if it never happened. *Be strong like dad. Keep it in.* Maybe, if her mother had talked about her feelings—Too much pride, that's the problem. The sin of pride. And, here she was, following the same script.

She threw herself onto the sofa, no longer able to hide the sorrow holing up inside her. "I have to be honest, Teen. Before the trip to Raleigh, I thought Murray and I wouldn't make it after the war. I didn't think we had much in common. It was all so quick."

Teen sat silent, her face registering no particular thought or emotion. She had no inkling Bobbie ever felt conflicted.

"When I met him in Raleigh," Bobbie continued, "I had a chance to see another side of him, a side I really admired. He told me about some of his experiences, and I thought we had really broken through that...web of silence. But when I tried to talk to him about our life together, about what he might want to do after the war, he'd clam up or change the subject." She couldn't stop herself. Feelings once so private were now gushing out. "The other night at his mother's apartment, he left me alone with his brothers and went to bed. Any day now, he could ship out, and he goes to sleep. Maybe, I'm crazy. I don't know. But I sometimes think...I'm just part of a life he wants to enjoy while he can because he knows..." She lowered her head. She was finally saying it — putting it out there within the grasp of that damn evil eye. "He knows he won't be coming home." She looked away. Tears were drenching her eyes, blurring her sight and grazing her cheeks.

The sisters had never shared any intimacies about their lives. Only four years apart in age, they seemed light years away in personality. Teen was the oldest, the bookworm, the one who stayed in college even though the depression was on. The one who had gone off to New York right after graduation, hoping to make her way in the world of journalism. It was 1933 and journalism jobs were hard to find, especially for women. She had married in 1938 and plans of making a living in her chosen field became a distant dream as she and her husband struggled to make ends meet. Bobbie, the closest to her in age, desperately craved her affection and hoped someday to follow her to the University of Michigan, but it never came to pass. They were sisters. They loved each other, but that inclusive family bond was missing. Now, Bobbie was making her privy to her deepest thoughts, and Teen was doing her best to comprehend.

"I seem to have a big mouth about everything, but when I'm alone with him, I clam up. I can't get him to say what he's really feeling. It's a difficult thing to ask. 'Hey, Murray do you really love me or—' It makes me sound like a dope. He wouldn't tell me the truth, anyway." Her voice was starting to break. "The thing is— I might never see him again...and I'm afraid."

Teen's expression suddenly softened and for the first time in her life, Bobbie felt the warmth of her sister's consoling touch. They sat together for a long moment until, sensing the need for a sisterly chide, Teen finally broke the silence and the embrace.

"You think too much, Bobbie. That's your problem. You're always trying to analyze everything — just like dad. It's a curse with you. And it's not healthy."

Maybe, Teen was right, but Bobbie had exposed the most vulnerable part of herself. She needed support, not a reprimand. *Why couldn't she listen and sympathize? Why did she have to be so…judgmental? What's so terrible about wanting answers?* Bobbie had been that way all her young life. How was she supposed to change now?

Suddenly, from the bedroom came a cry so piercing, it jolted them. *The baby!* Teen ran inside and carefully lifted the unhappy infant from her crib, tenderly rocking her back and forth until, safely sheltered in her mother's life affirming arms, her plaintive pleas subsided.

Bobbie stood in the doorway. How loving Teen was. She had never seen her sister show such affection. *If only I could have*—no. She mustn't think it. Just another hopeless longing.

Chapter Twenty-Four

*I*n a drab, little hotel room, Bobbie lay nestled in Murray's arms. Outside, a cold wind was howling with an eerie vengeance as the two of them were rapt, listening to the voice of Edward R. Murrow reporting from England:

> *"I turned and looked at that great ship lying in the harbor. The men were still coming ashore. Looking down at those brown tin hats was like looking down from a second story window at the cobblestones on the street. I hope never again to cross in that ship. Someday, there will be thick carpets, richly decorated state rooms, men in evening clothes and women in elaborate dresses. But for me, that ship will always carry the ghosts of men who slept on the floor, ate out of tin cans twice a day, carried their life belts night and day; the ghosts of men and boys who crossed the ocean to risk their lives as casually as if they had crossed the street at home."*

Murray turned off the radio and stared ahead, lost in a memory she could never hope to understand or share.

"The desk clerk didn't think we were really married," she said, hoping to gently coax him back.

He slowly turned to her with a look of playful benevolence. "You were so quick to show him the ring, the poor guy probably thought it wasn't real."

Bobbie glanced down at her wedding band. She couldn't ask. It wouldn't be kind.

"It's got sentimental value, Bob."

She smiled, flustered by his honesty. Sometimes, he would surprise her and grasp her unexpressed thoughts. Mostly, an ocean of frustrated needs continued to divide them.

He was studying every inch of her face, the way she had studied him that night in Raleigh as he lay sleeping in her arms.

"What's the matter?" she asked.

"Nothing. Just like to look at you."

"You know something I don't?" She was beginning to choke up. She held back.

He remembered the greedy guards who had taken his grandfather's watch. "I know it's getting harder to get off base. I know it'll be soon."

She needed to ask him. Now was finally the time. She braced herself. "Murray, each night, I wonder if it'll be the last. And I need to know — I need to know why—"

"Oh, my God," he cried, "I just remembered? We haven't seen that Broadway show Phil talked about. Can't go anywhere without doing that. Maybe, I can get a couple of passes. How about it?"

He was doing it again. She mustn't let him. "Sure, Murray. That'll be swell." She wanted to talk about tomorrow. Why couldn't he placate her? Pretend. *Yes, Bob, we'll have a wonderful life together with lots of children.* Why couldn't he say that?

Murray felt a flicker of tension. He knew what she was going to ask. Although the last few months had given his life more meaning than he ever thought possible, he couldn't bring himself to talk about it. Make plans. Make believe. It wouldn't be fair to her. Why was she always thirsting for answers he couldn't supply? She had her whole life ahead of her.

He saw the deep sadness that hung like a dark veil around her lovely face, and it filled him with an uncomfortable longing. "Bobbie, you've got to learn to enjoy life a little more. Try to cherish the good times."

Cherish the good times. Why did he have to say it like that— like today is all there is. He had burrowed his way into her heart, and now he was deserting her. *The war. The damn war!* She felt outraged. Her cautious, obliging nature taunting her, cutting into her like a knife – harsh and piercing. She had no right to feel this way. It made no sense at all. "How should I act, Murray? Tell me? Giddy and carefree? You're going off to war. You expect me to just ignore it? Push it all under the rug...like you do?"

There was a silence. He looked away, surprised by her outburst. "You know, Bob. It's not so bad sometimes, pushing things under the rug. Helps keep you sane."

Oh God. He had that look in his eyes. That same look

he had when he was holding her little niece in his arms. Like he knew something, but he couldn't say. She had promised herself she wouldn't get emotional. Wouldn't say anything to upset him. "I'm sorry, Murray. I didn't really mean to—"

"Forget it. I know how hard it must be for you. It's my fault. I never should have asked—"

"No. Please. I'm glad you're my— I'm so proud to know…" Her eyes glazed and she had to stop and catch her breath. She had tried so hard to be strong, but now her body was shaking with the turbulence of her unresolved fears.

He reached into his pocket and handed her a handkerchief. He seemed to always have one available for her these days.

She still couldn't say it. Couldn't tell him how frightened she was that she might never see him again. "I'm so sorry, Murray. It's just…those good times you talk about. The ones I'm supposed to— you know, cherish? I'm having some trouble understanding. Just, where are they?"

His face lit up. This was simple. This, he could tell her. He turned on the radio. His fingers rotated the dial until he found a music station and a song, "For All We Know". It happened to be her favorite. Strange. She never remembered telling him that.

He took her hand and led her onto the floor of their modest room, his sturdy arms moving slowly around her waist.

She could feel the strength of his body as he pulled her toward him. His cheek was now pressing gently against hers, and suddenly they were dancing. He had done it again! Changed the subject! Soon, her senses would be all muddled, and it would be too late. She had promised herself she wouldn't ask. But, he might die, and she would never know. She was desperate to understand. She wanted him to say it. Tell her why. *Why had he married her?* She broke from the embrace. "I need to ask something, and I want the truth."

"Sure, Bob. Shoot."

She looked into his eyes — past the silences and the doubts. The music seemed to be transporting him. No sadness, now — only a sublime serenity radiating from his every pore, infusing his whole body with a joy beyond the realm of words. *No. Leave it alone!* She took a guarded breath. "I guess — it's really not so important, after all." She lay her head on his solid shoulders and allowed the music to carry her, too.

—⁓—

For the next three days, she waited by the phone. On the morning of the fourth day, she awoke at 3 a.m. The sky was dark and overcast; the moaning wind pressed hard against the window pane. She thought she heard the ever-so-faint sound of a ship's horn. She sat up, frightened. After a moment, she lay back on her pillow, tears streaking like bullets down her ghostly pale cheeks.

—⁓—

In the blackened, misty hush of night, two troop carriers stealthily slipped past Lady Liberty and out of New York Harbor. Destination — England. The wind was blowing with an almost calculated fury, but Murray stood resolute on the deck of one of the ships, refusing to yield to its power, instead studying the graceful statue that stood brave and tall in front of him; remembering a time not long ago when her undaunted beacon welcomed him with the promise of a new life.

As his beloved New York skyline faded from view, his thoughts turned to Bobbie – to their last night together in that cramped, cold room, holding each other as if time and place had ceased to be. They made love with a passion he had never known before. He memorized every curve of her slim, lovely body and her sadly beautiful face. He would carry it with him. *That* is what he would remember. *That* is what he would see before he left this world. Not the nightmare of a child's memory in Lomza. Suddenly, he felt a strange yearning. He tried to brush it aside, but his brow furrowed with doubt. Had he done enough to calm her fears? To answer the unanswerable. He fervently hoped she would take his advice — the advice he had given so freely within the silence of their dance. *LIVE, BOBBIE. LIVE YOUR LIFE!*

—◦◦—

Before leaving for Detroit, she decided to fulfill a pledge she had casually made on their last night together. Teen saw how upset Bobbie seemed and argued against it, but she had promised him.

She took a bus to Manhattan and attended a matinee of *Something for the Boys*.

Sitting alone in the darkened theater, she felt herself go weak. As the curtain went up and the Army Air Force Band and glee club of servicemen filled the stage, she felt a calming presence that seemed to buoy her and give her strength. Her soul began to stir. *How Murray would have loved this!*

—⚊—

On the journey back home, the train was so cold, icicles were forming on the inside of the windows. Babies shrieked — their unhappy cries bellowing through the cars. There was no room at all to maneuver as passengers fought selfishly for any available space. Yet, Bobbie sat oblivious, with more important things on her mind. She was looking forward to getting back to her family and helping her father in the dress shop – and visiting Eunice, who had given birth to a healthy baby boy. But, mostly, she was thinking about an elusive, impetuous stranger she called *husband* who, in his quiet eloquence, taught her plenty about justice and tolerance — and action. Her father's prophetic words rang in her ear. *You never know someone until you live with them.* Would she ever get that chance? Despite her doubts, despite their differences, there were fundamental things she and Murray both believed in and *that* — might be a good beginning.

She grimaced as she reached into her purse for some pills Teen suggested she take to help settle her stomach on the long, turbulent ride.

The well-coiffed woman sitting in the aisle seat across from her glanced over. "You all right?"

"Sure. Just a little queasy. Probably something I ate. Can't hold anything down on these trains."

The woman winked in a gesture of tacit understanding. "Maybe, you're pregnant."

What a thing for a complete stranger to suggest! She quickly turned and stared out the window. After a moment, an impish grin slowly emerged on her flushed and flustered face.

Epilogue

Miami Beach, March 1994

*B*obbie sat in a patio chair around the pool of her home, waiting patiently for her daughter, Eileen, to locate the close-up button on her new video camera. She hadn't slept well the night before. Something had been troubling her, but she couldn't put her finger on it. All her jokes about going to bed with Ben Gay and waking up with Arthur Itis hadn't been able to ease a strange yearning that had awakened her at three in the morning. Of course, she knew full well what this day was. She thought she was fully prepared to reckon with it.

"Okay, Mom, I think I found it. The camera's rolling. What do you want to talk about?"

"I don't feel much like talking, today."

"Oh, great. It's your anniversary. So, be a sport."

"I'm entitled."

"No, you're not. Especially considering I bought this overpriced camera for the occasion. We might as well find some use for it while I'm here. So, how about the story?"

"Which one?"

"Which one? The famous one, of course."

"You never heard it before?"

"Are you kidding? A hundred times. But, this is your moment on film, you old ham."

"Fine way to talk to your ole ma," she said, her eyes crinkling in a mild chide.

"Just a figure of speech, Mom. You're younger than anyone I know."

"I'm older than anyone **I** know! Don't you think I've earned the right to do what I want?"

"Absolutely."

"Good. So, I don't feel like talking about it. Next case!"

"Mom. I hate to insult you, but whoever you are — you're the only one of its kind!"

Bobbie smiled. It had been one of Murray's favorite lines. Her daughter had remembered the story well.

"You have a right to your feelings," Eileen continued, "no matter how wrong they are. But, today, you are *very* wrong. Today, we need to hear it. Just once more."

Bobbie rolled her eyes. What a stubborn woman! She seemed to remember being rather willful herself once. Eileen seemed so like her father in so many ways. She had inherited his strong sense of purpose — a doer, not a talker like herself.

Suddenly, her attention was drawn to a frail figure slowly walking toward her, determined to navigate the few painful steps without assistance, his right arm tightly gripping a wood cane.

"Murray, get in here. You were part of this, I think."

She watched, agonizing with his every step as he carefully maneuvered his partially paralyzed body into the chair next to her. She would be ready to assist should he need her, but she knew not to appear too patronizing.

"She wants to know how we met, honey." She hoped to encourage his participation, but she didn't want to push.

For the last twenty years of his life, since a stroke had devastated his body, Murray had become progressively remote. But suddenly, his eyes brightened. "It's a big story, huh, Bob?"

Bobbie smiled as she pushed aside a stray hair that had fallen into his eye.

Focusing her new toy on her parents' time-worn faces, Eileen was preparing for her assault. "So—okay, here's the first question. Ready?"

"Oh, now, you don't want me to just talk. You want to ask questions, too? You go too far!"

"Yeah. I'm incorrigible. So here it is. Put on your seat belts. It's going to be a bumpy ride."

Bobbie and Murray shared a laugh. Somehow, Eileen's presence was helping to cushion the strange sadness she was feeling this day.

"Why did you jump into marriage after two weeks?"

"Oh. God! There you go, again. Three weeks!" Bobbie reprimanded. "Don't make it worse than it was."

"Sorry. Three weeks."

"Well, let's see. It was war time," she began, straining to remember. "I was twenty-six. Mama was bugging me because your Auntie Fay was engaged. Murray came along."

She paused and regarded her husband with wistful irony. "He said he had money in ten banks."

A mischievous smile saturated Murray's face.

"Oh, I see. My mother, the gold digger!"

"Some gold digger!"

"Were you deeply in love?"

She felt agitated by the question. After all the years talking about how they met, she had never been asked that. Why, now, should it bother her? "I don't really remember, except—I think your father was in a hurry to get married."

Eileen pointed the camera at her father. This was an important moment. She wanted to be sure to capture his response. "Why was that, Daddy?" The question would perhaps satisfy some forgotten conversation her mother had shared with her many years before.

Murray's face crackled with slight irritation. "I don't know. Why are you asking me? So many years ago."

"Fifty," offered Bobbie.

He turned to her in mock surprise. "Oh my God, that long? Think it'll last, Bob?"

Bobbie laughed. It delighted her when he responded to anything, especially humor. During the last difficult years since the stroke, she had seen him struggle against insurmountable odds. She labored to keep him from becoming more isolated and withdrawn. An eloquent thought or an honestly placed reflection – though rare now, gave her hope and strengthened her feeling that — although weakened and ravaged by a cruel accident inside his brain, the life force that was Murray still burned bright.

"I think I just wanted to go to bed with him!"

Murray's eyes widened. He quietly chuckled.

Eileen shook her head in a pretense of disgust. "I really didn't need to know that, Mom."

"Sorry, goodie two shoes. You asked."

The ease and comfort of that remark wasn't lost on her. Once, she would have cringed if someone had suggested she might want to sleep with a man, first. *She* was the goodie two shoes. Age, she understood had a way of melting away the pretense. Could she have ever imagined her mother saying that about her father? Of course, as Minnie grew older, she became much more open about her feelings. "He could put his slippers under my bed, anytime," Minnie once said after seeing a particularly attractive man on television. Many of Bobbie's old-world theories about both her parents fell by the wayside as time went on. Minnie and Morris had continued to amaze her as they moved seamlessly into a modern world. As for Eileen, Bobbie knew her comment hadn't delivered too much of a shock to her daughter's nervous system. Although technically a 'goodbye baby', Eileen was still considered part of the boomer generation. Nothing seemed to shock *them.*

Eileen turned to her father, determined. "So, Daddy, let's hear it. The whole sordid truth. We know why Mom married *you* or so she brags. Why did you marry *her* after just two weeks?"

"Three!" cried Bobbie, exasperation filling her lungs.

"Yeah. Yeah. Okay. Sure. Three."

Bobbie noticed that Murray had a faraway look in his

eyes. There he goes again, she thought. Some things never change.

"Daddy?" asked Eileen. "Did you hear the question?"

Bobbie felt the muscles of her face contract as she fixed her eyes on her husband. Eileen had unwittingly taken up the mantle of her own futile quest so long ago. How could she expect him to remember now, after all these years.

"Yeah. I heard it," he replied.

"So?"

Bobbie twitched in her chair and wiped a bead of perspiration from her brow. *Leave it alone. It doesn't matter. What could he say? So many years ago.* She thought he'd probably answer "Next case!" He used the term when something inconsequential became much too important, and she liked the expression so much, she adopted it herself.

Murray's face brightened, a gentle smile enveloping his gaunt, yet still handsome features.

Bobbie felt her pulse racing. Her body trembled with the memory of an unresolved issue. *This is ridiculous! What's happening to me? A schoolgirl about to be kissed on her first date.*

Murray looked at her, tenderly, as if seeing her for the first time. In a moment, the years peeled away. It was 1943. He was thirty again. The painful remnants of his illness evaporated from his face. His frail voice was now vibrant and full of hope. "Because when I kissed her, it was such a thrill, I knew she was the only girl for me."

Bobbie sat in stunned silence. *So simple!* Why couldn't she have allowed herself to believe it, then? It seemed so complicated, once — so curiously important. And now, she couldn't remember why. She brought her own doubts and insecurities to a relationship with a complicated stranger in an extraordinary time. He came home from war. Threw his uniform overboard as he sailed for America and came home to *her*. He did have a fairy godmother, just as he had joked. She must have watched over both of them.

They never talked much about that time. Mostly, it was ignored in the immediate task of getting on with their lives. Unspoken, but never forgotten, it lingered just below the realm of memory, somewhere between hope and despair. *He had seen so much. Leave it alone.*

Before the tragic stroke that was to change their lives irrevocably when he was only sixty-two, most of their time together was spent looking forward, never back — that she should feel such emotion over something locked away for so many years. *When I kissed her, it was such a thrill, I knew...* That he remembered at all!

Her eyes glistened as recognition of a lost time enveloped her, too. "Fifty years — still, it's nice to know." She leaned over, placed a loving kiss on his ashen cheek and quietly waved her daughter away.

Respectfully, Eileen's camcorder went to black.

Life is mostly froth and bubble.
Two things stand like stone.
Kindness in another's trouble,
Courage in your own.

Adam Lindsay Gordon

Made in United States
Orlando, FL
17 August 2023

36086007R00200